Lambs Dancing

Mary Johnson

To Karen —
Happy reading,
Hope you enjoy
this look at the
past. *Mac* 7/13/04

Beaver's Pond Press, Inc.
Edina, Minnesota

ISBN 1-59298-061-9

Library of Congress Catalog Number: 2004103393

Book design and typesetting: Mori Studio
Cover design: Mori Studio

Printed in the United States of America

First Printing: March 2004

07 06 05 04   6 5 4 3 2 1

Beaver's Pond Press, Inc.

7104 Ohms Lane, Suite 216
Edina, MN 55439
(952) 829-8818
www.BeaversPondPress.com

To order, visit www.BookHouseFulfillment.com or call 1-800-901-3480. Reseller and special sales discounts available.

To:

My strong mother and talented father who loved deeply and lived life fully.

1

WING AND A PRAYER

Jensine Neilsen tucked a damp strand of blond hair behind her ear and pressed a handkerchief to her nose to escape the odor of sour milk and ammonia. She supposed the restless baby in the next seat must be cutting a tooth for the diaper to be so strong. But, as her mother would be quick to assume, there was also the possibility someone had just been careless in the laundering, using tepid water and too little rinsing. The mother shifted to free herself and sighed as the baby eagerly nuzzled the dark nipple and began to nurse enthusiastically. Jensine quickly averted her face. "Gads, can't she at least cover herself!" she thought, suddenly remembering her mother's reaction last summer at the Jensen family reunion. Cousin Enid's five-year-old son had crawled onto his mother's lap, unbuttoned her dress, and latched on to her shriveled breast like a hungry newborn. Jensine's mother stewed about it all the way back to the farm until finally her father put up his hand in protest. "Johanne, I don't care if Enid lets Henry have a little titty until he's sixteen, just as long as I don't have to see those relatives of yours more than once a year." In the shocked silence that followed, he leaned forward, striking a match to light his pipe and preparing himself for the scolding he knew was on its way.

"Peder, you know I don't stand for that vulgar language!" Jensine held back a smile as she thought of the way her mother's lips had pursed tightly, and if looks could kill, Peder Neilsen would have been just a pile of ashes on the driver's seat of their Model T. Actually, death might have been easy compared to the silent treatment he got for the next week or two. But it didn't seem to bother her father much. He just went fishing to Beaver Lake more than usual, adding insult to injury as far as Johanne was concerned.

1

Then, of course, Johanne had given her usual disgusted sniff and added, "Humph, I don't know what this world's coming to." Jensine frowned at the thought of her mother's favorite expression. She had certainly heard it enough over the years. Right then it seemed to hit the nail on the head. Here she was on a dusty bus, sitting next to a stinky baby and a woman who didn't know enough to cover herself in public, bound for Lake Valley, a town she had never seen before, and a teaching position she knew nothing about except that it paid $125 a month. But then…it was 1927, and times were good, maybe not as good as '25, but still good. People were taking chances, and Jensine, too, had been caught up in the enthusiasm. Even she had found the nerve to spend some hard earned money on a flowered chiffon dress that barely touched the top of her knees and used a jelly from time to time to redden her lips a bit. It wasn't like Jensine to be so forward, as her mother would say, but her sister had talked her into it.

"You look like a regular flapper. Too bad you're so flat," Kirsten teased as Jensine tried on the new dress in their upstairs bedroom. Her younger sister lacked her own timidity and was always game to try something new. When Jensine told her about the teaching position in Lake Valley, Kirsten had rolled her eyes and laughed, "Ooh la la! Maybe you'll meet some suave farm boy." It didn't seem likely if Lake Valley folks were anything like the woman sitting next to her!

Her father had encouraged her, too, even when she fretted about the folly of signing on without seeing the school or town. "Wing and a prayer. Wing and a prayer, Jensine." That's what he'd said. But now again, she was having second thoughts about her quick willingness to sign Superintendent Kruse's contract. It didn't seem risky at the time, adding her name to a list of students available for on-campus interviews with superintendents looking for new teachers. She had immediately liked Mr. Kruse's quiet, direct manner, and the arrangement was simple really. She would teach seventh and eighth grade, board and room at the teacherage, and agree to immediate dismissal if she married. In Mr. Kruse's words, "We don't want any teacher in a family way." That was fine with Jensine. She couldn't imagine having a smelly little thing tugging at her breast anyway. The thought was nauseating. She glanced at the woman who was now burping the baby, clucking approvingly when an eruption of curdled milk took its place with numerous crusty spots of spit-up already on the shoulder of her blue dress.

Jensine controlled a gag and turned her eyes to the passing roadside. There was nothing except a ditch full of wild mustard and goldenrod, the sight of which made her sneeze, and across the fence, unending acres of tall corn broken by an occasional field of weedy oat stubble. At least in Steele County, there was a rolling pasture here and there. It was late August, and she knew the milk stage was over because her father had already laid the sweet corn by, and the cellar shelves were carefully lined with new newspaper and rows of Mason jars filled with every kind of vegetable Johanne could possibly think of planting in the garden down behind the chicken house. Just the week before, her mother had begun her annual cellar tours; that's what Kirsten called them. Every time relatives or neighbors dropped over, they were invited to carefully maneuver down the steep steps to view the plethora of canned goods. Johanne was especially proud of her pickles. There was no such thing as a bad pickle in her estimation, and every year she put up a good one hundred quarts of dill and sweet and at least twenty pints of the pickled beets her husband was partial to.

Jensine never said anything to her mother, but she couldn't help thinking she was a bit crazy about the whole business, mostly because when the next canning season rolled around, there was still enough food on the shelves to last through at least another year. But Johanne wasn't one to keep anything over; so come early July she sent Jensine and Kirsten to the cellar to bring up last year's canned goods to be dumped over the fence to the pigs. It was a job they both hated, and except for hoeing and weeding the garden, the only part of the process they were permitted to help with. Her mother thought one could never be too careful with the canning because of spoiling, botulism the extension people in the *Wallace Farmer* called it. Both her parents put great stock in the *Wallace*. Kirsten laughingly teased they should put the old issues, which they carefully stacked on the upstairs steps for reference, along side the family Bible on the lamp table in the front room.

Her mother also refused any help with the chicken and beef she canned. "If I do it myself, I know it's done right." That was her mother to a *T*. Nobody else could be trusted to do things quite right, including her daughters. "You've been off to college, but I expect I know more than you two will ever know about a lot of things." Jensine didn't doubt it one bit.

In 1902, Johanne Jensen had stayed behind in Denmark with a younger sister, Mena, while her mother, father, and little sister, Maren, sailed for America. They were to come later when things were settled with relatives in Maine and Minnesota and when Mena had finished reading for the minister. Johanne tried to keep in touch with her parents over the next three months, only to find the boy who was to post the mail had pocketed the money and tossed her letters in the nearest trash. Jensine had heard the story many times.

Her mother had been a dairy maid in the old country, and part of the arrangement between her parents and the mistress of the house was that young Johanne would be taught how to sew, do fancy work, and set a proper table. Her mother often spoke of the woman's harsh criticism, but the lessons stuck. Jensine's own hope chest was filled with her mother's beautiful needlework, and Johanne's children knew from an early age knives were always placed on the right side of the plate, cutting edge in. That was proper, and proper was an important word in her mother's vocabulary.

Accordingly, there were no nicknames. "People should give their children decent names and use them," her mother emphatically stated. (But sometimes when they were alone, Jensine's father would wink at her and call her Jensie.) Johanne felt the same way about how her children addressed her. "There isn't any Ma in this house. It's Mother, and you'd better remember it." Of course, her English was broken and mother came out sounding like mudder.

Jensine admired her mother even if she was hard to get along with sometimes. For one thing, she had plenty of pluck. Aunt Mena told the story of how eighteen-year-old Johanne had gone straight to the ship's purser when another passenger disputed their second class accommodations aboard the Gunnard Line. And when each family was put into a cage or stall according to their place of

4

emigration, Johanne had pulled fourteen-year-old Mena close to her side and into the center because the family next to them was picking lice like crazy.

Jensine knew her mother had gone to work as a hired girl for a neighbor, Jens Neilsen. A few months later, she married his brother, Peder, and within a year, in 1904, she had been born. By 1907, her brother Christian and her sister Kirsten had arrived.

Although Johanne had a narrow, old-country view of many things, Jensine knew she valued a good education, maybe because she herself had had so little. When the neighbor girls finished eighth grade, they got married or hired out to some bachelor or family in Albert Lea or Owatonna, but her mother was determined her daughters would go to high school. That was a problem because Ellendale didn't have a four-year high school. Resourceful as always, Johanne made arrangements for Jensine to live with the Lindquist family in Owatonna after she completed her freshman and sophomore year in Ellendale. She would do light housekeeping and tutor their small children in exchange for room and board.

Jensine would never forget her mother's words as she kissed her cheek goodbye. "Make us proud, Jensine." She knew she was expected to fulfill her mother's own dream.

Jensine thought back to that time with a shiver. After a few days, she realized she was not prepared for classes like chemistry and physics. The boy assigned as her chemistry laboratory partner quickly figured out she didn't know a test tube from a Bunsen burner and decided his best course of action was to ignore her existence. Jensine overheard him complain to his friends about being stuck with some dumb farm girl, and at the end of the second day, he turned to her and said, "If you're going to borrow my lab reports, you can at least wash up the equipment and put it away." Then he added snidely, "That's not too much for you to figure out, is it?"

Then shortly after she started working for the Lindquists, something happened she couldn't seem to forget no matter how hard she tried. It was a Saturday morning. Mrs. Lindquist was upstairs changing beds, and Jensine was finishing up the breakfast dishes when Mr. Lindquist called up the basement stairs. "Jensine, bring down the broom." She still wondered why she had taken the broom from its hook in the kitchen corner and hurried down the stairs without pausing to even think about why he didn't just use the old one kept down by the coal bin.

"Over here by the cistern, Jensine." It took a moment for her eyes to find him in the musty darkness, but then, instead of taking the broom from her, he grabbed her upper arms and pulled her towards him "How about a little kiss, Missy?"

Jensine remembered how frightened she had been—almost paralyzed in her fear, unable to move or speak. Finally, she had managed a strangled whisper. "Stop it!" But Mr. Lindquist quickly smothered her mouth with one hand and crudely squeezed a breast with the other. Jensine still believed the only thing that saved her that Saturday morning was Mrs. Lindquist's voice above them in the kitchen. She jerked away and fled up the stairs. Mrs. Lindquist looked at her in an odd, knowing way but said nothing.

Jensine always went home for Sunday. Usually, her father stopped for her early Saturday afternoon, and just the two of them enjoyed the ride home. "You're pretty quiet today, Jensie," her father had teased. She tried to smile and pretend nothing was wrong, but she felt dirty and ashamed. How could she tell her father? How could she tell anyone? She had grown up hearing stories about hired girls who got into trouble. Some even ended up pregnant and disgraced, abandoned by their families.

Once home, she immediately went upstairs. It wasn't long before her mother pushed open the door. "What's the matter, Jensine? You're not yourself." In a flood of tears, Jensine told her mother what had happened. She expected her mother to be angry, but surely not with her, so it was as if Johanne slapped her across the face when she scolded, "What on earth possessed you to take the broom down to him, anyway? You weren't using your head there, girl!"

"But it was Mr. Lindquist…!"

"Laus, Jensine, they never believe the girl. Mr. Lindquist is a banker and a big wig in the church. You're a little nobody! I can't tell you how many hired girls on the farms in the old country got taken advantage of by the mister. When they stopped hanging their monthly rags out in the wash, everybody knew they wouldn't be around long. You've got to be smart, Jensine. Don't put yourself in situations." She pulled her apron over her head and motioned for Jensine to get up. "Dry your eyes now and come down to the kitchen."

"Isn't there somebody we should tell?"

"Ah, Jensine, my girl, it will just make trouble for you and his family."

When Jensine felt presentable enough to go downstairs, her mother had gone to the barn. Kirsten looked at her curiously and asked, "What's wrong, Jens?"

"Nothing. I just had a bad week, that's all." Jensine was not stupid. She knew her mother expected her to keep a tight lip.

Later, when they came in from the barn, Jensine heard her parents exchanging angry words in the milk room.

"I'd like to take the strap to him, that's what I ought a do."

"Peder, that won't do a bit of good and you know it."

In the kitchen, Kirsten was all ears. "What's wrong?"

"Never you mind, Kirsten," her mother said as she came into the kitchen. "You girls clean up around here and wash the separator. Your father and I are going to Owatonna on business."

Whatever the business was, Jensine did not go back to the Lindquists. She stayed with Aunt Maren and Uncle Robert until her mother found another family. Then, as far as Johanne was concerned, the whole thing was over and done with. She never mentioned it again. It was not so easy for Jensine. The man's groping hands haunted her, and Aunt Maren said, as far as she knew, Mr. Lindquist was still an elder in the First Church of Christ.

The baby finally settled down to sleep, and the woman sighed in exhaustion. "Where you headed?" she asked.

"Lake Valley."

"There's no town, you know. It's just a school and a store with a dance hall tacked on, far as I know. Maybe a creamery, too, up the road a piece."

Jensine sat in stunned silence. Surely the woman must be wrong. There had to be a town. "But the superintendent talked as if…"

"No, it's just a place where a lot of Germans farm," The woman laughed. "And a lot of other folks come to carouse on Saturday nights." She seemed sure of herself, even a bit smug, so much that Jensine felt even more rattled. What had she done? Was it too late to change her mind? Oh, she could just hear her mother say, "Well, you've made your bed, girl. Now you've got to lie in it."

It seemed hours since they had passed through Blue Earth and Fairmont and two very small towns her father would have jokingly referred to as "wide spots in the road." But that didn't seem very humorous now that she was apparently headed for one. Superintendent Kruse had said she should watch for Spafford Store at the Lakefield corner and alert the driver. He would be waiting to pick her up. The bus normally went on to Worthington, fifteen miles to the west, and according to Mr. Kruse, a few miles out of the way. She stood up on wobbly legs and pulled herself to the front of bus.

"Remember, I have to get off at the Lakefield corner," she reminded the driver.

"Comin' right up, young lady." He pointed up the road and slowed the bus to swerve in front of a single building. "This is it." He swung the door open and stepped down to get her luggage. Jensine followed. There wasn't a soul in sight. The driver unloaded her steamer trunk and two black grips from the side of the bus and turned to her. "Anybody meetin' you? Kind of a lonely spot."

Jensine bent down to pick up the smallest grip so he wouldn't see her tears. "I'm sure my ride will be right along." As the bus pulled away, she glanced up to see the nursing mother, her sleepy baby's face close to her cheek, watching from the open bus window. Jensine smiled and lifted her hand in parting, but the woman simply turned away.

2

A MILE LONG

Jensine hadn't even thought about the possibility of Mr. Kruse not being there to meet her. His instructions had certainly been simple, but she suddenly realized he hadn't even given her a number to ring up. Surely he didn't expect her to stand there on the corner with her trunk and grips stacked around her like a gypsy waiting for God knows who. Jensine glanced at the little store behind her. Scrawled white tempera on the window advertised bananas for five cents a bunch, but a lopsided closed sign hung on the door. They couldn't be too hard up for business if they were closed at 2:00 in the afternoon, she thought. Her steamer trunk was too heavy, even to drag, so she tipped it on its side and sat down to wait in the sultry August afternoon

Jensine thought back to the morning when she had boarded the bus in Albert Lea. "You look like a million dollars, Jensie," her father had whispered in her ear. Her mother had straightened the blue tie on her white middy and reminded her to give the blouse a good hard shake before she hung it up that night. Gads, it was as though she had never been away from home. Oh, well, that was her mother's way of saying goodbye without getting too emotional. It had been hard to decide what to wear for the trip. She wanted to make a good impression, but still Mr. Kruse might wonder if she came too decked out. Her mother had thought the long-sleeved middy and dark skirt a bit too warm for August, and, of course, she had been right again. Then those stupid silk stockings! Perspiration pooled between her upper thighs. No doubt when she stood up, the back of her skirt would be damp and covered with the dust she had forgotten to wipe off the steamer. Oh, she was going to make a great impression all right. A first class hick with a wilted bob and dirty skirt!

What really took the cake, Jensine thought, was there was no reason under the sun for her to be plunked on her behind in such an exciting spot as Spafford Store, hoping someone remembered she existed.

After finishing normal school in Albert Lea, Jensine taught at District Thirty-four, the same little one-room country school near their farm that she had once attended. Jensine knew both students and parents had liked her, and she could have had her old job back in a minute or found another easily. Except for the old maids, most teachers only stayed a year or two until they found a man and got married, so there were bound to be openings.

But Jensine had her hopes set on a town school. There she wouldn't be passed around the district to be boarded like an unwanted shirttail relative. Her friend Violet Swedberg told horror stories about that…sleeping with bed-wetters, sheets that hadn't been washed for weeks, occasional bedbugs and full privies. In fact, that was the main reason Jensine took the job at District Thirty-four. It was so close to home she could politely refuse the free boarding part of her contract without seeming high hat.

And there were other things about the one-room school Jensine didn't like. One in particular was that the older boys only showed up in the winter. Their school year was from the time the manure pile froze in late fall to when it thawed in early spring. Some were well beyond the age any seventh- or eighth-grader should be, and their main goal seemed to be to cause trouble. They bullied the younger students and made life miserable for the teacher. Once, Jensine had lost her temper and pulled the red hair of Nels Jorgenson, a big lout who guffawed at everything she said. She sent him home, but his parents brought him back at the start of school the next day, promising a good whipping if he misbehaved again. They didn't want him at home either.

It was clear to Jensine that most of the school board members thought of her as a hired girl more than a teacher. She had to be at school early enough to stir up the coals she'd banked before leaving the day before and, of course, push the oil mop over the floor. And when one of the parents brought over the daily noon hot dish, it was her job to serve it. One board member, Alfred Peterson, who was also their neighbor, even had the gall to tell her she should let him know when the holes in the outhouse got filled up. "Isn't that just keen?" she complained sarcastically to her mother. "He probably wants me to take a shovel out there and knock off the piles of poop, too…"

Johanne's response was not unexpected. She shook her head disapprovingly at Jensine's choice of words and said, "Well, we're not here just to have a good time, my girl. We're here to work." That was about as much sympathy as she could expect from her mother.

But more than anything else, Jensine wanted to set her own course. If the truth were known, she thought, most people lived as if life were just a dress rehearsal for the real thing. Her father had told her more than once, "Plant your own garden, Jensie. Don't be lettin' your mother or anybody else be doin' it for you."

Jensine knew most town schools were looking for teachers who had more than a normal school education, so after a year and a half at District Thirty-four, she headed for Mankato State Teachers College. The two years she spent there were wonderful, living in Cooper Hall with girls from all over Minnesota and even a few from South Dakota, like Helen Turnquist from Watertown. She would miss the after-hours giggling and room parties. Even Jensine's job as dorm proctor hadn't stopped her from enjoying the fun.

It was also a relief to be away from her mother's nonstop advice and the constant squabbling. Much as she loved her sister, Kirsten was difficult to get along with. Always competitive, even in the little acts of living, she had to be the best…constantly comparing report cards, breast size, popularity, and even openly arguing she was their father's favorite. Everybody knew it and seemed to bow to her tantrums and demands, everybody except her mother. Jensine had learned a long time ago that it was better to just keep her mouth shut, but even then she couldn't always avoid the heated arguments between Johanne and her sister. Her father and Christian were lucky that way. They could head for the barn or the fields to escape the constant wrangling.

Jensine hoped the passing cars didn't think she was totally abandoned, maybe a hired girl thrown out by some family for unbecom-
ing behavior. She stood and felt her skirt stuck to her backside, just
as she had known it would. A cloud of dust approached from the
road to the south. It had to be Mr. Kruse. Soon, a Model A truck
pulled to a stop a few feet from her pile of luggage.

"I'll betcha yer Miss Neilsen." A small, wiry man in blue bib overalls stepped off the running board of the truck. He pulled off a faded
railroad cap to reveal a head of tightly kinked gray hair, tapped a
worn pipe on the heel of his shoe, and reached out his other callused
hand to Jensine.

"Sorry to keep you waitin'. Mr. Kruse sent me over at the last
minute on account of he had some school business to tend to." The
thick German accent was unmistakable, but somehow, the hand
reached out in welcome was exactly what she needed. Jensine took
it without hesitation, grateful for the warm strength. "Name's Emil
Ehrenberg...school janitor."

Emil grabbed the two grips and headed toward the open bed of the
truck. "Bet you're pretty hot and tired sittin' there in the sun. Well,
the missus has got some cold lemonade waitin' for you over at the
teacherage, and we'll be there before you know it. You just get right
up there in the truck, and I'll load your things. Looks like you're
plannin' on stayin' awhile."

"Can't I help with the steamer? It's heavy."

"Nah, I can get it." Emil turned the steamer upright and lugged it
over to the truck. One heave and it rested along side the grips. He
held the door for Jensine and walked around to the other side of the
truck. Before getting in, he packed and lit his pipe. The cloud of
smoky aroma made her suddenly homesick for her father. She wondered if Emil's wife had ever boiled his pipes like her mother once had
her father's. It was one of the few times, Jensine had seen him disgusted enough to slam the kitchen door on his way out to the barn.

The gravel road was full of potholes, and Emil Ehrenberg seemed
bent on hitting every one of them. Jensine pressed her feet to the
floorboard to keep from bouncing into the dash, but her driver

seemed unconcerned. He reached across her to roll down the window and catch the cross breeze. "Well, Miss Nielsen, I think you're gonna like Lake Valley."

"About how big is Lake Valley?" ventured Jensine.

Emil laughed. "Well, folks say main street is a mile long…mile from the school to the store, that is."

"Is the lake nearby?" Jensine swallowed hard, hoping for at least some small saving grace for this place that seemed to be nothing but a giant cornfield.

"Well, that's a funny thing, too. Can't rightly say how we came by the name. I'm thinkin' the closest thing we got to water in these parts is a mud slough over to the west of us a couple of miles. 'Course there's the big lakes, Spirit and Okoboji, but they're way south of here."

3

THE TEACHERAGE

E mil Ehrenberg couldn't have said it better, and, for that matter, the woman on the bus had been right, too. First, they passed the store, a small, somewhat shabby place with a larger building attached to the side and around the back. A lone green sedan was parked by the single gas pump.

About a mile up the road, sat the two-story brick school. A few tall evergreens provided a windbreak to the north and separated the school property from the surrounding cornfields. Emil shifted down to stop in front of a large square house, set back and to the right of the school and probably built around 1920 or shortly before, Jensine thought, judging from the dark green shingles which covered the upper story and set it apart from the traditional white boarding of the dormer attic and bottom story. Two overgrown spiraea nearly closed off the steps to the screened porch which wrapped around the front and side of the house—imposing by its size but somehow lonely in its flat cornfield surroundings, as if it better belonged on a farmstead with a big red hip-roofed barn or under a canopy of giant oak trees in a neighborhood with other big houses.

"Well, here's the teacherage where you'll be stayin'. The place on the other side of the school is where Superintendent Kruse and his wife live." Then he said apologetically, "Sorry the grass looks so danged bad. We need a good rain, that's fur sure."

"Oh, it's dry at home, too," Jensine replied and then waited for him to step down from the truck and tap his pipe on his heel before coming around to her side to open the door and lift her trunk and grips down from the truck bed. She climbed down, picked up the small grip, and followed him up a long sidewalk lined with faded peony bushes. Her stomach was a hard knot and felt as if it were directly attached to her pounding heart.

⚜

Jensine climbed the front steps and crossed the screened porch as Emil held open the front door for her. The dark, cool foyer smelled of Beacon wax, apple pie, and just a trace of cinnamon. "Bring her right in, Emil," a voice called from another room. "I'm right in the middle of takin' a pie from the oven." Then a heavyset, older woman shuffled energetically into the hall, wiping her hands on a faded apron. "You come right in, Miss Neilsen. I got a nice cold glass of lemonade waitin' for you and fresh apple pie a little later, soon as it cools a bit. I'm Ella, Emil's wife. My, you look awful hot and tired. Maybe you want to freshen up a bit first." The words fairly tumbled from her mouth. Then she pulled Jensine farther into the foyer, took the grip away and put it into Emil's hand in one quick move. "Now, no need for you to be car-ryin' that. Emil'l take it right up to your room."

Emil started for the open stairs, Jensine's grips in tow. "Ella, put the pot on and set that pie on the sill to cool. I'll be havin' a piece before I get back over to the school. I got floors to wax before the afternoon's done."

"You just go right up, Miss Neilsen. Emil'l show the way. I put fresh sheets on this morning and turned the covers back in case you might want to rest." Ella moved toward the kitchen but then turned to call up the stairway. "Frieda, she's here! Emil, don't forget Miss Neilsen's trunk out there in the driveway. She's gonna want to unpack her things 'fore they get too wrinkled."

"Yeah, yeah, Ella," Emil muttered. "I got things under control, so never you mind." Ella and Emil sounded so much like her mother and father Jensine couldn't resist a smile. They had reached the first landing when an upstairs door opened and footsteps clattered down the top flight of wooden stairs. A slender, black-haired woman thrust out her hand in a firm, businesslike manner to pull Jensine past Emil and up the last stairs.

"You must be Jensine Neilsen. I'm Frieda Bauer, high school sci-ence and math. Welcome to Lake Valley. I'll be right across the hall from you; if the room suits you, that is. The home economics teacher isn't coming until tomorrow, so Ella said you could take your pick." Jensine's attention was immediately drawn to the woman's eyes. They were dark brown, almost black, and even thick black-rimmed glasses couldn't hide their piercing intensity. Frieda turned to take one of the grips from Emil and led the way to the second bedroom.

The bedroom was papered in a small, blue flowered design. White French tieback sheers covered the double windows to the south. The furniture was sparse—white iron bed, oak chest of drawers, a small table with a mirror above it that needed resilvering, and a sewing rocker tucked back in the corner. And, as Ella had said, the pink chenille bedspread had been turned back to reveal starched white pillowcases trimmed in tatting. A colorful pieced quilt was folded across the end of the bed. Jensine felt the knot in her stomach untie.

By this time, Frieda had dropped Jensine's grip and opened the tiny closet. There was a big hook on the backside of the door and five others across the back wall. "It's not swell," she said, "but I manage. Of course, I'm not much of a clothes horse." She pushed the heavy bangs out of her eyes and headed for the door. "The bathroom's down the hall to your right. Why don't you wash up and come down for lunch? I think Ella just took a pie out of the oven." Then she smiled and added, "You might as well get used to the idea of eating frequently because that's the custom out here. No respectable housewife would let anyone set foot in her house without setting the table for lunch."

"I'm not really hungry," Jensine ventured.

But Frieda was already in the hall. "Come on, Emil, I'll help you with her trunk." The door closed after them, and Jensine was left in the silence to ponder her new home. She already knew she was going to like Ella and Emil Ehrenberg and Frieda Bauer.

Jensine didn't feel much like lemonade or apple pie either, but it would be unfriendly not to go down. Using the bathroom was a must and a quick comb through her bob might not hurt either. If she looked at all like she felt, she was a mess. She took a small comb from her purse and moved to the mirror. The face that stared back was thin and surprisingly pale considering the warmth of the room. "I look a fright!" Her mother always said she had nice features, angular, the kind of looks that don't fade when you get old. Jensine supposed they would have to do anyway, even though, in her estimation, her lips were too full. Her father said jokingly she had a real kisser. She combed through her short, blonde bob and tried to redo the finger waves, but the afternoon humidity had left a layer of frizz instead of soft waves. "Oh, well," Jensine thought, as her mother would say, "Pretty is as pretty does."

The bathroom was huge, no doubt a made-over bedroom. There was a footed tub, wash basin, toilet, wooden clothes rack, and enough room to camp out. Just having an indoor bathroom was a treat. It had been hard to go back to using the outdoor privy at home after living away at school. Jensine had been embarrassed when friends came home with her on a weekend. They hadn't said anything, of course, but she knew they didn't like the smell of biffy on their clothes any more than she did.

It was a relief to use the toilet. After tightening her garters to rescue her badly bagging stockings, she rinsed her face in cool water and wiped it with one of the coarse towels on the wooden bar. It smelled of homemade soap, the kind her father said had enough lye in it to take your hide right off.

Emil and Frieda were sitting in the kitchen at a round table covered with a flowered oilcloth. Ella was taking a pitcher of lemonade from the icebox. Hesitating at the door, Jensine waited until Ella turned and said, "You come right in. I'm just cuttin' the pie. Sit right here." She pulled back a chair and motioned for Jensine to sit.

"Serve it up, Ella. I ain't got all day, you know," prodded Emil impatiently.

"Oh, you," his wife retorted and put down a piece of warm pie in front of him, with a little extra force, Jensine thought. She served the rest of them and sat down with a tired sigh, tucking a loose strand of gray hair into her bun with a hairpin and resting her elbows on the table. "My bunions are sure givin' me trouble today. Maybe we'll finally get some rain. Shall we offer a little blessin'?"

Fork in hand, Emil frowned at his wife. "Now, Ella, we don't need to be sayin' grace every time we turn around. Next thing I know, you'll be wantin' me to pray over every dang dipper of water I take from the pail, and I ain't gonna do it." He ate two huge forkfuls of pie before Ella could even shake her head in disapproval.

The apple pie was heavy, not at all like the flaky Danish pastry Jensine was used to. Her mother would have brushed the top crust with a little beaten egg white or heavy cream to make it a nice golden brown. Ella's piecrust was thick, white, heavily laced with sugar, and liberally sprinkled with cinnamon. But what really seemed odd was the big wedge of hard cheese resting along side each slice of pie. Ella must have sensed Jensine's hesitation because she picked up the cheese with one hand and her fork with the other and said, "You probably don't eat cheese with your apple pie, but us German Lutherans like it that way. It makes the cheese and the pie taste good." Surprisingly, it did.

4

MOVETA OGLIRE

Moveta Ogilire, LakeValley's new home economics teacher, did indeed arrive from St. James the next day. Shortly before noon, her parents delivered her and enough luggage to fill not only the one remaining room in the teacherage but the dormer attic as well. She was literally stuffed into the back seat amidst bed pillows and quilts, but she leaned forward as best she could to wave at Jensine and Frieda while she waited for her father to come around and open the door. An armful of clothes spilled onto the driveway before Moveta could pull herself out of the car and straighten the short skirt, which had ridden up well past her knees. Plump is how Jensine's father would have diplomatically described her. Her brother Christian, however, would not have been so charitable. One quick look at Moveta's stout legs and straight brown hair, parted in the center and shingled up the back, and he would have flatly declared, "Homely as a mud fence!" Whatever that was. But Moveta had a friendly grin that even Christian would have had a hard time resisting. She grabbed Frieda's outstretched hand and exclaimed, "Well, this old pie face is finally here!" Jensine smiled, thinking she hadn't heard that expression since Kathryn Koopman back at Cooper Hall.

Moveta's father appeared to be a man of few words, just tipped his hat and immediately started loosening the ropes which tied the steamer to back of the car. Moveta's mother gave a sharp rap on the window to gain her husband's attention. It was abundantly clear she expected her husband to open the door for her because she waited, looking straight ahead, until he hurried to do her bidding. She checked her makeup and tightly waved hair in a small hand mirror before turning in the seat and stepping onto the running board. She paused, eyeing them critically, and Jensine wondered for a moment if she expected them to kneel.

Mrs. Ogilire was a big woman, tightly corseted, who appeared used to giving orders. She didn't waste a moment. "Moveta, don't just stand there, dear. Talk to the girls. Why in the world did you bring that old study lamp? Folks will think we don't have a nickel to our name!" She reached over, bent slightly, and tugged her daughter's skirt down in the front where it had ridden up because of her stomach, making it seem much shorter in front than in back. "Goodness, Moveta! Pull your dress down. You can be such a frump sometimes!"

Once the entourage followed Frieda and Jensine into the teacherage and up the stairs to Moveta's room, her mother immediately started rearranging. Mr. Ogilire quickly disappeared downstairs and, from the bedroom window, Jensine could see him rolling a smoke as he leaned against the car and prepared for a long wait. "Moveta, you don't want that bed against the west wall. It will be nothing but cold come winter. Of course, we brought those extra quilts just in case they don't have much heat upstairs." That said, she stripped off the white chenille bedspread, folded it and put it outside the door. Then, she took a pillow off the bed, brought it to her nose to smell and squeezed. "These are just feather, I believe. Good thing we brought our own down ones, Moveta." Ella's pillows and embroidered cases joined the bedspread in the hall. Jensine was glad their housekeeper had Saturdays and Sundays off. Poor Ella would have been beside herself.

❧

Jensine stood with Frieda in the doorway, realizing their help would definitely not be needed. She was embarrassed for Moveta, and for the first time, she was thankful her own parents had not been able to come, even though she knew they would never behave in such an ill-mannered way. It didn't seem to bother Moveta, though. She just rolled her eyes at them and pointed to the door. "Let me see your rooms. Can we use the kitchen at night? I love to cook, and I make fudge to die for." Jensine couldn't help laughing. Anyone who liked to make homemade fudge had to be all right. Chocolate was her own one weakness. It seemed she always found her way to the Fanny Farmer candy store when they drove into Albert Lea to shop.

By the time Moveta had seen their rooms and the bathroom, her mother, hammer in hand, was putting up a pole in the closet. She was driving nails into the wall with enough force to send them into the next room. "Moveta, I'm putting up a pole. You can't possibly hang all your things on these five hooks in here. Get your father up here. He doesn't need to be standing down there by the car waiting. We're not going until we get you settled here anyway. Give me a hand, Moveta. Don't just stand there!"

It was a good time for Jensine and Frieda to excuse themselves to the kitchen. Ella had set rolls the night before and instructed Jensine and Frieda to bake them the next morning to serve with the chicken salad. "They might want a bite to eat before they head back." Then she added, "Be sure you use the dining room in case the Ogilires are fancy folks. I laid out a nice cloth." Ella had also baked a rich chocolate cake and frosted it with some kind of brown sugar and coconut concoction that was unfamiliar to Jensine. Frieda said it was a German chocolate cake. "Why not?" she smiled as she cut pieces. "Everything else here is. Why not the cake?"

Mr. Ogilire seemed reluctant to stay for lunch. In fact, he spoke his first words of the day. "Agnes, we need to be getting back. I planned on doing some work at the bank before the day was over."

Agnes completely ignored him and settled quickly into a chair. "Oh, do sit down, Harold," she commanded. "Looks very tasty, girls. Did you make all this?" She heaped three big spoonfuls of salad on her plate along with two rolls, which she liberally spread with Ella's whipped butter.

"Oh, no," Frieda said. "Ella is the saint who gets the credit."

"I understand you girls pay her twenty-two dollars a month for meals and housekeeping. Let her earn her money, mind you. I think I'll have another spoonful of that salad. How about you, Harold?"

The very thought of anyone thinking Ella didn't earn her money was so unfair Jensine could hardly finish her lunch. Frieda must have felt the same way because she quickly removed the salad plates and served the cake. Mrs. Ogilire looked around expectedly for coffee, but Frieda offered only lemonade as if she wasn't about to give this unpleasant woman any excuse to stay longer.

By 4:00, Moveta was unpacked and settled in her room. Jensine liked her and couldn't help thinking she had to be a strong person to endure her mother's dominating personality without losing her own unique sense of humor. Moveta could laugh at herself, and that was something Jensine found difficult to do. She could learn a thing or two from Moveta.

Ella had left a hot dish in the icebox for supper. "Just needs to be warmed," she said. Frieda stirred up the coals in the cook stove a bit and put the hot dish in the oven. She said it was one of Ella's favorites—sausage, potatoes, and cabbage in a rich cream sauce. "Let's go over to the school and look around. Mr. Kruse gave me a key to the front door, and I think Emil is still there waxing floors. You can see your rooms."

Jensine felt the knot in her stomach return, but it was from pleas-ant excitement this time.

5

EMIL'S PRIDE AND JOY

As Frieda guided Jensine and Moveta through the front double doors of the school, she said with obvious pride, "Well, this is LakeValley School. I'll give you the free tour. Then you can check out your rooms while I see if Emil has had time to carry up my lab supplies."

"It smells like fresh wax and a whole lot cleaner than my last school," Moveta remarked. "That was a pig sty!"

Jensine knew Frieda had been teaching at Lake Valley the past two years, but she assumed for some reason Moveta had country school experience like herself or was even a first-year teacher. Frieda must have thought the same because she turned curiously and asked, "Oh really, where did you teach last year, Moveta?"

"A little burg in eastern South Dakota...a real dump. I tried everything in the book, but whether we were making muffins or sewing a seam, the only response I ever got from those stupid farm girls was 'My ma don't do it that way.' I thought I'd lose my marbles or at least pull some of my hair out before the year was over." Moveta crossed her eyes and grabbed her hair. "They didn't hire me back, but believe it, ladies, I was glad to go. It was a real hell hole!"

Jensine couldn't believe Moveta was talking so freely about her dismissal and she had actually used the word "hell." Jensine would have been absolutely mortified to even mention being let go, and hell was a word ladies didn't use unless they were sure of their company. Besides, her mother had taught her it was best not to share one's unfortunate experiences with others. "People tend to have big mouths, and you never know where or how your story will end up.

People can't talk about you if they don't know anything," Johanne often said.

Frieda looked over at Jensine and cleared her throat. "Well, let's get started. The closed door to your left is Superintendent Kruse's office. The library is to your right. And here we have the pride and joy of Emil Ehrenberg and Lake Valley School." She gestured grandly to the large gymnasium in front of them. The narrow oak boards gleamed in the late afternoon sunlight. At the end of the court, deep purple curtains were drawn across a stage.

"It's beautiful," Jensine said, "but where do people sit to watch the game?" There seemed to be room for only one row of chairs on either side of the basketball court.

"Well, there are elementary classrooms behind those roll-down walls on each side. So on nights they have games, they just roll up the walls and set up a couple of rows of chairs in each classroom. It works." Her voice echoed in the empty space. "You have to come early if you want a seat because Lake Valley always has a good team. Lots of tall kids here, and they know how to play basketball. Mr. Kruse expects his teachers to attend all of the games, so I hope you like basketball."

Jensine thought of her sister Kirsten. At five foot, ten inches she had been an outstanding basketball player. Besides being tall, she was competitive and had an aggressive quality about her that usually intimidated the opposition. Jensine wished she was more like that, but her father said it just wasn't her nature, and somehow, he made it seem like it was perfectly fine for her to be just the way she was.

"And for heaven's sake, don't step on the floor! Emil will have our heads if we do." Frieda pulled them down a short hallway to the left.

"Manual training's on the left, and here's your room, Moveta." She pushed open the door to the spotless home economics room. Three small kitchenettes and a dozen treadle Singers on opposite ends of the room were separated by several tables for bookwork.

Jensine thought the room was impressive, the crisp yellow gingham curtains at the windows probably Ella's work. And here again, the oak floors shone with a recent waxing and buffing. It was evident

Emil took great pride in his work. She suspected her room would be just as nice, and a small whirl of excitement turned in her stomach at the prospect.

Frieda went on to explain grades one through six were downstairs, and seventh, eighth, and high school were upstairs. Each grade room had its own cloak hall. She showed them the high school assembly where long strips of desks were bolted to the floor. "The high school students meet here in the morning for assembly. Study halls are in here, too. Jensine, when your seventh- and eighth-graders have manual training and home economics, you'll be supervising a high school study hall in here. And let me warn you, those seniors will test you every day. Don't give them an inch, especially at first."

Jensine's room was in the northwest corner of the school. Windows, reaching almost to the ceiling, lined the west wall, and only the top shades were half drawn, so the late afternoon sun poured through. The room was warm and stuffy, but Jensine imagined the breeze from the west would be enough to keep the room comfortable if the windows were opened on warm days. Four strips of ten desks each faced a scarred but polished teacher's desk and a front wall of cleaned blackboards. A doorway on the east wall led to the cloak hall. Except for rolled maps on the top of the blackboards and a mounted globe on the top of an old upright piano at the back, the room was bare. Jensine assumed the textbooks must be in the double closets just inside the door. She walked toward her desk, imagining the students who would soon be sitting in the room. Would they want to learn, or would they be like Moveta's students in Elkton? Well, Frieda seemed confident and excited about the year. That had to be a good sign because Jensine sensed Frieda was very sharp and an excellent teacher. She planned on taking any advice she had to offer.

Jensine sat down at her desk and opened the drawers one by one. They were empty except for a few pencils and some used chalk. They would probably get their supplies next Monday at the meeting Mr. Kruse had scheduled for all teachers. She heard footsteps in the hall. Emil poked his head in the door and smiled.

"Well, Miss. Neilsen, whatcha think of our school?"

27

"Oh, Emil, it's beautiful! I've never seen so many shiny oak floors in my life."

Emil's face broke into a proud grin. "Yah, I think we got one of the nicest schools around. We even put Worthington to shame, and that's a big school."

Jensine had to agree because she couldn't imagine any other school being lucky enough to have the loving care of an Emil Ehrenberg. She was reminded of what her parents often said about people from the old country. They weren't afraid to work, and they cared about what they did. Suddenly, Jensine felt proud of her immigrant parents. They were strong people despite their broken English and old-fashioned way of doing things.

Emil raised his hand in parting. "Well, if you ever need anything and don't see me in the halls, I'm down in the furnace room. It's where I keep my mops, buckets, and such. I'll be doin' your black-boards every night, so don't go worryin' about that. The way I see it, your job's teachin' the kids, not doin' the cleanin'." With that, he was gone. Jensine thought Emil had to be one of the nicest people she had ever met. She took one last look at her room and went to find Frieda and Moveta. Ella's hot dish was sounding more tempting by the moment

Frieda left for Round Lake early the next morning. It was a small town about seven miles to the west where her parents lived. She explained they were retired and expected her to attend the Presbyterian Church there with them and stay for dinner. It was a Sunday ritual which she enjoyed and also a chance to see her brothers and sister who farmed nearby. Lake Valley didn't have a church, but the German Lutherans worshipped and had Sunday School at the school gymnasium. Frieda said it was pretty much expected they attend. Otherwise, some people might think they were Catholic, and that, she said with a knowing smile, would not be a good thing.

Jensine supposed it wouldn't hurt to go and, after all, it wasn't as if going to church were foreign to her. She had been confirmed in the Lutheran church, and her family had been regular churchgoers until the terrible time of her grandfather's suicide when she was fourteen. He had never wanted to come to America, but his wife insisted they would never get ahead if they stayed in Denmark. Life in the new country proved difficult for him, mostly because there was no demand for stone masonry, his family's work for generations. Jensine had loved this gentle man and understood the sense of loss which gradually seemed to overwhelm him. She would never forget the night when Uncle Nels came to get her mother. Nothing was said, but she knew it had to be something bad. In the morning, though, her mother was up making breakfast as usual.

"Your grandfather's passed on," Johanne said, and that was it. But later that day, when they returned from making funeral arrangements, her mother's face was flushed with anger. Pots banged on the range top as she started supper. She directed Jensine to watch the potatoes in case they boiled over, tied a scarf over her head, and headed for the barn where Peder was doing the evening chores. Johanne didn't like the smell of barn on her clothes, so Jensine knew it had to be something serious to draw her mother there. When they returned to the house a good hour later, Johanne's shoulders were slumped and her eyes red from crying.

Jensine learned the story in bits and pieces over the years, mostly from relatives. The Geneva Lutheran Church they had attended since their arrival in America refused to bury her grandfather in the church cemetery because he had taken his own life. The church did offer a plot outside the iron fence, a spot generally reserved for the unchurched and local riffraff. Her mother's bitterness lasted ten years and through three pastors. "I don't need the church if that's the way of things," she said. Even after the iron fence was removed to enlarge the cemetery, and no one could tell who the fallen were, Johanne could not be persuaded to rejoin the ranks of the Geneva Lutherans.

When Jensine asked Moveta if she wanted to walk over to the school for the 10:30 service, Moveta scowled and shook her head. "Oh, poop, I like to sleep in on Sundays. It's the only day we can, you know."

"Please, Moveta, just this once. We can sit in the back. I hate going alone, especially this first time. Besides, Mr. and Mrs. Kruse will be there, and you know we're invited there for dinner. We might as well make a good impression."

The Lake Valley Lutherans were evidently serious about their religion. By the time Jensine and Moveta walked over from the teacherage, there were no back seats to be had. As they were ushered to the front, Jensine felt the curious stares. "Must be a couple of the new teachers," she heard a woman whisper.

6

CHOCOLATE-COVERED CHERRIES

Jensine and Moveta spent a lazy Sunday afternoon. After returning from dinner at the Kruses, they squeezed lemons for fresh lemonade and sat on the front porch. They had both liked Mrs. Kruse and were surprised to learn she was the high school English teacher and school librarian. It seemed odd since Mr. Kruse had clearly noted that their contracts did not permit them to be married.

"Probably one of those two-for-one deals," Moveta said. "Besides, she's definitely too old to get in 'a family way,' which, as you well know, is the sin of all sins." She drained her glass and added, "I noticed her bun right away. Did you ever know a librarian who didn't wear a bun?"

Jensine had to laugh because there was certainly some truth to what Moveta said. The librarian at Mankato State Teachers, Miss Wick, had her hair pulled so tightly into a bun her eyes looked slanted, at least that's what everyone said behind her back. She spent most of her time glaring over the tables and holding her forefinger to her lips in a permanent *shush* just in case anyone should dare to even think about whispering in her domain. And come to think of it, the librarian at Owatonna High School had sported a tight bun, too.

"Do you think they have older children?" Jensine asked.

"Who, librarians? Of course not; they get their jollies from books, don't you know?"

"Moveta, I'm talking about Mr. and Mrs. Kruse, you silly."

"Oh," Moveta said innocently, "the Kruses. I don't think so because she doesn't have the little baby belly most middle aged women have even if they wear a corset." Moveta pulled herself out of the wicker rocker. "Stay put, I have a box of chocolates in my room. I'll go get it. Then we can have our own little moment of rapturous delight," she added dramatically.

Jensine went to refill their glasses, thinking Moveta was proving to be an entertaining housemate, to say the least. She hadn't laughed so much since the pajama parties in the dorm. Jensine guessed there could be worse things than sipping lemonade and eating chocolates on a Sunday afternoon.

Moveta reappeared minus her pumps and stockings with a huge box of chocolate-covered cherries. She flopped in her chair and carefully removed the cellophane wrapping. Then she lifted the cover and folded back the tissue covering the candy. It seemed to Jensine there was almost a kind of reverence in her task. She passed the box to Jensine "Help yourself." Then she placed the box on the small table between them and settled back in her rocker. "I always start from the middle," Moveta said, selecting the center chocolate, and placing the whole piece in her mouth. She closed her eyes in sublime satisfaction. "Better than sex."

"Personally, I wouldn't know," Jensine responded, thinking immediately even her tone of voice sounded prudish.

"I would!" Moveta said wickedly. She reached for a second chocolate and raised it to Jensine in a toasting gesture. "Here's to Lake Valley, and here's to you and me. May we each meet some nice guy that fits us to a *T*."

"I'm not really looking for a man, Moveta."

"Oh, come on, Jensine, we're all looking for a man and you know it! Have another chocolate. I've got two more boxes upstairs."

"Moveta, we'll get fat."

"No, we won't. Trust me."

Jensine managed to eat two more and then, placing her hand on her stomach, she protested, "No more. Not after Mrs. Kruse's meatloaf and lemon pie."

"Suit yourself, but I'm going to have some more. Lots."

That was putting it mildly, to say the least. Moveta ate the whole box, carefully working her way from the center of the box to the corners. She seemed to enjoy touching the chocolates as much as eating them. When the box was empty, she refolded the tissue, put the cover back on, and sighed, "I hate myself when I do that. My mother would kill me! Well, I think I'll go upstairs for a quick nap. See you later."

Jensine sat on the porch wondering about Moveta and what had possessed her to eat the whole box of chocolates, but her thoughts were interrupted when Frieda's car pulled into the teacherage driveway. She joined Jensine on the porch and the two of them visited until it was time to think about a light supper. There was some of Ella's chicken salad left which would do fine. Moveta didn't join them. Frieda ran up to knock on her door, but she didn't answer.

"Must be sleeping," Frieda said.

"I don't think she's hungry," answered Jensine. She decided she wouldn't say anything about the box of chocolates. They ate their salad on the porch and talked about the coming week. Mr. Kruse had said all of the teachers would meet Monday morning at 7:00. He would go over some things they needed to know, and they could get their supplies. The rest of the week was to be spent getting ready for their classes.

"There's always plenty to do." Frieda sighed. "It takes me one day just to put the supplies away, but I love doing labs. The kids here are really good in science and math, so it's fun to plan experiments."

That surprised Jensine. It didn't seem like a bunch of farm kids would be that interested. "Even the girls?" she asked.

"Oh, the girls are tops. I know...I was surprised, too."

Except for using the bathroom several times, Moveta stayed in her bedroom all evening, but she seemed herself the next morning when she joined them at 6:30 for Ella's breakfast of cooked oatmeal, toast, and peach marmalade.

"Now, girls, you have to tell me what you like for breakfast. I'll be bringin' over a little lunch at noon. I got my bread set already, so you can have a nice hot bun with a little summer sausage. The peaches are still good, and there'll be oatmeal raisin cookies if I git to my bakin' after hangin' out the wash."

"Oh, Ella," Frieda laughed. "You're going to spoil us to death."

Jensine couldn't help but give Ella a hug as she left for the day. There was no doubt in her mind Ella was worth every penny of her wages and more.

7

FEELING LIKE HOME

Monday morning, Jensine, Frieda, and Moveta joined Lake Valley's six other teachers in the high school library. Black grade books and blue weekly lesson planners were neatly stacked in two piles in the middle of the big study table.

At exactly 7:00 A.M., Mr. Kruse began. He introduced himself, first telling them he was a native of North Dakota and this would be his fourth year at Lake Valley. Jensine was surprised to learn he was also the high school history and civics teacher and coached both the football and basketball team. She couldn't help noticing his wife seemed nervous, uncomfortable, and totally preoccupied with the fountain pen in her hands while he talked. Louella Kruse didn't raise her head to look at her husband until he had finished and nodded at her to begin the staff introductions. Then she merely said, "Louella Kruse...library and English," and looked to three older women, Marjorie Linn, Geraldine Carlson, and Florena Lindstrom, who were seated together to her left. "Old maids who've been sittin' on the shelf for quite a spell," Peder Neilsen would have said. Jensine had already noticed their sturdy black shoes, not much like her fashionable, soft leather pumps, which buttoned across the instep. They seemed friendly enough, though. In fact, Miss Linn, the first- and second- grade teacher, seemed to sense Jensine's nervousness when it was her turn to speak and reached over to squeeze her arm in support.

There wasn't much to tell, but it seemed all eyes were on her far too long. Jensine could feel her ears burn and the red creep up her neck. Across the table, Moveta leaned forward and whispered, "Jensine, you're blushing." Jensine stretched her foot under the table to nudge her, thinking what Moveta really deserved was a good swift kick.

The distinguished-looking man with the sandy hair and glasses sitting next to Frieda was Maurice Sheldon. Unlike the other two men, who were in rolled shirt sleeves in anticipation of a hot August day, Maurice was dapper in his gray summer suit, soft shirt, and bow tie. He was the music teacher and orchestra director and gave lessons, not only at Lake Valley but at neighboring Round Lake as well. Frieda told Jensine later he also played the piano in an area orchestra which occasionally played at the Lake Valley dance hall.

Clarence Voss, the manual training instructor, was the last to introduce himself. Jensine thought he was probably in his early forties and certainly nothing to write home about. He was quite bald except for a few long strands of greasy hair, which he had elaborately combed across the top of his head. And if his wrinkled shirt and pants were any indication, he had been working in his shop for a week already. Voss said he had been at Lake Valley longer than he wanted to remember. He seemed bored, almost to the point of rudeness, as Mr. Kruse went over the instructions he had outlined on the portable blackboard.

With a pointer, Mr. Kruse went down the list, adding brief comments along the way. Most of it Jensine had already heard from Frieda. Teachers were expected to be in their rooms at 7:00 in the morning and stay until 5:00 P.M. He explained the farmers put in long days, and they expected the teachers to do the same. All teachers had lunch and recess duty and were to go outside with the students as soon as they had eaten lunch. The men could smoke only in the boiler room of the school basement. Teachers were to handle their own discipline problems, but difficult students could be sent to the office. Frieda told Jensine later she should be very careful about sending any student to the office because Mr. Kruse would consider it an indication she couldn't handle her classroom. He had dismissed last year's seventh- and eighth-grade teacher for that very reason.

"Start out really strict," Frieda advised. "You can always lighten up later when you see what kind of students you have."

Mr. Kruse went on to suggest they attend Sunday services at the school if they were around, and their attendance at monthly community club was expected. In fact, the teachers would be serving lunch at one meeting during the year. Then he frowned and hesitated before continuing. "Last year, a few of you decided you were too busy to attend football and basketball games, so we were a little short on supervision, and the same people had to sell tickets at every game. The school board started asking where you were."

Mr. Kruse seemed to be looking directly at the manual training teacher, and Jensine couldn't help but think he was the guilty one. Mr. Voss tipped his chair back and met the superintendent's look with a cold stare. His dislike for Mr. Kruse was obvious and apparently something of which the other teachers were well aware. Frieda cleared her throat, and Mr. Sheldon reached to the center of the table for a grade book and thumbed through the empty pages as if he had never seen one before.

Clarence Voss dropped his chair to the floor with enough force to practically break the legs. "If that's it, I don't know about the rest of you, but I've got work to do before next Monday." He pushed his chair back, grabbed a grade book, and left the library. Across the table, Moveta raised her eyebrows until they almost completely disappeared under her bangs.

Jensine was uncomfortable for Mr. Kruse. In her estimation, the manual training teacher was not just plain rude, but arrogant as well. She felt sorry for Moveta who had to teach right across the hall from him and suddenly realized Mrs. Kruse's nervous behavior probably had a lot to do with Clarence Voss. But Mr. Kruse seemed calm as he motioned to the piles of grade books and planners on the table. "Take what you need. The rest of the supplies are in the closet across from Florena's room. Remember, they need to last the year." He turned and started erasing the board. The rest took this as dismissal and gathered their things to leave the room. Jensine noticed Louella Kruse stayed to put a comforting hand on her husband's arm.

Once down the hallway, Frieda threw up her hands in exasperation, "I am so sick and tired of that man I could scream. Mr. Kruse should can him, but Voss is so tight with a bunch of farmers out here, it would never happen. Let me give you a little advice, Jensine and Moveta, don't tell that man anything!"

"Jeepers!" Moveta exclaimed. "There were sparks flying there. What's the dope, Frieda?"

"I couldn't tell you in a month of Sundays, so I won't even start. You'll find out for yourselves soon enough. Come on, let's get our supplies."

That was just fine with Jensine. As far as she was concerned, Clarence Voss was a real drip, and she planned to stay as far away from him as possible.

The supply closet was small but filled to the top shelf with theme and construction paper, chalk, erasers, huge jars of paste, scissors, bottles of ink and paints. There wasn't enough room for all of them in the closet, so Jensine waited outside the door with Marjorie Linn while Frieda and Moveta went into the closet.

"If I were you, I'd take a little extra of everything, Jensine. Everybody else does. They hoard it in their rooms, so they don't run out. Like Florena, I swear she's in the supply closet every day. She's got enough to last until she retires and well into her eternal life, but it doesn't stop her from taking a little more. Honestly, that old crab apple!" Marjorie shook her head and laughed. "You just notice her book closet sometime. It's so full of supplies, she has to store her texts on the cloak hall shelves." Jensine spent the rest of the morning putting away supplies and setting out textbooks. The arithmetic books were a bit worn, but the readers and history books were fairly new and in good shape. She thought it was a good sign. Lake Valley must care about the education of its young people.

The Ehrenbergs brought over lunch at noon in a covered dishpan. On a table in the home economics room, Ella untied a white dish-towel to reveal fresh buns, oatmeal cookies, and ripe peaches while Emil unscrewed the lid of a large Mason jar of iced sun tea. Jensine couldn't remember when she had enjoyed such a delicious lunch in such good company. Lake Valley was starting to feel like home.

8

JOHNNY ATZEN

It was barely 6:00 A.M. when Ella hollered up the stairs that breakfast was on, but Jensine had already been up for a good hour. She bathed the night before, knowing Moveta always waited until the last possible minute and took her time and then some in the bathroom. The day promised to be very warm. "It's gonna be a hot one," Emil had warned as he and Jensine left the school the evening before. Even though she knew she was as ready as any teacher could be for the first day, she had walked over one last time to check her lesson plans. Dr. Wright, her methods professor at Mankato State, always stressed nothing took the place of good planning.

After her evening bath, she had laid out her short-sleeved crème silk. It seemed a good choice, simple but fashionable with its dropped waist and open collar, and Jensine knew it flattered her thin frame. Her matching silk summer stockings and buttoned pumps would both be uncomfortable before the end of the day, but she was more than willing to forego comfort for any measure of confidence gained by fashion. As Kirsten often said, "If you look good, you feel good." Of course, Jensine understood this was her sister's way of rationalizing her shopping sprees, but there were times when she thought there was some real truth to Kirsten's way of thinking.

"You look real pretty, Jensine," Ella smiled approvingly as Jensine took her place at the table. "Those eighth-grade boys are gonna be head over heels. I made a big breakfast for you girls, this being the first day and all. Thought some scrambled eggs and bacon might hit the spot."

Jensine's stomach was churning at the thought of any breakfast, to say nothing of the thresher's meal Ella was setting on the table. "I think I'll just have a peach, Ella. My stomach's a little nervous."

"Oh, you poor thing. Then a good hearty breakfast is just what you need. It'll settle it right down."

Moveta saved the day by sliding into a chair and promptly loading up her plate. "Ella, this looks wonderful! Where's Frieda? She wasn't upstairs."

"Oh, she's been up and gone since before 6:00. She's an early bird, that Frieda. Help yourself, Moveta. No sense it goin' to waste. I'll put some bread on the toastin' rack and then sit down and have a bite with you." Ella sat down with a soft sigh. She looked tired but smiled and said without complaining, "Mondays are always busy, what with beds to change, wash to hang out, rooms to clean, and then Emil comin' at 11:30 to help me bring over the noon lunch."

"Well, rest your dogs a bit after we go," Moveta encouraged.

Ella laughed and shook her head. "I don't know about you young girls and your way of sayin' things."

Moveta didn't seem in any particular hurry, but Jensine was anxious to start out for the school. It would be embarrassing to be the last teachers to arrive, especially when they lived right next door, and Jensine sensed Mr. Kruse kept a close eye on things like that. Finally, she couldn't wait any longer. "Moveta, I think I'm going to head over."

"Just a second. I'll just finish this last piece of toast and be right with you." She pushed her chair back and walked around the table to give Ella a quick hug. "Wish us luck, Ella. See you for lunch." As they walked across the dry lawn to the school, Jensine couldn't help wishing she were as cheerful and relaxed as Moveta seemed to be.

Mr. Kruse looked up and smiled in greeting as they passed his office. As they turned the corner, Moveta whispered, "I could swear he looked at the clock when we walked by. I think I'll use the side door from now on."

Jensine had to laugh. "Oh, Moveta, you're just imagining things." She headed up the stairs to unlock the door to her room. It was already stuffy, but before she could start opening the windows, Emil appeared out of nowhere.

"I'll git those for you, Miss Neilsen. Some of 'em are a little cranky, if you know what I mean. Might have to set an old book under a couple to keep 'em open." He slid the windows up easily, and only one needed propping. "You git a nice breeze from the west on this side of the building." Emil turned back to Jensine with a smile. He looked tired, and as he hurried out of the room, she suddenly realized this was a big day for him, too.

Jensine surveyed her room with pride. She had found a folded flag in the book cupboard, and Emil cheerfully put up a bracket to hang it off to the side of the front blackboard. And Louella Kruse was generous enough to share a large picture of George Washington from a crowded library wall. Red, yellow, and gold construction paper leaves formed a border around the large side bulletin board and divided it in the middle so one side could be used for seventh grade and the other for eighth. Jensine had decided to start the year with an inspirational quotation, something that would encourage her students to pursue lofty goals. It had taken her the good part of one afternoon to cut out the black letters for Longfellow's words, "And leave behind us footprints in the sands of time." It looked nice, boldly stretched across the top of the board, but she wondered if the meaning would be lost on her young students.

On the front blackboard, Jensine had written her name and 'Welcome Students.' It bothered her that Mr. Kruse hadn't given her a class list of her students, so she could practice pronouncing their names. Jensine knew from past experience it could prevent embarrassment, both for her and the students. Frieda told her, however, it made sense to wait until the first day to make a class list, especially in grades seven through twelve, because you never knew who would be returning the next year.

"Do that many students move?" Jensine asked.

"No, but lots of students still drop out, Jensine. The boys stay home to help with the farm work, and the girls get pregnant and marry early. Did you notice the pictures hanging in the library?

The graduating classes are small, but they don't start out that way. It seems like it begins at the end of eighth grade. A couple drop out each year. It's sad because the kids are smart here." There were forty desks in Jensine's room. She wondered how many of them would be empty.

Jensine had posted the daily schedule for both seventh and eighth grades on the bulletin board under the quotation. Of course, they would begin each day with the Pledge of Allegiance, and then seventh-graders would have arithmetic while the eighth grade read the assigned story from their literature book. Jensine was responsible for reading, spelling, penmanship, arithmetic, geography, and history, along with music or art, whichever one suited her interest. She knew it wouldn't be music because, as her father said, some people couldn't carry a tune in a bushel basket, and she was one of them. But she liked art and was good at it. It would be a good way to end the day. The boys and girls in both grades would leave her room twice a week to take manual training and home economics. Then, as Frieda had told her, she would go to the high school assembly to supervise the study hall. Jensine wasn't looking forward to that.

Frieda said students would begin arriving about 8:30 A.M., so Jensine went to stand by her door, planning to welcome each of them as they arrived. She hoped her smile wouldn't seem too stiff or that they could hear her heart pounding.

As she waited, Jensine's mind wandered back to her first day of country school and how frightened she had been. Her mother had walked with her up to the next farm where she met two little German girls, who didn't speak English either, and together they trudged the rest of the way, the two sisters holding hands and Jensine following behind.

The teacher quickly made them understand that foreign talk, especially German, just wouldn't do in her school. Jensine learned English from hearing other pupils and copying sentences and numbers from the book with the paper letters and numbers Miss Johnson put on her desk. She also had a small slate for numbers and beginning arithmetic. When the teacher worked with the older students, there was plenty of time to practice her letters and numbers and browse the small library, which was really nothing more than two shelves with a hundred or so books. Sometimes, one of the older girls would take Jensine into the cloakroom and help her with reading. Later, when she was in seventh and eighth grade, it was her turn to help the first- and second-graders. She also helped her mother learn the new language, but while Johanne learned to read English quickly, writing and speaking without her Danish accent were frustratingly difficult for her.

Jensine was still musing about the past when she heard the big double doors opening below and the chatter of voices. Although a few of her prospective students were obviously shy, most answered her greeting with a smile as they passed her to enter the classroom. The high school students also seemed friendly, but Jensine couldn't help being aware of their curious glances as they walked past on their way to assembly. She didn't doubt that by nightfall, every farmer and his wife in LakeValley would know all about the new seventh- and eighth-grade teacher.

The half-hour passed quickly, and a quick glance at the Elgin wrist watch her parents had given her as a graduation present showed only four minutes remaining until the first bell. Jensine closed the door and looked in dismay. Not only were all forty desks filled, but four students, all of them girls, remained standing at the back of the room, which had suddenly become very quiet except for three boys seated in the back who continued whispering. Actually, all of the boys were crowded into the back desks. That would change immediately, beginning with three young men who would quickly find themselves seated as near her desk as she could manage. Feeling weak in the knees, she walked to the front to face her students.

"When I close the door, all talking *and* whispering stops immediately." One of the noisy boys had the good sense to turn a little red, but the other two simply grinned and leaned back in their desks, giving Jensine the eye. She continued, "Will the student in the first row nearest the door please find Mr. Ehrenberg and tell him we need four more desks. The rest of you, please take out your pencils and sign your first and last names on the lists that are being passed back for attendance."

"Hey, Karl, you got a pencil? Didn't think we'd do any writing the first day."

Jensine wasn't surprised the question came from one of the grinning boys in the back. She walked swiftly down the aisle to his desk, knowing this kind of behavior had to be nipped in the bud. During practice teaching, she had learned a good way to get a student's attention was to move closer. "What is your name, young man?"

He was really grinning now, testing her, Jensine knew. "Well, my mom calls me John, and my old man calls me Johnny. Take your pick."

"What is your last name?"

He looked around the room, encouraged by forty-three other students who were openly enjoying the situation. "Christopherson." The boys laughed and the girls giggled.

"Well, John Christopherson, I will not permit this smart behavior in my classroom, so unless you want to bring a note home to your parents the first day of school, you had better get down to business. Wipe that smile off your face!"

"Yes, Ma'am." John raised his hand in a quick salute, his smile still lingering. He didn't seem at all intimidated. Jensine stared directly into the bluest eyes she had ever seen, and then returned to the front of the room, and said, "Please finish writing your names, and don't forget to include the students who are waiting for desks."

As the students wrote their names and passed on the lists, her eyes were drawn to a tall girl standing at the back who looked as if her most devout wish would be answered if the floor simply opened up and swallowed her. She was raw-boned, her long, tanned arms and chapped hands hanging out of her feed-sack dress. Jensine was sure about the dress because her father had brought home sacks of dairy feed in the same flowered print. The girl's face was windburned, except for the part that had obviously been covered with a kerchief when she worked in the field. Jensine felt a rush of sympathy for the plain, self-conscious student.

Emil quickly appeared with two desks in tow, promising two more as soon as he could bring them over from another classroom. The room was quiet as Jensine gathered up the lists and prepared to go over the names of her students. As she called the name of each student, she looked up to place the name with a face. When she came to John Christopherson, he raised his hand and grinned. This time the rest of the students didn't laugh; there were just a few snickers and suppressed giggles, and Jensine went on.

"Ethel...." She paused, feeling suddenly dry-mouthed. The last name was Fuchs. She had never heard of such a name in her whole life. How in the world should she pronounce it? There was a double consonant, but only a vowel on one side of it, so the *u* should be short. What about the *ch*? Hard or soft? She looked up, thinking that maybe Ethel would help her out of her dilemma, but she was not to be saved. Clearly, from the girl's stricken look, Ethel was the student in the feed sack dress. The room had become suspiciously quiet, and Jensine knew at once that this was her test. She cleared her throat.

"Ethel, how do you pronounce your last name?" Maybe it was because Ethel's reply was so quiet, nearly inarticulate—whatever the reason, Jensine could have sworn that Ethel said "Fucks." She could feel herself perspiring, something she never did. She hadn't even tried Mum, the new deodorant Kirsten and some of the girls in the dorm raved about. "Pardon?" Surely she had heard incorrectly.

"Fucks, Miss Neilsen. She said Fucks," the voice of John Christopherson rang out. The boys roared, and Ethel sat in paralyzed embarrassment. Never had Jensine been so tempted to march back and twist an ear as she was at that moment. Nothing in her practice teaching had prepared her for this unspeakable situation on the first day of school.

"Miss Neilsen." A dark-haired girl sitting near the front raised her hand. "Ethel's last name is said like *few*. Then just add a *ks*." Then she turned and looked at John. "There was no call for that, John *Christopherson*, and you know it."

Somehow, Jensine made it through the next two hours. She scrapped her plan to engage the students in an open discussion of what they would like to learn that year. "Wouldn't Johnny Christopherson have a heyday with that?" she thought. Instead she assigned a long division review assignment and doubled the number of problems she had originally planned to have them do. When they finished the review, Jensine told both grades to get out their readers, read the first story, and answer all of the questions at the end…in complete sentences. At first no one moved, but when she raised her voice and said "Now!" in no uncertain terms, even the boys scrambled for their books.

It wasn't at all what Jensine had planned for the first day of school. But her classroom was quiet… except for the sound of scratching pencils and rustling papers as her students tackled the fifty problems. To assign that many long division problems was a horrid, almost cruel thing to do to any class, but she needed time to gather her wits. Jensine sensed the girls were on her side. Johnny Christopherson had gone too far by embarrassing not just Ethel, but them, too. When the class left for a short recess and bathroom break, a thin girl with carrot-red hair stayed behind with some interesting news.

"Miss Neilsen, don't say I told you, but there isn't any John Christopherson in this class. He was just teasing. His name's Johnny Atzen."

At noon, Jensine could hardly wait to get to Moveta's room. Ella and Emil were already there covering one of the tables with a red-checkered picnic cloth. Throwing decorum to the winds, she kicked off her tight shoes and settled down to enjoy buns, hot from the oven, spread with ham salad, and ponder how she would deal with Johnny Atzen.

9

SERENDIPITY

The afternoon settled in nicely as Jensine made short homework assignments in each subject and collected the math review that had kept the students busy throughout the morning...except for Johnny Atzen, who flew through the problems, and then looked around as if to see what other trouble he could cause before getting out his reader. Jensine stopped to look over his shoulder several times while he was working and once asked if he had proven any of his answers. "You mean multiply 'em all out?" he asked, groaning loud enough to attract the attention of his classmates. "Why would I want to do that, Miss Neilsen? I know they're right."

"Well...we'll soon see, won't we?" she answered, sounding vengeful and tight-lipped even to herself.

After stacking the papers, Jensine went on to the oral reading she planned to have her students do the first day. It would be a welcome break from the long morning of seat work and give her a good assessment of their skill and confidence levels. Most seemed eager to volunteer, especially Johnny Atzen, whose hand shot up immediately. He read with a real flair for expression, Jensine noted, and played to his audience of classmates like an experienced performer. Ethel Fuchs did not raise her hand to read, and Jensine didn't call on her. She needed time to think of a way to gain the girl's trust and, above all, protect her from any further embarrassment. For now, it seemed best just to let Ethel be a quiet observer.

Johnny Atzen and most of the boys came back from recess red-faced and sweaty from playing Pump, Pump, Pull Away. "If we ever needed a nice breeze from the west, it's now," Jensine thought in dismay, struggling not to wrinkle her nose at the noticeable odor. She was about to hand out drawing paper when Johnny's hand shot up.

"Yes, Johnny?"

"You know, Miss Neilsen, that sayin' you got on the board's pretty stupid. I mean…how can you leave footprints in sand? They wouldn't stay cuz they'd wash away, wouldn't they?"

A boy in bib overalls across the aisle spoke up quickly, "Oh, shut up, John! Your big mouth already got us fifty long division problems."

"No, that's all right, Roger," Jensine interjected. "Let's talk about what Johnny said. What do the rest of you think?" The students looked surprised and not a hand went up. Jensine decided to wait, and finally a girl sitting in front of Ethel raised her hand hesitantly.

"Well, I know Longfellow is a famous poet, Miss Neilsen, and I don't think he meant for us to take it literally."

"Oh, nice big word, Delores," Roger scoffed.

Delores turned as red as her hair. "Well, I just think he's trying to say we should live our lives so we'll be remembered, that's all."

"Who doesn't know that, De*lores*?" Johnny interrupted, rudely emphasizing the second syllable of her name. "I still don't think it makes sense. He could've come up with a better way of sayin' it."

"Well, let's vote," Jensine suggested. "How many agree with Johnny? Raise your hands." Every boy put up a hand in support, but there were six more girls in the room, and their vote carried. Johnny was obviously disappointed.

"What about you, Miss Neilsen?" he asked, definitely not willing to give up his argument. "What do you think? 'Course you put it up there, so you probably like it."

"I think both you and Delores make good points." Then, she looked directly at Johnny and asked, "How would you rewrite Longfellow's line, Johnny?"

"I don't know offhand, but I'd come up with somethin' better than that."

"Oh, give it up, John!" Roger grumbled, "I'm sick of doin' problems."

"Be sure to let us know when you come up with just the right words," Jensine encouraged in smug amusement.

Jensine knew her students were as glad as she was when the closing bell rang at 4:00. The room was hot and stuffy, and a definite back-to-school lethargy had set in, but as they filed past her at the door, every girl except for Ethel left with a friendly "Good night, Miss Neilsen." In a spontaneous gesture, Jensine reached out and touched the quiet girl's arm. "Have a good evening, Ethel. See you tomorrow. Hope it's not quite so warm." Ethel didn't raise her eyes or respond, but Jensine was sure she saw a brief smile touch her lips. It was a start. Jensine noticed most of the eighth-grade boys lagged behind and left together with Johnny Atzen in their midst. Clearly, he was their leader. They passed her to head down the stairs, then looked back and grinned as if they shared some secret. She was sure she knew what it was and was tempted to let them know she was in on their little joke, but there was a better time for that revelation.

"Boys, get a move on. You don't want to miss the bus."

As they thumped down the stairs, Jensine heard one of them mutter, "What a crab!"

It was 5:30 by the time Jensine finished correcting papers and recording the scores in her grade book. She was delighted to note Johnny "Christopherson" had forgotten his little disguise at least once during the day and written his real name on his mathematics paper. It gave her a splendid idea for squelching his mischief once and for all. "Just wait until tomorrow, John *Christopherson*, you little smarty pants!"

As Jensine turned back from closing the windows and raising the shades, she was startled to see Clarence Voss standing just inside the door.

"Just stopped by to see how things went your first day."

Jensine didn't think for one moment he had just stopped by. There had to be some other reason he climbed two flights of stairs at the end of a hot day. As he moved down the row between the desks towards her, she couldn't help but notice his wet armpits and the sour smell of perspiration. "Actually, quite well, I think, this being the first day and all."

"Well, just thought I'd tell you there's a big wedding party at the Log Cabin Saturday night. If you're interested and like dancin', I could pick you up. I just live out south of here."

As far as Jensine was concerned, hell would freeze over before she went anywhere with Clarence Voss, even if he decided to wash his hair and underarms. She thought of what Kirsten had said when one of the homely Nelson boys from Blooming Prairie had asked her out, "Pass on this one, Jens!" Clarence Voss was definitely a pass, but her instincts told her he needed to be handled carefully. Just her brief hesitation was enough for him to sarcastically add, "Of course, you probably go for the new swing stuff instead of the old time polkas and schottisches folks out Lake Valley way like to jig to."

"You know, Clarence, thanks for asking, but I think I'd better keep my nose to the grindstone for right now. Maybe later in the year when I'm not quite so busy." Jensine could have bitten her tongue. Why had she given him any hope when she knew perfectly well she would never accept an invitation from him?

"Well, think on it," he said. "You can always change your mind. Course, for all I know you're carryin' a torch for someone back home." He turned to go and then, glancing at the windows, remarked "You'd better pull that one shade even with the others or old Kruse will be on your tail." He gave a derisive snort and strolled out of the room.

What an unpleasant man! Surely Mr. Kruse didn't spend his time checking to see if the window shades were evenly drawn. Jensine shook her head in disbelief as she massaged the back of her tired neck and began to tidy up her desk. She felt literally drained. Tomorrow would be a full day of lessons, and Wednesday she would have her first high school study hall supervision. Just the thought of it made her nervous. As she closed her door, she noticed Frieda was just locking her door.

"Jensine, hold up. I'll walk back to the teacherage with you. Should we check to see if Moveta is still in her room?"

Jensine laughed, "Not a chance, Frieda. I saw her come around the building from the side door and head for the teacherage an hour ago, when I was at the window emptying out the pencil sharpener. She told me last night she didn't plan on burning any midnight oil on this job."

"Between you and me, Jensine, putting in long hours pretty much comes with the job, but to each his own, I guess."

"Say, Frieda, do you by chance know Johnny Atzen?"

"Doesn't everybody? What's our dear little Johnny up to now?"

After Jensine explained the events of the day, Frieda threw up her hands, shook her head, and chuckled, "That's Johnny Atzen, all right. But really, Jensine, he's a good kid and smart, too. I think part of his problem is his older brother Leslie was killed in a horrible farm accident two years ago. The horse he was riding must have spooked because it threw him, and somehow his foot got caught in the stirrup. Anyway, it dragged him across the whole section and right up into the barnyard where Mr. Atzen and Johnny were doing chores. I guess the body was barely recognizable...Well, Johnny's been pretty much a handful ever since. I guess you can understand his parents doting on him, but I do know that they'll support you all the way. I think they expect you to be strict with Johnny." Frieda paused, "Have you decided how you're going to handle his little charade?"

"I think so, Frieda. Actually Johnny cooked his own goose. I can hardly wait to pass back papers tomorrow."

As they walked back to the teacherage, Jensine felt a sudden sense of contentment. The dreaded first day was over, and she had survived. The late afternoon sun was pleasantly warm, but a cool breeze from the northwest bespoke of the crisp autumn days ahead, her favorite time of the year. Frieda, Moveta, and the Ehrenbergs were already dear to her. Perhaps she had found a bit of serendipity in this unlikely place.

Ella served a hearty goulash of homemade egg noodles, fresh tomatoes, and tender chunks of beef for supper, and there was warm apple crisp topped with whipped cream for dessert. "I just picked a few big Wealthys off the tree by the side of our house. Thought they'd make a nice tart crisp. I know Emil likes it that way. Hope it's not too sour for you girls."

"Ella, it's out of this world!" said Frieda.

Ella beamed at Frieda's compliment and went to get the pan. "There's more. Might as well have a second helping. It don't make good leftovers."

Moveta didn't eat with her usual gusto. She left goulash on her plate and passed on the apple crisp altogether. Jensine was fairly sure she knew why. She had noticed an empty box of chocolate-covered cherries and several small foil wrappers in the bathroom wastebasket when she washed up for supper, and was pretty sure they hadn't been there in the morning. To Ella, preparing and serving food was a simple act of love, and she was obviously hurt by Moveta's lack of appetite. "Maybe I shouldn't have fixed goulash. I know some folks don't care for it. You girls have to tell me what you like now, and I'll be sure to fix it."

"Oh, Ella, you know I could eat the whole blame thing by myself, but I spoiled my appetite by having a couple of chocolates when I got home. Put it in the warming oven and I'll have some later." Then Moveta excused herself quickly and ran up the stairs. Jensine heard the bathroom door shut. After she and Frieda helped Ella clear the table, she shooed them out of the kitchen.

"Don't you be doin' my job now. Sit on the front porch a bit, and I'll bring you a cup of hot tea."

The early evening was quiet except for a cicada finishing its afternoon buzzing concert and a cow blatting for a calf in some distant pasture.

"Oh, I forgot to tell you, Frieda," Jensine said as she remembered Clarence Voss's invitation. You're not going to believe this, but Voss asked to take me to the dance Saturday night. Isn't that a hoot!"

"Oh gad! I hope you had the good sense to say no. That man's nothing but trouble!"

"I told him I had to keep my nose to the grindstone for a while."

"Good!" Frieda stopped rocking and then gave Jensine a rueful smile. "Darn, though, I thought maybe the three of us could go together, so you could check out the Log Cabin, but it won't do to have Voss see us. Oh, well, we'll drive down to Arnold's Park instead."

"What's that?"

"It's a big amusement park by Lake Okoboji—roller coasters, the whole bit. There's also a swanky ballroom, no old-time stuff. A fellow I went to high school with, Will Mosher, has an orchestra, and it plays there sometimes, maybe even this weekend."

"Sounds fun."

"Well, I've still got some papers to correct, and then I'm ready to hit the sack. I'm pooped. How about you?" Then Frieda laughed, "Remember, you've got Johnny Atzen to deal with tomorrow. You'll need all the rest you can get."

After her bath, Jensine knocked lightly on Moveta's door. "Good night, Moveta." There was no answer. She decided to write a letter home before turning in. Her family would welcome any news from faraway Lake Valley.

10
STUDY HALL

In the morning Ella's leftover goulash was gone and the Dutch oven left soaking in the sink. "Moveta must have gotten hungry in the night. Bless her heart," Ella clucked as she poured hot coffee for Frieda and Jensine. "Sometimes food tastes better a little later on, and like she said, she spoiled her appetite with those chocolates she ate. I think I'll put a nice pot roast in the oven for tonight. Does that sound good to you girls?"

"Oh, Ella, it's going to be hot again today. You don't want to heat up the kitchen. Just a slice of your wonderful bread and some salad would be plenty," Frieda suggested just as Moveta slid into a chair and reached for the warm toast.

"For sure, Ella. I'm still full from my midnight raid on your goulash."

Ella patted Moveta's shoulder, obviously pleased she had liked her goulash after all. Before returning the pot to a small back burner, she poured coffee into the stained cup which always rested on top of the warming oven and then sat down beside Moveta, sighing as she stirred cream and two heaping spoons of sugar into her coffee.

"Don't know why it has to stay so warm. Emil says it's a cooker over to the school on these days, too."

Jensine wished Ella would forget about the pot roast for supper. She seemed worn out. Frieda must have had the same thought.

"Ella, please, just fix a cold salad for tonight. Go home early and rest."

"Oh, you girls are going to spoil me. It's just my arthritis acting up. I'll be fine once I get goin'. Like Emil says, we're both gettin' old."

"Well, I've got to get going if I intend to have that lab set up for my chemistry class." Frieda pushed her glasses up on her nose and took one last sip of coffee.

"Wait, Frieda, I'll walk over with you. I can use the extra time to correct a few papers," Jensine said.

Moveta reached for another piece of toast and spread a thick layer of peach marmalade before glancing up. "You girls go right ahead. Ella needs company, and I'll just sneak in the side door."

Jensine's room was already warm and stuffy, and she was glad she had worn her light gingham. As she pushed up the windows and pulled the shades, she noticed Emil had been hard at work. The blackboards had been wiped down and even the erasers dusted. Frieda said Emil and Ella were both in their seventies and had farmed south of Lake Valley for nearly fifty years before their son took over the home place. Their energy was amazing, Jensine thought.

It seemed she barely had time to check the day's lessons and correct a few remaining arithmetic papers before the halls started to fill with students. Jensine went to stand by her door. She particularly wanted to greet Ethel. It seemed important to get the day started right for this shy student. She got curious stares and some downright open grins from the high school boys as they walked by on their way to the assembly. It seemed Johnny Atzen's admirers extended well beyond the eighth grade. He arrived with his buddies just before the bell rang and slid into his seat with a grin. Ethel's desk remained empty. Jensine felt sick. Had she lost Ethel before the year even began?

"I believe just Ethel is absent today," she began.

"She's probably pickin' rocks, Miss Neilsen. Old man Fuchs is plowin' under his timothy, and he's got the kids walkin' behind, throwin' rocks in the wagon or sliding 'em on the stone boat." Of course it was Johnny Atzen who blurted out this information. "You know they've got seventeen kids in their family, don't you, Miss Neilsen. My dad says Ida Fuchs pops one out every year."

Jensine was literally aghast. "Johnny, that was a totally inappropriate comment!" But even as she scolded, she thought of her own father who felt strongly the barn and field were no place for his daughters and wife. Then, refocusing on her class, she said, "We need a volunteer to write down Ethel's assignments for the day, so who would like to..." The words weren't out of her mouth before Johnny's hand shot up.

"I'll do it, Miss Neilsen."

Somehow, this spontaneous act of kindness seemed out of character for Johnny Atzen. What did he have up his sleeve?

"Thank you, Johnny. Perhaps just place the assignments on her desk at the end of the day."

Jensine felt a huge sense of relief as she plunged into the lessons of the day. Frieda was right about Lake Valley students being bright and eager to learn. They seemed anxious to get their corrected papers back, even Johnny. When she passed back their arithmetic papers at the end of the day, Johnny looked perplexed when his wasn't returned. He furiously waved his arm to get her attention, and she purposely avoided looking at him. Finally, he couldn't contain himself any longer.

"Miss. Neilsen, I didn't get my paper back."

Here was her golden opportunity to put Johnny Atzen in his place once and for all. "I don't believe you handed one in, Johnny. I know I didn't see yours when I corrected them last night. There was a paper for a Johnny Atzen, but I threw it in the wastebasket because obviously there's no Johnny Atzen in the class. Too bad, too, it was a perfect paper." The room was suddenly dead quiet, and all eyes locked on Johnny.

"She's gotcha, Atzen!" one of Johnny's cohorts hollered, and the class erupted in laughter. Jensine actually felt a little sorry for Johnny. Blotches of red moved up his neck, and he seemed to literally shrink before her eyes.

"But..." he managed to stutter, "but..."

"It's almost time for dismissal, students. Don't forget to do your homework assignment." At the bell, the students filed out, still laughing, all except Johnny Atzen, that is. He made a pretense of straightening up the inside of his desk until everyone was gone and then came to stand by Jensine's desk.

"I'm sorry, Miss, Neilsen. I was just kidding. I didn't mean anything bad. I could do my paper over to get credit."

"Johnny, you and I aren't off to a very good start."

"I suppose you're gonna tell my folks."

"No, I think this is just between you and me. You need to redo your paper, but as to credit, I don't think so."

Blue eyes stared back at her. "That's okay, Miss Neilsen, I don't deserve a grade."

"Well, I need to get busy here."

"I gotta get home to do chores, too. Say, Miss Neilsen, I could help Ethel with her makeup tomorrow. Then she wouldn't get so far behind in her work. I'm really pretty good at math." He fidgeted a bit, and then said, "Well, see you tomorrow."

Later, Frieda poked her head in the door and asked, "How did it go with little Johnny?"

"I think Johnny Atzen and I are going to get along just fine, Frieda…just fine." Jensine couldn't help thinking that except for Ethel's absence, the day had been an overwhelming success. Now, if she could just get through her first high school assembly the next day, life would be good.

Jensine and Frieda could smell Ella's pot roast the minute they opened the front door to the teacherage. "Supper's almost ready, girls. If you want to freshen up a bit, I'll mash the potatoes while you're doin' that and then you can sit down to a nice hot meal. Moveta's up in her room, so give her door a knock."

Ella joined them at the table with a cup of coffee. After dishes, she usually went home to eat with Emil, and something told Jensine she probably made another big meal for him. Ella looked tired, but she smiled cheerfully. "I'm gonna fry up a mess of bullheads when I get home. One of my boys caught a big stringer of 'em over at Plum Slough."

Jensine gagged at the thought. Her mother wouldn't let a bullhead near the house, let alone think of eating one. "Might as well eat mud as eat a bullhead," Johanne always said. But then, Jensine thought, Ella Ehrenberg's bullheads were probably as good as her pot roast.

⁕

Ethel was back on Wednesday wearing the same feed-sack dress she had worn the first day of school. And if possible, her face was sunburned even a deeper red. She seemed anxious to get caught up with the work she had missed, and true to his word, Johnny Atzen not only made sure she had the class assignments, but he also skipped his lunch recess time to help Ethel with her math. Jensine felt regretful for having judged him so quickly.

Jensine's first high school study hall was right after lunch, so she ate quickly and left her noon recess supervision early in order to be in the assembly before any of the students arrived. Except for the gymnasium, it was easily the largest room in the school. A battered desk on a raised podium faced eight long rows of desks, enough for a hundred or so students. Jensine knew freshmen were assigned to rows on the left and seniors to the right. Frieda said their seats had been alphabetically assigned the first day, and she should just use the chart on the desk to check attendance. She waited by the door until the second bell rang and then stepped up to the desk. She remembered Frieda's advice about being strict, at least to begin with.

There were only juniors and seniors in the study hall, and they didn't seem to pay any attention to the fact the second bell had rung. Most were still out of their seats laughing and talking with other students. Jensine cleared her throat and when the noise continued, sharply tapped the desk bell. To her relief, they slid into their seats.

"This *will* be a study hall, students, so get out your books and begin your work." There were some heavy groans, but most pulled out their books.

"What if you don't have anything to do, teacher?" Jensine looked quickly to the back of the assembly and the huge young man who could barely fit into his desk. He was one of the few students wearing a tie, albeit an ugly one, and he didn't look about to get busy,

59

now or anytime soon. His eyes opened in surprise as she quickly walked between the rows to his seat. How satisfying it would be to give that frightful tie a good hard jerk!

"Then find something and right now! And please do not call me 'teacher.' I have a name."

"Yeah, Duane, find something, you big tub of lard." This unkind remark was delivered along with a solid punch from another student across the aisle.

"Young men, that will be quite enough!" Jensine could feel her underarms getting wet. Good lord! Was perspiring a built-in part of teaching?

"Oh, come on, Duane and Harold. Stop being so stupid. She's just doing her job."

Jensine turned to face the pretty girl who had come to her defense. It wasn't she didn't appreciate it, but she knew it was important for her to get control of the assembly on her own. Otherwise, it would be a very long year.

"And you are?"

"Betty Kramer."

"Betty, thank you, but please tend to your own work. This is not your business."

"Sorry, Miss Neilsen," Betty apologized. "I was just trying to help."

"And I appreciate it." Jensine thought she needed to add that because Betty had turned beet red and looked on the verge of tears

Duane was still not moving. The thought crossed her mind that perhaps he was literally stuck in his desk and couldn't move. His big mouth still worked though. "Hey, my brother saw you in church with that other new teacher. You know, the home ec lady with the bad haircut and the dresses that are shorter in front than they are in back. Betty says she keeps a box of chocolate-covered cherries in her desk and snitches them during class."

"That will be just enough!" How dare he talk about a teacher that way!

"My brother says you're a real looker, and he might ask you out sometime."

"Young man, you are one step from being out on your ear!" Jensine knew this was a foolish threat because there was no possible way she could remove him from his desk, let alone drag him out of the room. Apparently, though, Duane was out of words because he shifted slightly and appeared to be groping in his desk for a book. Thank God he wasn't stuck there for eternity after all! He pulled out what looked to be a novel and thumbed through to find his place before he glanced up at Jensine and grinned.

"It's okay, Miss Neilsen. I'll be good."

Then she turned to face Harold. "And you, young man, can move forward and take the empty seat in back of Betty." There was some oohing and aahing, but Jensine decided to leave well enough alone and walked back to her desk. Duane had to be a chemistry student, so she made a mental note to ask Frieda about him. She also decided it would be a wise investment to buy some dress shields or maybe even try that new Mum. Never in her whole life had she perspired as much as she had over the past few days.

When she asked Frieda about her unruly student, Frieda just smiled and said, "Duane's a very bright young man. He could put Lake Valley on the map some day. He's just testing you, Jensine. He likes attention, and that's one way to get it. I don't think he'll give you any more trouble." Jensine didn't want to bet on it.

Early Saturday evening, Moveta, Frieda, and Jensine headed for Arnold's Park. It was everything Frieda had promised, two huge roller coasters and, of course, the usual amusement park rides—a Ferris wheel, merry-go-round, and bumper cars. But there was also an open-air roller skating rink and a ballroom. It didn't seem possible to Jensine anything as wonderful as this could be just twenty-five miles from a school, gas pump, and creamery in the middle of nowhere.

They spent most of their time in the ballroom. Frieda was disappointed Will Mosher's orchestra wasn't playing. "I wanted you to meet Will. He's really special."

Moveta seemed to have the time of her life. She was surprisingly light on her feet, a good dancer, Jensine thought. Frieda and she didn't dance nearly as often as Moveta did. Of course, they didn't accept every invitation either.

11

A Nice View

Her mother would have told her to keep her nose out of it, but Jensine was worried about Moveta. She spent more time in the bathroom than she did her bedroom; vomiting and filling up the waste basket with her little foil wrappers and empty candy boxes. Jensine finally decided to share her concern with Frieda, but her response, "That's really her business, Jensine," was so matter-of-fact Jensine was embarrassed for even bringing it up.

Ella said something, though, toward the end of September, while she and Jensine were clearing the table after the evening meal. "Too bad Moveta didn't come down for supper. The pork roast was real tender, and my lemon pie is her favorite." Then she added, "She shouldn't be takin' all those laxatives unless she's really bound up. It ain't good for her."

"I know, Ella. I feel like I should say something to her. Or you could, Ella. She loves you...maybe you...."

But Ella shook her head emphatically, "No, I wouldn't want her thinkin' I was snoopin' in the wastebasket or meddlin' in her affairs." She brushed the crumbs from the tablecloth before she said hopefully, "She'll probably get over it?"

❧

School was going well. Even Johnny Atzen had settled down. He was a bright student, eager to participate, and usually helpful. But there was something definitely conspiratorial about him, like the morning he raised his hand and said, "Roger and me are sure glad you moved us up to the front, Miss Neilsen. We can see lots better from here." Then he looked across the aisle at Roger Krueger, who was smirking broadly, and grinned. "Right, Roger?"

"Yah, Miss Neilson, it's *lots* better sittin' up here."

And as they had done since the first day of school, all the eighth-grade boys gathered around Johnny as they left for lunch and recess, laughing at something he said and then looking back at Jensine before they headed out the door and down the stairs. Jensine couldn't help but be suspicious. Johnny was up to something; she was sure of that, but she couldn't put her finger on what it might be.

Jensine was further bewildered in study hall the same day when Duane Finnern raised his hand and asked if all the boys could move up to the front of the assembly. "I think us fellows would get a lot more done if we were sitting right there in front of you, Miss Neilsen," Duane explained, arguing his case. "For one thing, the girls wouldn't be bothering us...and..."

"Duane, that is such baloney!" Betty interrupted, turning around to glare at him.

"Now, now, Betty," Duane teased smoothly, "remember our little secret."

Jensine lost her patience. She was in no mood for their bickering. Besides, she had spelling papers to correct. She struck the desk bell sharply several times and motioned the boys to come forward. "Come up here then and sit. And please get busy! You have work to do, and so do I." The boys, except Harold, who stayed in his desk behind Betty, moved quickly to their new seats, even shoving a bit as they vied for the very front ones. For rest of the hour, whenever Jensine looked up, they seemed to be leaning slightly out of their desks, staring at her, but quickly feigning curiosity in the empty blackboard behind her when she caught them looking.

After the bell ended the hour, Jensine looked up to see Betty standing by her desk. "I'm sorry, Miss Neilsen."

It was all she got out before Harold pushed her along into the hall scolding, "Jeez, Betty! What are you doin'…lettin' the cat out of the bag?"

Jensine unlocked her classroom the following Monday to find a large, unfinished board nailed across the opening in the front of her desk. It was so appallingly ugly she didn't even take off her coat before storming off to look for Emil. When she found him in the furnace room oiling mops, he looked up sheepishly. "I know what's on your mind, Jensine, but you'd best go ask Mr. Kruse about it." As Jensine went up the steps, she heard him mutter, "Darn fool kids anyway!"

"Mr. Kruse, I need to talk with you." Jensine knew her voice was trembling as she stepped into Mr. Kruse's office.

He got up from behind his desk and shut the door behind her, admonishing, "I know you're upset, Miss Neilson, but just sit down and let's talk about…" He paused, clearing his throat before adding, "…about it."

It! Jensine's temper flared. The almighty *IT*…how she disliked that word! *It* was Johanne Neilsen's euphemism for sex and anything connected with it, a word her mother couldn't bring herself to say aloud; instead… "*It* will get you into trouble…don't let any boy talk you into *it*…nice girls don't talk about *it*…" And now Mr. Kruse wanted to talk about… *it*.

"I don't want to talk about anything, especially not *it*, whatever you mean by that. And please don't give me the runaround. All I want to know is who decided that ugly board should be nailed to the front of my desk."

Mr. Kruse almost lost his balance as he leaned back in his chair, clearly surprised at her emotional outburst. He cleared his throat again and reached forward to drum his pencil on the desk before answering. "First of all, Emil will be putting up a finished board the first chance he gets." Then he continued, "Usually, desks have what they call a modesty panel…for the ladies, you know…but apparently the one in your room and the one in the assembly don't."

Jensine's hands flew to her hot cheeks. "Oh…Oh…!" Johnny's comments and Duane's study hall request became as obvious as her mother's phobia about sex.

Mr. Kruse was trying to explain something, but his voice sounded far away. Finally, she focused enough to hear him say. "I normally stay out of the way if I know a teacher is doing a good job. And that's the case with you, Miss Neilsen."

He paused, uncomfortable in what he was about to say. "But last Friday after lunch, Ethel Fuchs stopped by the office. It was a hard thing for her to do, but she finally got out that Johnny Atzen and Roger Krueger were picking on you."

"Picking on me?"

"Well, to use her words…looking up your dress." There was no way to adequately describe Jensine's absolute mortification. Had she been that careless about the way she sat at her desk…choosing not to cross her ankles because of the heat? And all the while the boys were ogling!

Then she realized Mr. Kruse was still talking, although seemingly preoccupied with his pencil. "After the football game Friday afternoon, I put two and two together when I heard Duane Finnern talking with the other players about the 'nice view' in study hall." He waited as Jensine struggled to regain her composure. "Now, I think the best way to handle this situation is for you to just ignore it. I'll have a little talk with Duane. He knows better. And Johnny and Roger…I'll give them a few chores after school."

Somehow Jensine found her way upstairs to her room. Emil had already been there, opening the windows and shades to let in as much breeze as possible, as if in humble apology for the ugly remodeling of her desk. As usual, she stood by her door, greeting students until the last bell. The conversation in her room was definitely hushed except for Johnny's loud, "Who ratted?"

Jensine didn't say anything to Moveta or Frieda at lunch; it was too embarrassing. But Emil must have told Ella because she patted her shoulder sympathetically as she unpacked the lunch and said, "I baked some sugar cookies this morning...nice and crisp, the way you like 'em, Jensine."

Jensine went to her room right after supper. She had a pounding headache, and she certainly wasn't in the mood to talk. Shortly before bedtime, Moveta knocked lightly and then pushed open her door just enough to offer a big square of fresh fudge resting on a paper doily in the middle of a fancy plate. "Remember what I said, Jensine...better than...you know what."

Jensine couldn't help but laugh. "Oh, come on in, Moveta." Then she said in embarrassment, "I suppose you heard about what happened."

Moveta plopped on the bed. "So the buggers got a peek at your panties, Kiddo...good thing you were wearing some."

"Moveta!"

Moveta just shrugged and grinned. "Aren't you going try the fudge?"

12
THANKSGIVING AT THE BAUERS

Jensine wasn't looking forward to Thanksgiving. Both Moveta and Frieda were going home for the holiday, and Ella had already given notice she was having all of the relatives at her house, and her girls at the teacherage would just have to get along without her for a few days. There was nothing Jensine would have liked better than to spend a few days with her own family. There was so much to tell them, things that just couldn't really be shared in the weekly letters they exchanged. But, as her mother said, it was a long way to go for just four days, and if the weather should get bad, she'd be in a real pickle. "Best wait until Christmas, Jensine. It'll be here before you know it," her mother advised. So that was the end of that. Frieda said she was more than welcome at their family gathering in Round Lake, and maybe she would go after all even though she had refused Frieda's first invitation. She and Moveta had enjoyed several meals at the Bauers throughout the fall. They were warm and welcoming people, but Jensine felt guilty taking advantage of their hospitality when she couldn't repay it.

"Oh, phooey," Frieda objected. "They love you." When Jensine told her it would be a good time to get caught up on her paper correcting, Frieda was quick to say she would drive her home in the evening.

As it turned out, it was a very pleasant day, wonderful food and good company. Of course, they spent a lot of time visiting about people Jensine didn't know, but even that was not without some interest when the conversation turned to Frieda's friend Will.

"By the way, Frieda, I talked with Lottie Mosher the middle of the week, and she says they're thinking about moving into town in a couple of years. Suppose one of the boys will take over the farm," Mrs. Bauer remarked as she served afternoon coffee and pumpkin pie.

"Wouldn't think it'd be Francis," Frieda's father added. "He's teaching at the country school out in Indian Lake. Don't think he cares much for farming anyway. More of a suit-and-tie fellow," He reached for the bowl of whipped cream and spooned an extra dollop on his pie. Jacob Bauer was a small man with a shock of coarse gray hair and a drooping walrus mustache. Jensine had never seen him without his heavy sweater; an oversized, curved pipe; and a book. He seemed to spend most of his time in an old rocking chair near the south window, his ornate cane always within easy reach.

"Keep an eye on my neighbors that way," he said. Jensine loved his sense of humor and gentle tolerance of his wife's sharp tongue. Lizzie Bauer argued about everything. She was one to split hairs and obviously was not pleased unless she had the last word, and that could be on any subject from how to pronounce *calm* correctly—without the *l*, of course—to the price of seed potatoes three years before. Jacob usually didn't object, but once in a while, Jensine noticed, he did venture to say, "Oh, Lizzie, don't know if that's the truth," but then he would quickly escape back into the pages of his book before she had time to send a cross look his way.

Aside from her obvious tendency toward contrariness, Lizzie was an imposing woman, tall and ramrod straight even though in her early seventies, and there could be no doubt how Frieda came by her penetrating black eyes. They were her mother's. Jensine thought it unusual Lizzie was never without the same large gold loops in her pierced ears. She wondered what her own mother would think of that. To Johanne's way of thinking, only loose women pierced their ears. Once, when Jensine had remarked about the earrings, Frieda explained her grandmother had given them to her mother as a parting gift when she left Germany with Jacob. It reminded Jensine of the story her mother had told her about her own grandmother throwing her apron over her face and crying the day they left Denmark. She knew she would never see her daughter again. It was easy to understand why the worn jewelry was so precious to Lizzie Bauer.

"Well, I'm thinking it will be William, the younger one. He's been doing the farming out there anyway for the most part. He went to the Farm School up at the University, so he's probably got all kinds of new ideas. 'Course Lottie wants him to give up playing for dances. She's never liked that, you know, all the smoking and drinking that goes on in those places."

"That doesn't mean Will does it, Mother. I think it would be a shame if he ever gave up his music. He loves it so much, and you have to admit, he has a wonderful voice."

"Don't get on your high horse, Frieda. I never said he wasn't good. You can have him sing for my funeral any day; your dad's, too. That would be fine by us. I'm just repeating what Lottie said. We've been friends for a long time, and she usually tells me what's on her mind." Clearly, the discussion was over as far as Lizzie Bauer was concerned, but then she suddenly added, "You should introduce Jensine to William. They'd be a good match, don't you think?"

"Now you're talkin,' Lizzie. William's a real nice fellow. He's gonna go places, if I'm any judge of people. You'd like him, Jensine." Jensine could feel herself blush, something she never failed to do when attention turned to her. Jacob apparently noticed and chuckled as he added even more cream to his coffee. "Yes, sir, that might be just the ticket for you, Jensine." Of course, everyone around the table laughed and voiced their approval.

"How about a blind date? You're good at arranging things, Frieda. Fix 'em up. Of course, maybe you don't want to do that since you and William are such good *friends* and all."

Frieda turned, threw her napkin at her younger brother, and quickly carried her plate to the kitchen, saying over her shoulder, "What do you know about it, Bill? Come on, Jensine, I'd better get you back to the teacherage."

The ride back to Lake Valley was quiet, too quiet, Jensine thought. She couldn't think of anything to say that wouldn't sound stupid. For heaven's sake, she didn't expect Frieda to fix her up with someone she was stuck on herself, and she certainly wasn't game for a blind date anyway. She wasn't that desperate! Finally, she just smiled at Frieda, and said, "Thanks for the wonderful day." Frieda seemed to relax.

"Guess I'm just a little grumpy today," she said turning into the teacherage driveway. "Sometimes Mother is such a know-it-all. I think I'll stay overnight, as long as I'm here, and keep you company. Too bad Moveta isn't here. We could have homemade fudge. I'll give her credit. It's the best I've ever eaten, next to her divinity and peanut brittle, of course."

Frieda was up and gone before Jensine was out of bed the next morning. Normally, she was an early riser, something her mother insisted on in her house, but there seemed no need to face any sooner than necessary what was sure to be a lonely weekend at the teacherage. But, she thought, maybe it was good in a way; it helped her appreciate the comforting friendship of Moveta and Frieda and just how much Ella meant to their daily lives.

Snuggled warmly under the soft quilt, she thought about Frieda's reaction to her brother's teasing. As far as Jensine knew, Frieda didn't date, or at least if she did, she never talked about it. Moveta, on the other hand, was always flapping about the boys she dated, and ever since her dancing debut at Arnold's Park, hadn't been without a Saturday night date. It seemed strange because she certainly wasn't a knockout by any stretch of the imagination. Jensine hoped Moveta didn't have a reputation for being fast. She never missed a wedding dance at the Log Cabin, Lake Valley's infamous dance hall; even though Mr. Kruse had mentioned several times that it wasn't a good idea to be a steady there. Jensine herself had never set foot in the place; probably, because she lived in mortal fear Clarence Voss would be there, and there would be no getting out of at least one dance with him. Fortunately, though, he had given up asking her out. In fact, he usually didn't even acknowledge her when he passed her in the hall, which she didn't mind at all. He was a pompous ass as far as she was concerned.

Suddenly, the quiet of the morning was broken by the thud of the front door closing. Maybe Frieda was back because of car trouble or Ella had decided to come over after all.

"Jensine, get your lazy rear end out of bed." Moveta laughingly pushed open the bedroom door as she went by to her room.

"I thought you weren't coming back until Sunday, Moveta." Shoving back the covers, Jensine padded barefoot down the chilly hall to Moveta's room.

"No, silly. I've got a date with a guy from Brewster tomorrow night."

"Since when? You didn't say anything about it before you left."

"You don't think I tell you and Frieda everything, do you? I met him the last time I was at the Cabin."

"But weren't you there with somebody else?"

"That doesn't mean I didn't dance with other fellows, you goose. The only problem is I'm sure he's Catholic, being from Brewster and all and with a name like O'Connor. My God, what else could he be? My mother would have a cow if she knew. You know, the only thing worse than a Catholic is an Irish Catholic," she said, sarcastically mimicking her mother's disapproval. "But who cares? I certainly don't. He's fun and can really cut a rug. Say, he's probably got a friend he could bring with for you, Jensine. It's not too late to give him a ring."

"No thanks, Moveta. I'm not game for any blind date."

"Suit yourself. I'm not sitting around in this godforsaken place any more than I have to. It beats me how you can be so content doing nothing except lesson plans. Make some whoopee, Jensine!"

"I just haven't met the right person, that's all."

"Well, and it's not going to happen anytime soon, Jensine, if you don't get your fanny in gear and meet some men. You can be so standoffish! Get dressed, will you? Let's cook. I brought back some groceries, so we can eat even if Ella isn't here."

Moveta's date was right on time Saturday night and, of course, Moveta dragged him into the front room to meet Jensine. Albert O'Connor was a huge man, in all honesty, not only tall, but heavy and almost dwarfing Moveta. He fit perfectly the stereotype most people seemed to have of the Irish: red hair and plenty of freckles.

He was friendly enough, Jensine thought, and obviously taken with Moveta. In fact, every time she opened her mouth, which Moveta did fairly often, and no matter how trivial the remark coming out of it, Albert threw back his head and roared as if it was the most amusing thing he'd ever heard. Then he gave her a quick squeeze around the waist, his hand lingering a little too close and long under her breast, to Jensine's way of thinking anyway. She was beginning to wonder if they had done more than just dance at the Log Cabin.

"Say, Jens, why don't you come along? It'll be a good time."

"Thanks for asking, Albert, but I don't want to intrude." She didn't doubt for one minute that it would be a good time, for Albert and Moveta, that is. After they left, the teacherage was so quiet and lonely Jensine couldn't bring herself to finish the papers she was correcting. There wasn't a lot to do except write another letter home. Then she had the sudden inspiration to try the homemade fudge recipe Moveta had hastily scribbled on the back of an envelope one night…just in case, she said, Jensine or Frieda felt brave enough to try it on their own. "Just follow the recipe, Jens. That's the secret, and be really careful when you do the soft ball test. Put a little cold water in a sauce dish, drop in a bit of the boiling chocolate and see if you can form it into a soft ball with your finger. If it just barely hangs together, it'll set without being sugary." It must have been beginner's luck because the fudge was perfect. As she enjoyed a big piece before wrapping the rest in wax paper to save for Moveta and Frieda, Jensine wished that life could be more like making a batch of fudge.

Frieda returned to the teacherage Sunday afternoon her usual self and even a bit excited about a missionary who had spoken at her church. "It was so interesting, Jensine. She's a nurse and missionary on a Navajo Indian Reservation in New Mexico. I'd give anything for a chance to do something like that."

No such grand ideas of good deeds for Moveta, not that she didn't have plans, however. After one date, she was head over heels in love with Albert O'Connor, and she made no bones about the fact she was setting her cap for him. Frieda said poor Al didn't stand a chance. He was a doomed man. Oddly enough, Moveta suddenly stopped hanging out in the bathroom after every meal, and there were no more foil wrappers in the wastebasket. By Christmas, she had gained a good ten pounds, seemed blissfully happy, and Ella was almost overcome with gratitude at the welcome gift of her hearty appetite. Albert O'Connor was a frequent caller at the teacherage and nearly always stayed beyond any hour of respectability, sometimes in the privacy of Moveta's bedroom. They always waited until they thought Jensine and Frieda were asleep to tiptoe up the stairs and down the hall, but as Frieda said, "Those squeaky stairs are a dead giveaway."

All of the teachers were invited to a Christmas tea at the Kruses Sunday afternoon of the last week before vacation. Moveta grumbled about having to spend a boring afternoon with the same people she saw all week when she could be doing something fun with Albert. Jensine was sure she knew what that "fun" might be when Moveta said, "I think I'll just stay home and take a nap...maybe see if Albert wants to drive over later. Anything would be better than an afternoon of sipping tea, listening to Marjorie giggle, and watching dear Florena push her glasses up her nose and then blink her watery eyes a mile a minute."

Frieda wasn't amused. "You know, Moveta, sometime we have to do things to please other people, not just ourselves. Louella will be disappointed if you don't come, and, knowing her, she'll go to a lot of work to make it really nice."

"Oh, I suppose..." Moveta sighed and went to change her clothes.

By 2:00, everyone was at the Kruses except Clarence Voss, but nobody mentioned his absence or seemed to miss him. Mr. Kruse welcomed them at the door, sporting festive red braces. Louella Kruse was wearing a deep burgundy velvet dress trimmed at the neckline with ecru lace, and she had loosened her usually tight bun, so her auburn hair was soft around her face. She was striking woman, though fragile, Jensine thought, and certainly a gracious hostess. Her

dining room table was absolutely elegant—linen cloth, crystal punch bowl, polished silver service, and fancy plates laden with sweet breads, cookies, and homemade candy. Moveta quickly filled a plate. "You do want us to sample everything, don't you, Louella?"

It wasn't long before Maurice Sheldon found his way to the piano in the front room and everyone gathered around to listen and join in the carols. Jensine was surprised at Mr. Kruse's booming bass voice and Louella's clear soprano and impressed that both Frieda and Moveta could sing the alto parts without any music to read. She wished she felt comfortable singing at all, instead of being relegated to the davenport with Florena, Marjorie, and Geraldine. She felt like an old maid. And Moveta...well, she seemed to be having a wonderful time for someone who didn't want to be there.

Later, as they visited, Moveta walked over to the fireplace mantel and looked curiously at a small picture in an ornate silver frame tucked in amongst the fresh evergreen boughs. "What a cutie! Who is he?" she asked admiring the small boy posing by his wagon.

Louella's eyes were suddenly misty, and Martin Kruse crossed the room to put his arm around his wife's waist before he cleared his voice and said, "That's our Glen. We always put his picture there during the holidays...seems like he's a little part of our Christmas that way."

"Me and my big mouth!" Moveta burst out disgustedly as they followed the snowy path back to the teacherage.

Jensine went home for Christmas. In her homesickness, she found she had conveniently forgotten the realities of her family life and the problems that had stirred her to move away in the first place. Nothing had really changed, same old squabbling, except her father seemed tired and thin, frail almost, and his eyesight had failed to the point he was having a difficult time reading his *Danish Brotherhood* news. When Jensine asked her mother about it, she said they had an appointment with the doctor in Owatonna after Christmas. Her mother was having a conniption because Kirsten was dating a traveling salesman she had met in Albert Lea. Johanne was convinced nothing good could come of it. "Those kind of men are nothing but trouble. Mark my word," she warned, "nothing but trouble. Here today, gone tomorrow. Fly-by-nighters, like Dad used to say."

But in the privacy of their upstairs bedroom, Kirsten confided, "Jensine, he is so suave, not one of your country duds. I just know when he gives me a diamond, it'll be a real rock."

Jensine was shocked. "But you barely know him, Kirsten. Have you even met his family?"

"His father's dead, and I'm not marrying his mother, Jensine. For God's sake, it isn't as if he were the Fuller Brush man. He sells farm machinery to implement dealers. Honestly, sometimes you are just as 'old country' as Mother. I'll bet you haven't even had a date since you've been gone."

Kirsten was right. She hadn't, but she did decide to splurge a bit when they drove into Albert Lea. A soft brown wool coat with a beautiful fox shawl collar caught her eye, and without a second thought, Jensine spent a sizable part of her savings on it. When she modeled it for her parents, her father whistled approvingly, "Pretty ritzy, Jensine." Her mother examined the inside seams critically for loose threads and then agreed it was a lovely coat.

13

A SIMPLE INVITATION

The winter of '28 was bitterly cold. There was seldom relief from the raw wind that blew across the cornfields and piled up snow on the backside of snow fences. Even so, folks crammed into the gymnasium every Friday night to cheer both the boys' and girls' basketball teams to victory, and they usually had no trouble soundly defeating most of the nearby schools, including Frieda's hometown. She admitted the Lake Valley teams were good, but not nearly as good as Round Lake's '21 team when her friend Will Mosher played. Jensine had to smile at Frieda's obvious admiration and wondered again if there weren't a bit more to it than that. She and Fieda usually sold tickets at the door. Actually, it helped make the weekends a little shorter, and besides, nobody else seemed to want to do it, certainly not Marjorie Linn and the other two elementary teachers; and Moveta was far too busy with Albert O'Connor to be bothered. Clarence Voss didn't show up at all, no doubt in open defiance of Mr. Kruse's request. Once Jensine asked Frieda for particulars and was told that Voss had expected to be named superintendent after the last one left and was actively supported by a few of his farm cronies. When the board chose Mr. Kruse instead, it had been a hard pill for him to swallow. He took out his resentment on Mr. Kruse and, according to Frieda, never lost an opportunity to back-stab him. "Don't kid yourself," she warned. "There's dirty politics even here in Lake Valley."

If the weather were decent, they went ice skating on Rodenberg's Pond Saturday and Sunday afternoons. Then, too, they were frequently invited to their students' homes after church for Sunday dinner. Frieda and Jensine usually accepted, but Moveta flatly refused, saying she wouldn't be caught dead wasting her Sundays with the students she saw every day of the week in school. Actually, Jensine rather looked forward to the invitations and thought years later, when Lake Valley would be just a part of the distant past, she would still appreciate that these people so graciously welcomed her into their homes. Often the dining room table was covered with white Damask and the wedding china. But once in awhile, the home was more humble, like when she was invited to the Fuchs. Moveta thought she was crazy. "God, Jens, you aren't going to accept that one, are you? Voss says the little ones poop in the closets when it's too cold to go outside! Can you imagine?" She rolled her eyes and looked at Jensine as if she had lost her mind.

The fact Clarence Voss had even opened his mouth to gossip with Moveta about the Fuchs encouraged Jensine to quickly accept Ethel's handwritten invitation to Sunday dinner in late March. "Good for you," Frieda said in approval. "I don't think any teacher has ever been invited to the Fuchs."

Ethel said she and her father would pick Jensine up after church. Sure enough, a muddy truck pulled up in front of the teacherage promptly at 12:00. Frieda had warned her Bill Fuchs was a rough German with a reputation for swearing a blue streak, so she wasn't totally shocked when he gruffly ordered, "You get in the back, Ethel, so the lady has a little room. Be too crowded up here with all three of us." Ethel quickly slid across the seat with an embarrassed smile.

"Hi, Miss Neilsen."

"Oh, for heaven's sake! We can squeeze together to make room for all of us." Jensine cringed at the thought of Ethel riding in the back like a calf on the way to market. Besides, the March wind was raw; it was downright cold.

"Well, let's go then. Had to bring the truck on account of the lane bein' so muddy. The missus's been cookin' all morning, and Ethel's been dustin' and cleanin' ever since she finished with the milkin'." Then, quite unexpectedly, he added, almost gently, Jensine thought, "Nice you could come. Ethel here's been really countin' on it."

As the pickup churned up the muddy lane, it struggled in first gear to get through the deep ruts. Jensine prayed they wouldn't get stuck. How on earth had she ever forgotten what a farmyard was like in the spring? Stupidly, she had worn her good pumps, and they didn't fare well as she tried to balance herself on the narrow planks which had been laid down to form a path through the mud to the house. They entered through a small back shanty attached to the kitchen. Manure-covered overshoes lined the back wall, and across from it, on one side of the kitchen door, dirty work coats hung on spikes pounded into rough wall cleats. On the other side of the door, there was an old, narrow table, fold-up leaves long gone, with a water pail and chipped enamel wash basin resting on the top.

"Don't smell too hot out here. We been tryin' to get most of the manure pile pitched before the fields get too soft," Ethel's father apologized. "Ethel says your folks are farmers, so it probably ain't no new smell."

"Oh, it's fine, Mr. Fuchs," Jensine answered. Her mother would have hit her father over the head with the house broom if he had even dared to enter the milk room off the kitchen without rinsing off his barn boots out by the stock tank. She smiled to herself when she thought of the time her mother had actually swung the broom in his direction and scolded, "Don't you step foot in this house with those dirty boots. I won't put up with it, and you know it." Obviously, Mrs. Fuchs didn't have her mother's gumption, or knew it was a losing battle. It probably was a little of both.

The kitchen had no linoleum, just oak planking, and was bare except for a cookstove, a sink and pump along the south wall, a huge, old rocker, and a long trestle table covered with at least three checkered tablecloths needed to span the length. An assortment of painted and varnished chairs surrounded the table, not nearly enough for the family, Jensine thought. And there was no wedding china or Fostoria, just unmatched plates of every pattern, tarnished silverware, and cheap flowered glasses, probably given as premiums at the local creamery. Only Mrs. Fuchs and two little ones, a baby and a toddler, both tied into their high chairs with dishtowels, were in the kitchen.

"She's here, Ida. Don't worry about bringin' a little mud in, Miss Neilsen. There'll be plenty more 'fore the end of the day." Ethel's father made a half-hearted attempt to wipe some of the mud from his own shoes on the dirty hooked rug by the door before helping her with her coat.

Ida Fuchs turned from the cookstove and wiped her hands on her apron, made of the same feed-sack as the dress Ethel wore to school almost every day. "We're so glad you could come, Miss Neilsen. The kids could hardly wait. I told them to stay in the front room and give you a chance to breathe before they crowded in to meet you." Jensine was shocked. Ida Fuchs was not at all what she expected. She was a thin, but pretty woman, barely out of her thirties. How had she ever ended up with this coarse German farmer obviously considerably older than herself and more than a dozen children? My word! Johnny Atzen had been right after all. She must have married very young and had a child every year since. When she spoke, her voice was quiet and refined. "I think we're almost ready to eat. The roast is done, and the gravy is simmering. I hope I got all of the lumps out. Bill, should I mash the potatoes or...?

"Nah, don't bother with the mashin', Ida. Boiled's fine. Don't make much difference either way to my way of thinkin'. Potatoes is potatoes. But suit yourself. You're the cook." Then he walked to the door joining the kitchen to the front room and said, "Darlene, you stay in there with the little ones. This is Ethel's company, and she oughta be at the table for the first round today. Come on, let's eat 'fore it gets cold."

Nine boys, ranging from the late teens to six or so, and all wearing bib overalls, took their places around the table. Mr. Fuchs went to the head of the table and pulled out a chair to his right for Jensine. Then, with his wife standing by her chair at the foot, he bowed his head for grace. It was short, just "Bless the bread. Amen." His wife hurried to the stove to dish up the food, which she handed to Ethel to serve, her husband first, of course. As he piled food onto his plate, he frowned and looked toward an older son seated next to Jensine. "Karl, you move on down a chair. Ethel should sit next to her teacher, not you." Karl quickly shifted to the next chair.

Jensine had never seen such a big platter of roast beef in her whole life, but by the time it made its way around the table, it was empty except for a few small slivers. She wondered if there was any left for the "second round" eaters who could be heard giggling in the front room. After serving the rest of the meal—potatoes and gravy, boiled parsnips, thick slices of heavy bread, and peach sauce, Ethel took her place beside Jensine, and her mother joined them. Jensine waited while they passed the food back and forth between them and shared whatever was left, but Mr. Fuchs and the older sons were almost finished with their meals by that time.

"Good roast, Ida. I knew I picked a good one to butcher. Got the coffee on?"

"Good heavens," Jensine thought, "can't he at least wait until his wife has her first bite?" Besides eating herself, Ida Fuchs was also trying to feed the baby and toddler. But she quickly jumped up and went to the range to set the pot on a front burner. It was certainly easy to understand why she was such a rail. The poor thing never had time to eat, not with this demanding man bossing her around and giving her a new baby every year. Over coffee and pie, though, he settled back in his chair and carried on a surprisingly informed conversation. Jensine realized immediately Bill Fuchs was not a stupid man by any means. He asked about her parents and their farm and said his own probably came to this country about the same time as hers; then he moved on to weightier matters.

"Don't like what's happenin' to farm prices. My corn wasn't worth a damn thing last fall! And the roast we just ate? Hell, I was ahead to butcher the damn thing 'stead a sendin' it to market." Jensine had heard her father voice the same concerns, not in such colorful language, of course. Her mother would have been beside herself.

"Bill, do you want a little more coffee?" Ida's face was red with embarrassment, and she was clearly trying to steer her husband to higher ground.

"Yah, you can warm it up a bit, Ida. Say, Miss Neilsen, what's your idea of some of them teachers up there at the school? I tell you one thing. That fella you got teachin' manual training don't know his ass from a hole in the ground. He spends most of his time up at the store

83

jawin' about the superintendent." His wife cleared her throat loudly, and Ethel squirmed in her chair, but he wasn't finished yet. "I think the sonofabitch should git a job somewhere else if he don't like this one." Jensine had no idea how to respond. She wanted to laugh because it was good to know she and Frieda evidently weren't the only ones who didn't like Clarence Voss.

"Well, boys, let's pitch a little shit. We can git out a few loads before dark." He nodded his head in Jensine's direction and added, "Mighty nice of you to come. Darlene kin bring you back when you're ready." Ida Fuchs was visibly relieved, but lifted her cheek for a quick kiss as he left the table.

"Miss Neilsen, you and Ethel can visit in the front room while Darlene and I feed the little ones. I hope you can stay awhile. It's fun to have you here with your pretty clothes and nice manners. You're Ethel's favorite teacher, you know."

Jensine remembered Darlene from school, a shy girl who, except for meeting Ethel at lunch recess, was always alone. The two of them stood together, backs hunched against the east brick wall and as far away from the other students as they could get without disappearing around the corner. Darlene was two years older than Ethel and the only other Fuchs in attendance except for the younger ones. The older boys who gathered around the table had all dropped out to help their father farm. With such a crew, it didn't seem necessary that Ethel and Darlene had to help outside as well. God knows, their mother most certainly needed help with inside chores.

Jensine was sure most of the little ones were boys, too, and all of them resembled their mother. It didn't seem fair only Ethel and Darlene were spitting images of their homely father. As Ethel struggled with conversation while they sat on the saggy couch in the front room, waiting for her mother to join them, Jensine couldn't help noticing the geraniums potted in tin cans crowding the west window sills. They were spindly in their reach for sunlight, but full of red blossoms. She also made a mental note to ask Mrs. Fuchs, if she had a moment in private with her, about Ethel's poor articulation. She always sounded like she had a mouth full of mashed potatoes. Frieda said she thought Ethel was just terribly tongue-tied and a simple clip under the tongue would probably make a world of difference, but how to broach the subject could be tricky.

Ida Fuchs joined them once the little children were put down for their afternoon naps. The older ones stayed in the kitchen to help Darlene with the dishes. "Usually, we all pitch in, but we don't get company much. It'll be nice to just sit and visit for once." Jensine felt sorry for poor Darlene. She couldn't imagine doing dishes and scrubbing pots and pans for this army of people. Good God, Jensine's mother was cranky for a month before the threshing ring even started, and that only meant ten or so extra mouths to feed for a couple of days.

"Ethel just loves school this year. I know it's because of you. I always liked school. I finished the first two years of high school and thought I'd like to be a teacher, but then I met Bill when he bought the farm next to ours. And you know how it is when you're fifteen and in love. All I could think about was getting married and having babies. Of course, I never thought I'd have quite so many." Then she shrugged and added ruefully, "Bill says we make babies so easy all it takes is washing our underwear in the same water."

Jensine didn't know whether to laugh or cry. She sensed Ida Fuchs felt the same way. "The funny thing is I'm an only child. My mother died in childbirth when I was five. They couldn't stop the hemorrhaging, I guess. The baby died, too."

"I didn't realize your father lived on the next farm."

"Oh, no, Miss Neilsen, we needed more land, so we sold the other farm and bought this one about eleven years ago. My dad remarried, but we don't see them much since we moved. His new wife is nice enough, I guess, but she says it's a crime to have as many children as we do. Bill says nobody's asking her to take care of them, so she can just mind her own business. My goodness, here I am talking about myself so much. Ethel, you should show Miss Neilson your stories."

Ethel blushed in embarrassment. "They're just farm stories. She'd probably think they're dumb."

"Oh, Ethel, I would love to see them. I didn't know you liked to write. Go get them."

"See, Ethel, I knew she would want to see your writing. While you're up, tell Darlene to put on some water for tea and take out a plate of sugar cookies from the pantry. And not to wash the crystal pitcher. Just set it aside, and I'll do it myself later." Jensine had noticed the lovely lead glass water pitcher and had fully intended to remark about it. It was obviously a prized possession.

"It is a wonderful piece, Mrs. Fuchs. "The etching is so delicate. Is it a keepsake?"

"It's all I have of my mother's. She had beautiful things. I thought when my dad remarried, he would ask if I wanted any of them because Marian, that's his new wife, has her own china and silver, but he never said a word. Guess he thought I didn't care about it. Bill says I should just come right out and ask for it because it's my due, but I hate to be too forward."

Jensine broke the uncomfortable silence that followed by commenting, "Your geraniums are just beautiful. I've never seen so many big blossoms. You must have a green thumb, Mrs. Fuchs."

"Oh, no. I don't have time for flowers and such. That's Bill's doing. He loves seeing anything grow.

Over tea and crisp sugar cookies, Ethel shared her stories. Jensine thought they were delightful and surprisingly well written for an eighth grader. And each story was illustrated with fine black ink drawings. "These are wonderful, Ethel. And your drawings! You're a real artist." She couldn't help giving her a quick hug when she handed back the notebook. "You have to share these with your classmates." The look of warm pleasure on Ethel's face was almost Jensine's undoing. Thankfully, the baby started to fuss, and she was able to hide the quick tears.

"Hungry baby, I guess." Ida Fuchs sighed and quickly left the room. When she returned, the baby was nursing under a blanket that discreetly covered her shoulder and breast. "I suppose Darlene should take you back into town, Miss Neilsen. I know you have things to do for tomorrow. I always thought it would be fun to correct papers, but I suppose that gets old after awhile, too. Ethel, you take the baby for a minute. I'll walk out with Miss Neilson."

Jensine and Ida stood on the back step while Darlene brought the pickup as close to the door as she could get. "Miss Neilsen, I wanted to ask you something. It seems like Ethel doesn't talk very plain. She's hard to understand, and that makes her embarrassed. We'd like to help her if there's some way..."

"You know, Mrs. Fuchs, I'm going to talk with Miss Bauer about Ethel. She might have some ideas. I'll send a note home with Ethel, and we can go from there."

"Oh, that would be wonderful! Bill and I'll do whatever needs doing. He's that way, you know. I know people around here think we're quite a tribe with all our kids, but we're good people. We work hard, pay our bills, and don't expect any hand-outs." Jensine didn't doubt it.

The following Saturday, Frieda and Jensine picked up Ethel at the end of her lane and drove down to Lake Park where Doc Evans clipped her tongue. He said he couldn't believe the doctor who delivered her hadn't discovered it. It was a wonder she had even been able to nurse. Neither Frieda nor Jensine bothered to tell him what they suspected: Bill Fuchs had delivered all of their seventeen children himself.

14
OUT IN THE WASH

According to Frieda, as they visited over a cup of cocoa in the teacherage kitchen one evening in late March, the biggest event of the school year was the banquet and prom held in the middle of May. "You won't believe it. It's the craziest thing. Only juniors and seniors and faculty members are invited to the banquet at the school, of course, and they always ask Ella to head up the food committee, so you know that's got to be wonderful. But afterwards, everybody in Lake Valley, and I mean everybody, turns out at the Log Cabin to watch the grand march and then join in the dancing. The old codgers wouldn't miss it on a bet, and even the little kids come and make a nuisance of themselves, running around."

"I'm surprised they have it at the Log Cabin. Don't they drink liquor there? Jensine questioned. "That's what Marjorie says anyway."

"Yes, Jensine," Moveta answered sarcastically, "they do sell 3.2 beer at the Log Cabin and a lot of people drink it, and some even bring their own bottles, too, and buy set-ups. Imagine that! People do drink, you know, even if it is Prohibition. Anybody with a half a brain knows that's not going to last. God, you are such a prude! The Cabin isn't the den of iniquity you seem to think it is. You really should go some time and see for yourself. I doubt you'll rot in purgatory for one quick peek." With that, Moveta abruptly emptied her cup in the sink and left the kitchen.

Jensine was stung by Moveta's sharp words. Had she sounded that sanctimonious? Well, she thought huffily, Moveta and Albert practically lived at the Log Cabin, spending every Friday and Saturday night there, so no doubt she was an expert on what went on there.

Frieda cleared her throat. "I know what you're thinking, Jens, and normally I would agree with you. But life is a little different here. I'm sure most of the farmers make home brew out in their granaries, and the kids probably have their first sips as babies. It's not a big deal."

"I guess it's just different from what I'm used to, Frieda. For heaven's sake, my mother thinks it's a crime to even keep apple cider in the house if it starts to ferment a bit. I certainly didn't mean to offend Moveta. She was so touchy about it."

"Oh, she'll get over it. Maybe she and Albert had a little tiff. She's seems a little edgy. Anyway, Jensine, dig out your party dress. You'll have a grand time, and I know you'll love the music. Will's orchestra is playing, so it won't be your typical Lake Valley old-time dance. We can go together, if you want."

"I'm game if you are, Frieda. Moveta's probably right in saying I should get out more. Maybe I am a real flat tire like my sister Kirsten always says."

⁓

Easter was late that year, not until the middle of April. Jensine hadn't planned to go home for the week of vacation because it was so close to the end of the school year, and her mother had already voiced the opinion it would be a waste of good money. But when Moveta offered her a ride as far as St. James, and Emil volunteered to meet her bus coming back, she changed her mind. The teacherage would be a lonely place with both Frieda and Moveta gone and Ella busy with her own family. Besides, maybe she could convince Kirsten to drive her to Albert Lea to shop for a party dress for the prom. Now, she thought, that would really throw her mother into a tizzy.

As it turned out, shopping for a new dress was small potatoes. Jensine was disappointed Christian, not her father, met her at the bus depot. She was looking forward to the ride home, just the two of them, visiting and sharing things as they always had. As they climbed into the car she couldn't help asking, "Where's Dad?"

"He's not doin' so good, Jensine. It's the diabetes. Remember how he was havin' a hard time readin' when you were home over

Christmas? Well, it seems like he can hardly see at all now, and he's got this big ulcer on his leg, right down to the bone, that won't heal no matter what Ma tries. She's pretty upset and worried, and, of course, it don't help much with Kirsten and her fightin' all the time over her datin' that guy from Albert Lea. She says she's gonna marry him. I'm glad you're home, Jens. Maybe you can calm the waters a bit. Right now, they're pretty rough." Then Christian grinned. You know, Sis, I never thought I'd rather be spendin' time in the barn 'stead of the house, but when Ma and Kristen go at it, all hell breaks loose. Christ, Jens! Ma's gotten so sour; it's like she was weaned on one of her own pickles. And poor Dad, he's stuck there in the house with the two of 'em."

Christian wasn't exaggerating. Things were more than tense at home. Johanne was vigorously blacking the top of the kitchen range with a crumpled newspaper when Jensine came through the milk house into the kitchen. Her mother's lips were so tightly pursed Jensine had to look twice to see if they existed or had permanently disappeared into her mouth.

"Don't be comin' too close, Jensine. You'll get your nice things all dirty with what I'm doin' here."

Jensine felt a quick spark of exasperation. For heaven' sake, she hadn't seen her mother since Christmas! Why was it Johanne couldn't put her anger and hard feelings aside even for a minute? But no, the world revolved around Kirsten. It always had.

"Where's Dad?"

Johanne's face suddenly crumpled into tears. "Oh, Jensine, he's so sick." Jensine stepped forward and pulled her mother into her arms, smeared newsprint and all.

"Why didn't you tell me? I would have come home."

"There wasn't a bit of use, Jensine. What could you do? Your coming home would just make the neighbors think the worst. You know how nosey the Petersons are anyway. It's probably all over the county by now."

"Mother, you make it sound like Dad's being sick is a sin or something."

91

"It's our business, Jensine, and nobody else's."

Later, when Jensine quietly opened the door to her parent's bedroom, her father was still asleep, his shallow breathing filling the room. He was in his pajamas, his right leg propped on two feather pillows. There was a pervasive sick smell in the room, but something else, too, which Jensine quickly recognized as the sweet rotting odor of gangrene. A few years ago, she had helped her mother care for a neighbor who had lost his arm, and she would never forget the horrid smell as Johanne changed the bandage, or the doctor's dire prediction that a little more of the stump would probably have to come off before it settled down to heal. "God," Jensine prayed, "please don't let that happen to Dad."

Her father had always had such big, strong hands. He frequently joked it was from over fifty years of squeezin' and pullin' cow tits. But now, lying folded on his chest, they just looked old, blue veins standing out on parchment thin skin. Jensine covered them with her own as she leaned over the bed, whispering softly, "Dad, it's me, Jensie."

His eyelids fluttered as he struggled to rouse himself and focus on her face. Then he smiled. "Hell, Jensie, you don't have to tell me who you are. I'm not that much of a goner."

"Good, because I'm going to spend the rest of the afternoon sitting right here. We've got a lot of visiting to catch up on. Should I put some pillows behind your back, so you can sit up a bit?"

"Just as long as you don't jar my leg. It's a sore one and don't smell none too good neither. Give me a little bit of that water over there on the dresser, will you? Seems like I'm thirsty all the time."

Her father seemed to perk up as they visited, and Jensine was heartened his same old sense of humor was still there. But when her mother came in later to change his bandage and see if he needed to use the bedpan, it was more than she could bear. She left on wobbly legs to sit at the dining room table in the next room while Johanne tended her husband. Even so, Jensine knew the exact moment when the gangrenous leg was exposed. She covered her mouth and convulsively gagged.

When her mother was finished and came into the dining room, she sighed and stopped to pat Jensine on the back. "No sense gettin' yourself all upset, Jensine. That won't do a thing except get your father down more than he already is. Suppose we should have Doc Ertel come out again. Seems like it smells worse than it did yesterday." She paused before adding, "Don't know what he can do though. He just pats your father on the arm and shakes his head at me as he goes out the door. I tried to pay him a little something when he was out last time, but he said he hadn't done anything to get paid for."

"But there's got to be something we can do. We can't just let him lie there and rot away."

"What should I do? You tell me what I should do, Jensine, and I'll do it." She could hear the fear behind the anger in her mother's voice. "I wasn't going to tell you until I had to, but Doc Ertel says he'll probably have to take the leg if things keep lookin' the way they do now."

"Oh, God, Mother! No!"

"Shush now. He'll hear you. Go back in there and visit. It'll give me time to do a few chores around the house."

"Where's Kirsten?"

"Off with that fellow. Spends night and day with him. It's got trouble written all over it, if you ask me. Course, your sister is never one to take my advice, so I might as well keep my mouth shut, all the good it does to talk about it."

Fat chance of that, Jensine couldn't help thinking. She knew from hard experience her mother wasn't one to ever give up on her notion of how things should go.

The putrid odor still lingered in the bedroom even though her mother had lifted a window a bit. "Sorry about the smell," her father apologized.

"Dad, it's fine. We'll have you better in no time."

"Well, don't know about that, Jensie, but I'll tell you one thing, if that sister of yours gets married like she says she's gonna, I wouldn't miss the chance to give her away for love or money. I'll get her down the aisle if I have to crawl." Then he laughed, "That man's got his work cut out for him. Hope he knows that."

"Oh, Dad, we all love Kirsten. She's just got a mind of her own, that's all."

"Sure we do, Jensie, but she's a handful, and we both know it." Then he chuckled and patted her hand. "How about you? You still like it there in Lake Valley? Tell me all about it."

Jensine spent the next hour talking about Lake Valley, mostly about her students—Ethel's skill in capturing farm life in her essays and illustrations, and, of course, Johnny Atzen's latest escapade. Emil had caught him making giant wet wads from the paper towels and flinging them up on the bathroom ceiling, where they stuck like glue. When she told her father about her Sunday dinner at the Fuchs, he observed, "People surprise you sometimes, don't they, Jensie. Things ain't always the way we think they're goin' to be." And the image of Bill Fuchs potting geraniums to brighten his wife's front room came immediately to mind.

Kirsten didn't come home for supper. "Guess she had more important things to do than spend a little time with her sister," Johanne grumbled.

"Mother, for heaven's sake, Kirsten's almost twenty-three years old."

"That doesn't mean she's got any brains when it comes to men. I know a loser when I see one. They act like a couple of lovesick fools whenever they're together. It almost makes me sick."

Christian had been right. The waters were rough at home, but at the moment, Jensine couldn't think of one thing to do that would help. Kirsten came home after midnight. Johanne must have waited up for her because she could hear arguing downstairs before Kirsten ran up the stairs, opened the bedroom door, and grabbed a pillow to throw at Jensine before flopping on the bed.

"I know you're not sleeping, not with all that yelling downstairs. Sit up! I've got something to show you." Kirsten grabbed Jensine's hand and placed her own left hand over it. "It's a diamond! He gave me a diamond! It's huge! Mother's having a cow, but I don't care. It's not her life."

"She just doesn't want you to get hurt, Kirsten. You know Mother's always had a hard time letting go. She'll get used to the idea. Just give her time."

"I want you to meet Thor when you're home. He's so good looking, and I like it that he's older. I think we'll probably get married in the fall. He might be transferred to Fargo, so we want to do it before that happens. I'll be so glad to get out of here. Mother is just impossible!" She rolled over and held her left hand up in the light to admire her engagement ring. "How's things in Lake Valley? Are you dating anyone?"

Jensine ignored Kirsten's question. Somehow, she didn't feel like telling her sister she still hadn't managed a date.

Kirsten and Jensine drove to Albert Lea the next afternoon. Thor met them at a restaurant for lunch. He was nice looking, Jensine thought, definitely older. But her mother was right; they did act a little silly with their hand-holding and outright smooching. After lunch, Jensine excused herself to go shopping. She didn't feel much like a new dress, but maybe it would be just the thing to raise her spirits. The shop on Mainstreet had something that caught her eye immediately. It was a two-piece, tea-length party dress of pale blue embroidered rayon georgette, and its dropped waist and short bolero jacket definitely flattered her slim frame. The clerk said the color was marvelous with her blond hair.

❧

Christian took her to the bus depot on Saturday. It was difficult to leave her father. Before she boarded the bus, she hugged her brother. "Thanks for being there for Mother and Dad. They need you, Christian."

"We'll be all right, Jensie. Ma's a tough old bird. She'll get Dad through this if anyone can." How Jensine wanted to believe that.

Emil met her at the Spafford Store as he had promised. Such a spot of sunshine, Jensine couldn't help thinking. The world could definitely use a few more Emil Ehrenbergs. Jensine relaxed for the drive back to the teacherage, enjoying the smoky fragrance of his pipe until she suddenly remembered her father had not lit up his beloved pipe once in the week she had been home. Emil must have sensed her thoughts because he leaned over to pat her knee sympathetically.

"Take it things ain't so good at home. It'll all come out in the wash, Jensine. Always does."

15
WILL MOSHER

As it turned out, Jensine had much more to do with the prom than just showing up in her blue chiffon. Shortly after her return from Easter vacation, Duane Finnern, the senior class president, stopped by her room after school to ask if she would consider being the faculty advisor for the big event. "Just thought I'd tell you, Miss Neilsen, when we had our class meeting, everybody thought you'd be the best one for the job. I know we give you a hard time in study hall sometimes, but it's just because we know you're a good sport."

Jensine couldn't help but smile. She had come to enjoy the big senior and realize he was not only smart, but also quite gifted when it came to leadership. There was an honesty about Duane that earned him the respect of students and teachers alike, but it was his sense of humor and natural wit, often self-deprecating, that made him everybody's favorite. That and the fact he carried both the football and basketball team to near perfect seasons, even skunking Frieda's beloved Round Lake forty-two to nothing on a beautiful October afternoon.

Duane was the center on the six-man team and literally pushed at least three of his opponents back on their behinds every play. In basketball, his soft touch and arching set shot accounted for most of Lake Valley's points. He liked to visit with Jensine about the games and often came to study hall early just for that purpose, especially after she told him about Kirsten. She remembered one of their conversations.

"I feel sorry for the girls playing that dumb half-court game in those long-sleeved middies and baggy bloomers. It seems downright stupid to come to a dead stop at mid-court and throw the ball across the line to another player. They should change the rules."

"That's what my sister thinks, too, Duane, but there are some folks who don't think girls should be playing any competitive sports."

"Why not?"

"Well, you know… rough play…"

"Yeah, and sweating…that's probably a really bad thing for girls to do. That's all wet baloney if I ever heard it."

And another time he asked her if she knew Betty Kramer and Harold Ahrens were struck on each other. "That's why we all laughed when you moved Harold to the desk right behind her," he said. "They've been pretty tight for a couple of years. You might want to walk down the aisle once in awhile during study hall, Miss Neilson, and see what Harold's up to." To Jensine's dismay, she found Harold spent most of study hall gently massaging Betty's underarm and other soft parts. From the smirks of the surrounding students, apparently Jensine was the only person in the dark.

Jensine put down her pencil and leaned back in her chair. "Duane, are you putting me on about being faculty advisor?"

"Wouldn't think of it, Miss Neilsen, especially when I'm working you for a favor. How about this for a little added incentive? The senior class will pay for your way into the dance."

"Oh, come on, Duane. You'll have to do better than that. Teachers get in free anyway because we're all supposed to chaperone."

"Guess that won't work then. He paused as if in deep thought, then snapped his fingers. "I have it! You can sit by me at the banquet and give me half of your meat and all of your dessert. Wouldn't it be special to share your meal with the class president?"

"Duane, you are such a ninny! I'll do it just to get rid of you. My spelling papers will never get corrected otherwise."

Jensine shooed him out of her room, but not before he added, "Have you got a date lined up? My brother said he'd be glad to do the honors."

The student committee, headed by Duane, seemed to welcome Jensine's organizing skills. "Why not invite Mrs. Ehrenberg to attend our committee meetings instead of just telling her what we want served?" she suggested. "She might have some menu ideas we haven't thought of."

"You mean Ella, Miss Neilsen?" one of the boys interjected dubiously. "What's the use of botherin' her? We have the same thing every year anyway, fried chicken, and for punch, that orange nectar my ma buys from the Watkins man. That's no big…"

"Miss Neilsen's point exactly, Arnie," interrupted Duane. "We don't have to always serve the same food. Hey, let's be a little creative this year and have roast beef and maybe something pink to drink. Of course, we could have a little fried chicken, too, for those who might get their undies in a bundle over a change in the menu." The rest of the committee laughed and quickly agreed with Duane

Ella was absolutely thrilled! She came to the next meeting prepared with all kinds of ideas—beef burgundy and stuffed chicken breasts for the main course, along with garlic mashed potatoes, glazed carrots, and a light lemon dessert she insisted was absolutely wonderful. Even Arnold was impressed, and her menu passed with a unanimous vote. Once the committee got past the notion things had to be to be the same way they'd been for the past ten years, ideas begin to fly.

"I think we should have more of a program," Lucille Birch, argued. "The banquet's always so short. We just eat and that's it. It would be more special for the kids who don't have dates. They get all dressed up, too, you know, and they're just as much a part of the class as anyone else even though they're not going with anyone."

"Got any ideas, Lucille?" Duane asked. "We're listening."

"Well, my cousin goes to a big school, and they have the senior class history and will at their banquet."

"What do we have to will anybody, Lucy-Ducy?" Arnold scoffed. "Sounds pretty stupid to me."

Once again Duane came to the rescue. "I could will my appetite and ugly ties to Harry Atz. He's so skinny you can't see him when he stands sideways, and he wouldn't be caught dead in any tie, much less mine. It could be a hoot! How about if you and me take a crack at writing it, Lucille? I think it sounds like a great idea. Maybe the blame thing won't be so boring."

Before the meeting was over, the Lake Valley banquet and prom had taken on a whole new look.

~❦~

Jensine prayed for good weather. Emil had said several times over the past weeks the farmers needed a good sod soaker. To use his words, it was drier than a popcorn fart, but as far as she was concerned, the rain could hold off for one more day. The morning of the prom dawned sunny and almost unseasonably warm, but by noon clouds were gathering in the west. She and Duane kept their fingers crossed as they decorated for the banquet. So far, so good. The only wet blanket was Emil. He was not happy about setting up tables in the gymnasium. "Suppose the floor will get all sticky," he grumbled. "It'll be a mess to clean up. Don't see why you couldn't have it in the home economics room like always. There's plenty of room in there without messin' up the gym."

"But it's just not very festive having it in a classroom. Besides, Emil, the committee will be here bright and early tomorrow morning to help clean up. We surely appreciate that it's extra work for you," Jensine added putting her arm around his shoulder.

Emil seemed somewhat placated, but he couldn't help one last bit of fussing. "Just seems a shame to ruin a good floor."

By four o'clock the aroma coming from the home economics room where Ella and her helpers were cooking promised an absolutely divine meal. The tables were beautiful with long ribbons of purple and gold crepe paper running down the middle and Lucille's tasseled programs at every place setting. Everything was falling into place just as Jensine had hoped it would. She felt a quick surge of pride at her successful efforts, and then remembered another of her mother's favorite axioms; "Pride goeth before the fall," of course, always followed by "Mark my words."

After one last check, Jensine hurried across the schoolyard to the teacherage to take a quick bath and dress for the evening. Overhead, the sky was dark and thunder rumbled in the distance. "Darn," she thought. "Why can't the weather ever cooperate?" By five o'clock, it was raining buckets. Frieda, Moveta, and she would be absolutely drenched just getting to the banquet. Her dress would be ruined, and it would be silly to even think of wearing the matching blue hair band that made her look quite glamorous, at least according to her roommates. They had experimented with it one evening and decided it looked best when Jensine wore it more down in the middle of her forehead with the bow off to the side. "Definitely hot," Moveta exclaimed. "Now push your arm bangle up past your elbow, and you'll look like a regular fashion plate."

"Fat chance," Jensine thought, remembering the evening. "A drowned rat would be more like it!"

But leave it to divine providence and an Irish Catholic. Albert O'Connor wasn't invited to the banquet and didn't have to show up for at least another two hours, but he arrived early, cheerful as always, with a small grain tarpaulin. "It ain't pretty," he said, 'but in this downpour, no umbrella's goin' keep you from gettin'" soaked. "I'll hold it up over you and deliver you gals one at a time right to the front door. Who wants to be first?"

Jensine could have kissed him silly. "I should go as soon as I can, just to make sure everything's ready."

Albert took one look at her cream pumps and shook his head. "Got anything else to wear? Put those flimsy things under your arm until we get to the school." Frieda ran up the stairs to get Jensine's everyday shoes while he situated the tarp over the two of them. Then he tucked her hand under his arm and led her across the yard peeking out from the tarp just enough to avoid the growing puddles of water.

Mr. Kruse and Louella were already at the school. He smiled his approval at Jensine and was quick to add, "Looks and smells wonderful, Miss Neilsen, but hope we don't have to build an ark before the night's over. Still I bet the farmers are celebrating. This rain is just what the doctor ordered."

By 6:30, all of the students had arrived. They came holding blankets and old coats over their heads, completely undaunted by the torrential rainfall. Emil stood guard by the door making sure nothing wet was carried past the front entry. Two hours later, everybody agreed it was the best banquet ever. Not only was the dinner delicious, but Duane and Lucille's class history and will had everybody in stitches, even the prudish Florena who actually laughed outright on one occasion. When Duane willed his appetite and ties to Harry Atz, Harry brought down the house by standing up and saying, "I accept. It's the only way I can get him to stop begging at lunch, and I know I can make some money sellin' those ugly ties for tail switchers. Just tie one on the end of the cow's tail and watch the flies disappear."

Harold and Betty willed their two seats in study hall to any loving couple in the junior class. Jensine knew what that was all about and apparently so did everybody else because she caught Florena sniffing her nose in disapproval and whispering behind her hand to Marjorie.

Jensine and Frieda stayed until all of the students were on their way to the Log Cabin for the dance and then set off in Frieda's car after telling Emil to grab Ella and leave the cleanup to the next day.

Frieda was right. Everybody was there. The Log Cabin was so crowded they could hardly squeeze their way in to find a spot to watch the grand march. "There's Will," Frieda whispered. "Right there in the front, getting ready to call the grand march. I'll introduce you after the first set." Before Jensine could decide which of the band members was Will, Duane Finnern was at her side and offering her his arm.

"Miss Neilsen, may I have the pleasure of your company to lead the grand march?" Jensine felt herself being guided onto the dance floor before she could muster a response. She sensed the students knew this was going to happen because they started to clap and cheer wildly, and the rest of the crowd joined in.

"Way to go, Finnern," one older man called out. "You know how to pick 'em." Everyone laughed and clapped even louder as Frieda's friend started to call the grand march.

"Find your partner and line up two by two after the young man escorting the lovely lady in blue." Frieda's friend smoothly called the march until couples stretched across the entire dance floor, and Duane finally swung Jensine into the first dance, a lively fox trot. When it was over, she looked for Frieda but was immediately claimed by another senior boy and then another until the set was over, and Jensine was positively breathless. She spotted Frieda sitting with Moveta and Albert and made a quick beeline for the side booth.

"Didn't know you were such a twinkle toes, Jens," Moveta teased as she slid into the booth to sit by Frieda.

"I can't believe how well the kids dance. It's like they've been doing it all their lives,"

"They have," Freida said. "You should see them polka. Then you'd be truly amazed." She paused and then asked, "What do you think of Will? Doesn't he have a great voice? I was going to introduce you, but he looks busy getting ready for the next set. Maybe at intermission."

Albert changed the subject to more practical matters. "Jens, you look thirsty. How about a little nip? I've got a pint of hooch right here I'd be happy to share."

"Just some water would be great." Both Moveta and Albert laughed as if it was the funniest thing they had ever heard, and Moveta reached across the booth to pat Jensine's hand.

"Oh come on! Let your hair down and have some fun. Even Frieda's having malt, and I'm certainly not going to march into Kruse's office on Monday and say 'Mr. Kruse, I must tell you that Miss Neilsen, yes, your little pet, Miss Neilsen, had a drink at the junior-senior prom.' Honestly, Jens, live it up a little! I'm serious."

By this time Albert was already pouring a generous shot into a glass and pushing it across the table to Jensine. "This'll loosen ya up. A little nip never hurt anybody." Jensine threw her customary caution and twenty-odd years of her mother's preaching on the evils of liquor to the wind and took a small sip.

"Really, Jensine," Frieda said in disapproval, "I'm surprised at you. I know I'm drinking malt, but that's hard liquor." Something about her censoring tone hit a raw spot.

"And you're not my mother, Frieda. I'm twenty-four years old."

"Slide out a minute, Jensine. I'm going to talk to some friends across the way." Spots of color showed on Frieda's cheeks as she literally sailed from the booth and skirted around the edge of the dance floor."

Jensine felt terrible. Why on earth had she made such a rude remark to Frieda? Moveta seemed unconcerned. "Frieda had that coming, Jens. She's pretty judgmental, if you ask me. Right, Albert?" But Albert was so nearly ossified he didn't know or care about such a small unpleasantry.

Somewhere in the middle of the second set, Jensine looked up to see the bandleader, Frieda's friend Will, heading directly toward her. Her first thought was he should be up there directing his band, or singing, or playing the trumpet or the violin and whatever else he did. As he approached the booth, Moveta's eyes widened, and she kicked Jensine under the table. "Don't you dare say no!" she mouthed behind her hand.

Up close, he was very tall and very dark. Jensine had never felt so affected by anyone of the opposite sex or so nervous about it. He didn't beat around the bush. She had to give him credit for that: he just smiled and said, "My drummer bet me a buck I couldn't get a dance with the little lady in blue. How about it? It's a great little fox trot, even if the grammar's bad, and I promise not to step on your toes." Moveta chose this moment to deliver another kick. He held out his hand and pulled Jensine out of the booth and onto the dance floor. "I'm Will Mosher, and you must be the Jensine Frieda Bauer's always talking about." He was a superb dancer, graceful for a big man. Afterwards, she couldn't for the life of her remember one thing they talked about, except he might drive over some Sunday afternoon. That and the song—"Ain't She Sweet."

"Well?" Moveta waited expectedly as Jensine slid into the booth and took another sip of her drink. "Did he ask you for a date? He's absolutely gorgeous—tall, dark, and handsome. He's the bee's knees, if you ask me."

"He's a good dancer."

"Jensine, you goose, forget the dancing and think about the man." Moveta did her customary eye-roll and moved even closer to Albert, who put his hand under the table and apparently squeezed something because Moveta jumped, giggled, and playfully asked, "Albert, whatever are you doing under there?"

"Where's Frieda? I don't see her."

"Oh, Albert and I are going to give you a ride home. She's got a headache or something, so she went back to the teacherage." Jensine was pretty sure that wasn't the reason Frieda disappeared so early in the evening.

⚜

Jensine was tired the next morning, but her job as advisor wouldn't be over until the gymnasium met with Emil's approval. "No doubt he's already bemoaning a few sticky spots on his beloved floor," she thought as she quickly dressed and headed down the stairs. She couldn't remember hearing Moveta come in last night, but she didn't have time to check, so her curiosity on that matter would have to wait. Ella didn't come on the weekends, so the quiet kitchen was no surprise, but Jensine half expected to see Frieda up and about. Maybe she had had a headache after all, she decided. But Frieda's car was not parked in its usual spot in the teacherage driveway.

⚜

"He's more long-winded than usual," Jensine thought as she waited patiently for Reverend Miller to finish his sermon and move on to the weekly communion. She had come to really dislike that part of the service, mostly because his attempt to chant the liturgy was so God-awful. Even she could tell that. He started out flat and by the end, he was so off key most of the congregation was totally lost, and those who weren't had to be praying for the final amen. Then, of course, everyone would traipse, row by row, to the front and kneel down at the portable altar rails for the cup and the bread. It took forever. The gym was packed as always. "Really," Jensine thought as her mind wandered, "who would know if I didn't come every Sunday?" Moveta hadn't attended the Lutheran service since last winter, and as far as Jensine knew, Mr. Kruse hadn't called her on the carpet for it.

"And he'd better not," Moveta had warned. "If and where I go to church is my own business, and I'll tell him so." But the local parishioners apparently noticed because, a few Sundays before, Jensine had heard two women behind her whispering about Moveta.

"Yah," one said, "I heard she's goin' with some Catholic from Brewster. Bet her folks wouldn't take to it if they knew." Jensine mentioned it to Moveta, not to be a gossip, but to prevent trouble for her friend. Moveta was typically unconcerned.

"Who cares, Jensine? Besides, for their information, the old bags, Catholics aren't keen on Lutherans either." She snorted, "And the ones out here aren't all that holy. They're even too damned tight to build a church."

"What do the O'Connors think about you and Albert, Moveta? You've met them, haven't you?"

Moveta shrugged. "Just once. They weren't real friendly, but Albert says they'll come around when they get used to the idea. His mother's the worst, and she's a convert for God's sake! But I'm not worried. We'll work it out when the time comes."

When Jensine heard a car in the driveway in mid-afternoon, she assumed Frieda had returned from Round Lake. "Hopefully, she's not still put out about Friday night," she thought. Somehow, it seemed totally out of character for Frieda, but then maybe her brother Bill was right about Will Mosher being more than just an old family friend. Jensine heard steps on the stairs and prepared to mend her friendship with Frieda, but it was Moveta who barely knocked before pushing open the door. She was rumpled from necking on the downstairs couch with Albert and obviously excited about something more than that.

"Jensine, that Will is here. Run a comb through your bob and pinch your cheeks. Albert and I'll keep him company until you get downstairs." Moveta paused and then added, "Do me a favor and shuck that baggy old sweater. It fits you like a sack. This guy needs to see some curves."

"Oh, Moveta, I look a mess. I never thought he'd come this Sunday, maybe in a few weeks or so..."

"Oh, for God's sake, Jens, here's your chance. This guy is the cat's pajamas, and you're just standing there in a funk. Get moving!"

Albert and Moveta were entertaining Will Mosher in the front room when Jensine appeared several minutes later minus the baggy sweater. She felt suddenly shy and nervous until he turned to her and smiled. "Hey, you're a pretty lady even when you aren't wearing blue." Albert chose this moment to let out his usual guffaw and squeeze Moveta, who was grinning like she had arranged the whole affair. Jensine felt like strangling them both.

"It's too nice an afternoon to sit in the house. I borrowed my drummer's new car and thought we could go for a little ride. Albert and Moveta, there's plenty of room if you want to come along."

Like that would ever happen, Jensine thought. She knew Moveta wouldn't miss the opportunity afforded by a deserted teacherage. "Oh, no, just the two of you go. Albert has to get back to do chores anyway." As she walked to the front door with them, she added, "Have a good time, and don't hurry back."

As Will backed out of the driveway, he looked over at Jensine and chuckled. "How long do you think it'll be before Albert gets to the chores?"

16
KIRSTEN'S WEDDING

Once Johanne Neilsen accepted the fact that no amount of scolding and argument would persuade her younger daughter not to marry a traveling salesman, she threw herself full-bore into the wedding plans. It was going to be proper, no doubt about that, and the ceremony most definitely was not going to be in the Geneva Lutheran Church. In her words, "The United Methodist in Ellendale will be plenty good." That was fine with Kirsten since it had a larger fellowship hall for the reception, and, more importantly, a center aisle in the sanctuary, which, according to her, would make the bridal procession much more stunning.

Jensine spent two weeks at home in June before heading off to Mankato for summer school, but visiting with her mother was pretty much out of the question. Johanne was totally absorbed in sewing the wedding gown and the green voile dresses for the bridesmaids. The sewing machine treadle hummed day and night. Jensine tried several times to bring up the subject of Will, but neither her mother nor Kirsten seemed particularly interested in hearing any details about her life. Clearly, everybody and everything was on the back burner until Kirsten walked up the aisle the third Sunday of August on the arm of her brother. Jensine remembered ruefully her father had said he would crawl on his knees if he had to, but in the end, he agreed his leg probably wouldn't hold up. Jensine just hoped his failing eyesight would permit him to at least glimpse Kirsten in her bridal finery. He spent most of his time now in the big chair in the front room with his leg elevated and was delighted Jensine spent hours every day at his side visiting about the wedding plans, Lake Valley, and Will Mosher. Unlike her mother and Kirsten, he was interested, and Jensine happily shared her new relationship, which had blossomed since that first Sunday afternoon in early May. She couldn't help bragging about Will's wonderful voice and orchestra.

"Don't sound like much of a way to make a living, Jensie. A man's got to have something solid, especially these days."

"Oh, Will's orchestra just plays on the weekends. Otherwise, he farms his folks' place. When they retire in another year, he's going to take it over. But I think that's why I like him so much. He loves music and even recites poetry, but he's not afraid to roll up his sleeves and get his hands dirty either." She paused to reflect for a minute before continuing, "It's hard to explain, but there's something so alive and honest about him. And, Dad, he has the most wonderful sense of humor."

"So you like this fellow, do you? Sounds like it could be a bit more than that," her father teased. Then he added, "I hear he might be comin' to the wedding? I'm anxious to meet this farmin' musician and see if he's good enough for my favorite school marm."

"Actually, Dad, he is going to come. He said there should be a little lull in the farm work about then."

"Well, if he comes, he can keep me and my leg company. Damn thing anyway. Thought it'd be better by now.

To Jensine, it seemed the summer flew by. Maybe it was because she found herself so looking forward to the weekly exchange of letters with Will. By the time the last session of summer school was over, August was half past and Kirsten's wedding only a few days away. The sewing machine was finally quiet—they were all giving thanks for that, especially her father—and the second batch of homemade mints was carefully stacked between sheets of waxed paper in the pantry. According to her mother, the first attempt wasn't creamy enough to offer guests, especially those on the groom's side from Albert Lea.

The only real worries were the big floppy hats ordered to match the bridesmaid dresses that were late in coming, and the hot argument between the prospective bride and groom about honeymoon plans. Because Thor was being transferred and would be covering new territory, he foolishly suggested they get settled in Fargo first and take their honeymoon later in the fall. Kirsten had a royal fit over this possible change in plans, and told him in no uncertain terms she was not about to do anything of the sort. Her main objection was that her trousseau would be out of season by then. She sulked, argued, and slammed doors until he finally couldn't take any more and agreed their North Woods honeymoon wouldn't be delayed. He wasn't happy about it; that was clear. When Jensine found him on the back steps rolling a cigarette, he looked up and muttered, "I hope the damn mosquitoes eat her alive." Jensine laughed and thought he was learning fast just what life with Kirsten would be like if she didn't get her way. She almost felt sorry for him.

It had been one of those unusually dry summers. The corn started firing in early August, and the sumac had already turned a deep crimson. Even Sunday morning prayers and the clumsily painted sign in the Methodist parking lot pleading "Pray for Rain!" had no effect. But it really didn't come as a surprise when they awoke the third Sunday of August to a violent thunderstorm accompanied by sizable hail. As Peder said, "That's pretty much the way of things." Jensine just hoped the weather didn't foreshadow a stormy marriage. Kirsten wailed throughout the morning that her wedding was ruined. "Sure, it couldn't piss a drop all summer, but come my wedding day..." And that, understandably, quickly brought her mother from the pantry.

"Now you listen to me, Kirsten Marie, and I mean business. I won't have that kind of talk in this house. Maybe your Norwegian traveling salesman will put up with it, but I won't, and you know it!" Kirsten stormed upstairs and Johanne returned to the pantry where Jensine was helping with last-minute chores. She knew Mrs. Adolph Peterson, their farm neighbor to the south, had offered to come over and help, but her mother quickly refused, making the excuse Clara had enough to do without helping with a wedding. Jensine knew otherwise. Clara simply wouldn't do things quite right. She had heard her mother say more than once Clara Peterson didn't have the sense God gave lettuce. As they worked in the pantry, putting the chicken salad together, Johanne sighed, "Your sister's hopeless sometimes, Jensine. Her complaining isn't going to change a thing except make her eyes puffy and red. Then we'll have to listen to that, I suppose."

"Oh, she'll get over it. I just hope Will doesn't get stranded in this miserable weather."

"He'll be fine, Jensine. Hope we have some time to do some visiting with him, coming all this way and such." Jensine glanced at her mother in surprise. Johanne had barely acknowledged Will's existence to this point.

"I think he'll stay overnight at least. He wants me to ride back to Lake Valley with him."

"That makes sense. It'd save the expense of taking the bus, and as long as you have to be there in a week anyway...Is his car reliable? I wouldn't want you stranded out in the middle of nowhere with some man you barely know. It wouldn't be proper." Johanne sniffed a bit with that opinion, and Jensine quickly decided not to tell her mother she knew Will more than a little. There would be plenty of time later to share any plans because they weren't rushing into anything. Both Will and she agreed on that. Besides, Johanne looked exhausted. She hoped Kirsten appreciated how much work had gone into making the wedding everything her sister wanted it to be. Her mother added a pinch more salt to the salad and turned her attention to stacking the dozens of fresh buns she had baked early that morning into towel-lined dishpans. It reminded Jensine of Ella's noon lunches.

"Are we going to take the food into the church this morning?"

"Suppose we should. Just hope Mabel isn't too generous with the salad when she makes up the buns. It'd be the talk of the town if we ran out. We need to straighten up a bit before your Will gets here. Wouldn't want him thinking we don't keep house."

"Oh, Mom, that would be the last thing he'd care about. You spend some time on yourself now. I'll finish the buns." Jensine shook her head as her mother left the pantry. This whole wedding thing had gotten out of hand. It would be so much simpler just to get married at the parsonage and avoid all this foofaraw, to say nothing of the expense.

Jensine knew her parents couldn't afford the extra dollars, especially with her father's ill health and the fall crop outlook so poor. Her mother had stretched the wedding budget to its limits, even suggesting she would make do with her best dress instead of sewing a new one, but Kirsten totally threw up her hands at the suggested possibility. "For God's sake, Mother. It's black! You can't wear that to a wedding."

Peder settled that argument. "Johanne, you have Christian drive you into Owatonna and pick out something nice. You don't get much, and the mother of the bride should be decked out a little bit." Her mother grumbled about where the money would come from for that, but Jensine knew she was pleased. Her father was right. This should be a special day for Johanne, too. In the end, she took her sister Maren with her, and together they picked out a flowered lavender dress with a matching cloche. Even Kirsten forgot her self-preoccupation long enough to compliment her mother.

Jensine had just finished the buns when Kirsten hollered from upstairs. "I think he's here, Jens. There's a car coming up the lane."

Jensine quickly pulled her apron over her head and smoothed her hair in front of the small mirror over the sink. She wanted to be the first to greet Will, and she knew that would take some doing with her sister already at the kitchen door. "For heaven's sake," she thought, "can't I even have this one moment…just for me." She put her hand over Kirsten's. "I want to see him before he meets everyone, Kirsten. It's been more than two months."

Kirsten relinquished her hold on the doorknob and grinned, "He's all yours."

Thankfully, at least the downpour had turned into light drizzle as she stood on the front step and watched the car churn up the sticky lane and pull along side the door. Even through the mud splattered windows, Jensine could see Will's smile, and that was all it took for her to dismiss her promise not to rush into anything,

Jensine was sure Kirsten and her mother were watching through the small pantry window when Will got out of the car and gathered her into his arms. "I've missed you, Jens," he said softly, holding her close. Then he laughed, "I think I'll give whoever's peeking out that window a real eyeful." He kissed Jensine deeply, pressing her tightly to his body and caressing her back, even letting his hands drop over her bottom. "How's that?" he whispered. "What will your mother think?"

"Will Mosher!" Jensine warned laughingly. "Stop that!"

Within minutes, Will Mosher had Johanne Neilsen's full approval, and she had him at the kitchen table sampling the food for the wedding lunch. "Help yourself to the pickles," she encouraged, putting an opened quart of dills on the table. "They're this year's batch and nice and solid, even if I do say so myself." By the time Will had eaten three buns liberally spread with chicken salad and a half jar of solid dill pickles, Johanne was practically cooing over him. "I should probably have you try the pickles we're taking to the church. Be a shame if some of them weren't good." Will happily obliged even though Jensine's stomach turned at the thought. He was going to be darn sick if he didn't stop.

Later, after he visited with her father, Will suggested Jensine and he drive the food to the church. "Give us a chance to be alone," he whispered. They packed the dishpans of buns, two big crocks of chicken salad, and five quarts of dills into one side of the back seat and draped Jensine's bridesmaid dress over the other. Then she ran up the stairs to tell Kirsten she would see her at the church. "Well?" she asked.

"Well what?"

"What do you think of him?"

Kirsten shrugged. "He's okay. Not what I thought." Then she added, "I hope he has a suit coat along and knows enough not come in those rolled-up shirt sleeves."

Jensine almost laughed. She knew her sister well enough to recognize envy. So be it. Will definitely had a masculinity about him that made Thor seem soft and a little too smooth. "See you at the church then." She turned to go downstairs and then added, "Be happy, Kirsten, please be happy."

Her father had moved from the table to the big kitchen rocker, and she stopped to kiss his cheek on her way out the door. He grabbed her hand and squeezed it tight. "I like him, Jensie. He's a smart fellow, too. Knows he's got to pet the cow to get the calf."

17

In a Family Way

By November, Kirsten had left her husband three times, Moveta was back to spending inordinate amounts of time, especially in the morning, in the teacherage bathroom, Frieda was writing weekly letters to a missionary nurse in New Mexico, and Jensine was in love. In fact, she and Will Mosher spent nearly every Sunday together. Moveta joked they were competing with Albert and her for the front room davenport. Frieda always managed to be conveniently gone, over at the school working on labs, according to her, when Will came to spend the afternoon. At first Jensine felt guilty, almost as if she had stolen him from Frieda, but he seemed so unaware of her feelings for him that Jensine couldn't believe he felt anything more than warm friendship for her friend. Sunday nights were uncomfortable, though, she had to admit. Frieda always seemed a bit cold and kept to herself. But as the week progressed, she warmed and things were pretty much back to normal.

Moveta was another story. She seemed happy but sick most of the time. One evening while Jensine was helping clear the supper table, the bathroom door slammed particularly hard for the third time in less than a half-hour. She handed her stack of plates to Ella apologizing, "I really should finish helping you, Ella, but I have to check on Moveta. I wish she would get over her flu bug. She's been throwing up for the past week."

Ella laughed sympathetically, "Oh, she'll get over it. Just takes a bit."

"I'm surprised she still has such a good appetite."

"Yah," Ella replied, "that's the way it is sometimes."

Jensine could hear Moveta retching in the bathroom, dry heaves, as her mother called it, when there was nothing more to come up, but still the gagging kept on. The door was slightly ajar, so she pushed it opened enough to stick in her head. Moveta was on her knees over the toilet. "Moveta, can I get you anything? Maybe if you put a wet towel to your forehead…"

"God, Jensine, mind your own business!" Moveta managed to reply before her head went back into the toilet bowl. Finally, after a few more desperate attempts to vomit, she struggled to her feet, looking, Jensine thought, like the wrath of God.

"Maybe you should see a doctor, Moveta."

"You are so dumb sometimes, Jensine. Don't you get it? I'm knocked up, or as you would probably say, being so proper and all, *with child*. I wouldn't think it would take a farm girl so long to catch on." Moveta bent over the sink, splashing cold water on her red face.

"But you can't be, Moveta," Jensine stammered, embarrassed she had been so clueless. "You'll have to resign. It's right in our contracts."

"And that's a bad thing, Jens? Albert and I are going to get married as soon as we can. The only problem will be telling our folks. I know my mother will have an absolute fit and so will his, but we'll work it out."

Jensine could hear Ella coming up the stairs and put a cautionary finger to her lips, but Moveta seemed unconcerned. "Come on in, Ella."

Carrying a plate of soda crackers, Ella came into the bathroom. "Sometimes a few crackers helps your tummy. Just munch on 'em real slow," Ella encouraged.

"Thanks, Ella, you're a peach." Moveta took a cracker and headed for her bedroom. "I'm going to hit the sack or at least lie down until the next wave hits me. I thought it was a morning thing, not all day."

"Usually is, but I know with my last one, it was pretty much day and night until the fourth month was over."

"Oh, God, I'll die before then!"

Ella put a comforting hand on Moveta's back. "Nah, you won't and when the little one gets here, you won't even remember it. Well, 'spose I'd better be gettin' home. Emil'l be expectin' supper. Course, he wouldn't ever think to fill his own plate. That'd be askin' too much."

Jensine followed Ella down the steps. She wondered if Frieda knew, or if she herself was the only one who was so dumb? For gad's sake, Will probably even had it figured out. Ella must have sensed her discomfort because after she tugged on her worn winter coat, she reached up to pat Jensine's cheek. "Oh, it's not the end of the world, Jensine. Lots of babies come a little early. And like Emil says, it'll all come out in the wash. Always does."

Jensine went back up to her bedroom to correct papers and wait for Frieda, but her usual self-discipline failed after the first two papers. Who really cared if John Cramer could successfully diagram a sentence anyway? It sure as the world wouldn't help Moveta out of her fix. Finally, she decided to go down to the kitchen and make a batch of fudge. Over the past year, that had become a real comfort, and even Moveta, the master fudge maker, admitted Jensine's had reached a level of perfection generally allowed only to home economics teachers. "You're catching on, Jensine. The secret is not to push it along. Just a soft rolling boil over medium heat. Fire up the stove and it sugars every time." By the time Frieda was back from the school, Jensine was spreading the creamy stuff on wax paper to cool.

"What's up, Jensine? You've gone to making fudge in the middle of the week? I thought that was a Sunday night ritual for you and Moveta."

"Oh, Frieda, I'm just worried about what's going to happen to Moveta. You knew she was pregnant, didn't you? Why didn't you say something? I feel really stupid, you know."

Frieda pulled out a chair and reached for a butter knife to cut herself a generous piece of fudge. "I thought you knew, Jensine. Besides, it wasn't really my news to share."

"Do you think Mr. Kruse knows?"

"I don't think so, but I think some of the kids are suspicious."

"How do you know that? How embarrassing for Moveta!"

Frieda laughed, "Oh, they're quick to pick up on anything. Sometimes there's a little visiting during lab time, and I heard Mary Anne tell Johnny that Miss Ogilire hit the door running again during Foods."

"I feel so sorry for Moveta, Frieda. Her mother is such a witch, and Albert's mother doesn't sound like a picnic either."

Frieda sighed. "I've always wondered what the big deal is. I'm sure most of the people out here have sex before marriage. Nobody says much about that, but let a girl get pregnant and the tongues really start wagging. I don't think the kids will be mean, though. Moveta is popular with her students." Jensine was surprised. She had thought Frieda would be more judgmental.

"Do you think there's anything we can do to help Moveta?"

"Not really, Jens. It's something she and Albert will have to work out. Say, this fudge is really good."

Jensine was excited for Thanksgiving. According to her mother's rare letters, her father was better, the sore almost healed on his leg. Her brother was anxious for her to meet Hannah Lipinski, a young hired girl he was seeing from the farm across the section. Kirsten and her husband would be home, and most important of all, Will was going with her. Her only misgiving was leaving Moveta, who decided at the last minute not to go to St. James. Later, Jensine couldn't help wonder about Moveta's farewell. She'd hugged her tightly at the door and whispered, "Thanks for everything, Jens. You're the best." What was that all about?

There were light snow flurries on Thanksgiving morning as they headed east on Highway 16. Even with an extra blanket tucked around her legs and feet, it was chilly, and Will pulled her close. "Snuggle up, Jens. It's drafty." A good excuse, anyway, Jensine thought, as she slid across the seat. The trip actually seemed short.

They visited nonstop, and when there was a lull in the conversation, Will was humming or singing a tune. Like her father always said, she couldn't carry a tune in a basket, but there was something about Will's absolute joy in music that warmed her inner being. Once she turned to him and asked in amazement. "How do you remember the words to all of those songs?"

"Oh, if I like a song, I pretty much remember it after I hear it a few times." By 11:00, they were turning north out of Albert Lea and home was less than an hour away. Suddenly, Will slowed down and pulled to the side of the road. "Guess this is as good a time as any." He reached into an inner pocket, took out a small blue box, and placed it in Jensine's palm. "Guess I'm supposed to pop the question now. Not enough room in the car to get down on my knees, though, and we'd probably look pretty silly standing out in the corn field , but how about it?"

"Will, I never expected…" and she started to cry.

"Hey, don't cry! If I'm the right fellow, you're supposed to be happy."

"Oh, Will, I am! I just don't know what to say."

"How about yes?"

"I don't mean that, you silly. Of course, I'll marry you. It's just I didn't expect it to happen right now." She slipped the ring out its satin bed and handed it to Will. "Here, you put it on my finger."

"It's not much. Pretty small, but maybe when times are better, we can get you a real sparkler."

"Will, it's beautiful!"

"I know things aren't settled enough to set a date, but maybe by spring, we'll have a handle on it."

Christian met them at the door with a plump, glowing Hannah by his side. The house was warm and filled with the aroma of Jensine's father's pipe tobacco, baking turkey, and sage dressing. Pumpkin pies cooled on the kitchen table, and Jensine thought she spied mincemeat as well. She had mentioned to her mother it was one of Will's favorites. It pleased her Johanne had remembered. The room quickly filled with her family. Jensine was overjoyed to see her father walking, aided only by a small cane. His eyes, though, were not improved; he seemed to feel his way to his usual high-backed rocker in the corner. There was no sign of Kirsten and Thor.

"You're lookin' pretty happy, Sis," Christian said as he took her coat. "Got some news for us?" And her mother, about to baste the turkey again, turned to her expectantly.

"Actually, we do," Jensine smiled and held out her left hand. Christian whooped and grabbed Will's hand in a strong clasp, and her mother, in an uncharacteristic show of emotion, left the turkey roaster open on the oven door, dropped her basting spoon, and hugged her.

"I was thinkin' it was about time for this to happen. You can only court for so long. Like my father said, it's either tie the knot or cut line." She turned to her husband, "Peder, Jensine's got herself a diamond." Then she opened the door to the upstairs, "Kirsten," she hollered, "Are you and Thor coming down or not? We've got big news!"

There was no answer at first, but then an unenthusiastic "Be right down." When Kirsten finally appeared, Jensine was surprised to see how thin and pale her sister was. She seemed sick and unhappy. "What's up?" Kirsten asked.

Christian grabbed Jensine's left hand and held it out to Kirsten. "Jens and Will are engaged."

Kirsten glanced at the ring and then held her own hand along side her sister's. "Look how small it is compared to mine." The room was suddenly quiet until Johanne slammed the oven door shut and said with tight lips, "What an awful thing to say, Kirsten. You should be ashamed of yourself. Just because you're not happy, doesn't mean you have to spoil things for the rest of us."

Jensine was used to Kirsten's meanness, but she never expected her to be downright cruel. What she really wanted to do was to grab Will, get back into the car, and head for Lake Valley, but that wouldn't be fair to her parents and Christian. She wondered what Hannah and Will thought of her family. When Jensine finally brought herself to look at him, she expected to see hurt embarrassment, but he just shrugged and winked at her. He handed his jacket to Christian, took Jensine's hand in a tight squeeze and said, "Say, Johanne, I bet you've got one of those good dill pickles for me."

Jensine felt a sudden sense of relief as the tension left the room as quickly as it had come with Kirsten's nasty remark. Her sister turned to stomp up the stairs, muttering as she went, "Nobody gives a rat's ass that I'm pregnant and feeling like shit." For once, her mother simply ignored her.

❧

They got back to Lake Valley Sunday afternoon. Will just dropped her off and drove on to Round Lake. The teacherage was quiet, so Moveta was probably resting. Her door was open, though, so Jensine peeked in and then pushed the door open. Moveta's room was completely empty, the bed stripped and the closet cleaned out. Jensine sat down on the unmade bed and wept. She hadn't even said goodbye to Moveta.

Later, when Jensine went down to the teacherage kitchen, she found a note propped up against the sugar bowl on the table. It was short and to the point, just like Moveta. *"Dear Jens, Frieda, and Ella... Albert and I decided to elope. Be happy for us. Jens, make yourself a batch of fudge tonight and remember to take it nice and slow. Stay in touch. Moveta."*

❧

Betty Kramer didn't return after Thanksgiving either. Jensine thought she must have the flu going round, but when her absence lasted through the whole week, she decided to ask in study hall. "Has anybody heard anything about Betty? She's been gone all week."

There was a long uncomfortable silence. Still Jensine didn't catch on. "Maybe one of you who lives near her could see she gets the assignments. That way she won't be so far behind..."

121

There was still no response until finally Leona Kepka cleared her throat and said, "Miss Neilsen, Betty's folks sent her to Minneapolis... to live with her aunt." A couple of boys in the back snickered, and when Jensine shot a reproving glance their way, she couldn't help noticing Harold's ears were so red, they were almost purple; and later, much to her chagrin, that he was still practicing with the basketball team, even though Betty had been sent away in disgrace.

18

HOLIDAY VISIT

Life at the teacherage wasn't the same without Moveta. Truthfully, it was more than a little bit dull without her humor and straightforward manner of speaking. As Emil often observed, "That girl ain't afraid to call a spade a spade."

Even Ella seemed subdued and after the first few quiet evening meals, she sighed, "Moveta spiced things up around here, Jensine. That's for sure. It's too quiet somehow, and Emil says he misses her somethin' terrible. She was always good to talk to when he cleaned her room after school. He don't care too much for the teacher they hired to take her place. Kind of a nitpicker, Emil says. Always findin' fault." Jensine didn't say anything, but Emil hit the nail squarely on head. Moveta's replacement, Miss Emerson, was indeed a tightlaced sourpuss. Jensine wondered why Mr. Kruse had given her the job, but knew it was probably because there wasn't anybody else available. Thankfully, though, Miss Emerson drove from Lake Park where she lived with her mother, so there was no need for her to stay at the teacherage. That would have been the last straw. The students weren't happy with the replacement either. Moveta was a popular teacher who made her classes a practical living experience.

Even shy Ethel Fuchs stopped by one morning before school to lament Moveta's absence. "My ma says it's a stupid rule. Just because you get married and have a baby doesn't mean you're softheaded and can't do your job." Jensine marveled at how her articulation, and along with it, her confidence, had improved. Ethel had managed to find her own little niche in high school, writing and illustrating for the school newspaper. It was an afterschool activity, but surprisingly, Bill Fuchs agreed she could stay a couple of hours each week to do her part. Other staff members commented how out of character it was for the colorful farmer to allow such a thing, but Jensine knew, even though he would never admit it, he was proud of his daughter. And Ida positively glowed when Jensine visited with her after Sunday services. Of course, she was pregnant again, her belly an enormous bulge on her otherwise thin body.

Shortly before Christmas, Moveta invited Ella, Frieda, and Jensine to Brewster for what she called a little Saturday afternoon get-together. Ella was waiting by the door ready to go when they stopped at the farm to pick her up. "Emil kinda wishes he could go, too," she laughed as she got into the car. "But I told him this was just for us lady folks."

The O'Connors were living on the family farm in a small house usually reserved for the single hired man. Moveta, already showing her pregnancy, met them at the door with an enthusiastic hug when they arrived shortly after 2:00, bearing gifts for the marriage that hadn't really been celebrated. "You shouldn't have, but I love it!" she exclaimed as she eyed the presents and then took their wraps to put in the tiny bedroom just off the front room. "Just make yourselves comfortable while I take a cake out of the oven. I'm trying out a new recipe, something special. Hope you'll like it."

"It smells real good, Moveta," Ella sniffed in approval.

"And you have to sample my Christmas baking," Moveta encouraged as she returned from the small nook that served as the kitchen bearing two huge plates of cookies, candy, and sweet breads. "Jensine, I made fudge just for you and peanut brittle for Ella. I know it's her favorite. Frieda, the divinity is for you. I even shelled black walnuts to put in it."

"It all looks wonderful, Moveta," Jensine complimented, settling for a big piece of fudge. "And your house is so festive." It was true; Moveta's little home was absolutely delightful and certainly reflected her flair for decorating, from the soft, colorful toss pillows on the davenport to a small Christmas tree dotted with crimson velvet bows.

Ella leaned forward, offering a small package to Moveta. "Here, Moveta, I made you a little somethin' for your wedding."

"Oh, Ella, you are such a dear!" Moveta carefully unwrapped the set of pillowcases trimmed in tatting and gently smoothed the soft linen with her hands before looking up, tears in her eyes. "I love them! I want to put them on right now."

"Oh, it's not much," Ella said modestly. "I tucked a little somethin' between the cases for the baby, too. Don't know about the color, but it should fit whether it's a boy or girl." Moveta lifted the top case to reveal a pair of yellow knitted booties. There was no holding back the tears then.

Frieda cleared her throat and probably saved them from a wet afternoon by passing the candy plate around again and placing her own gift in Moveta's lap. "I hope you have a cedar chest, Moveta. Otherwise, I botched it."

"Knowing you," Moveta smiled, wiping her cheeks with the back of her hand, "it will be something different and beautiful, and you bet I have a cedar chest." Frieda's gift was an elegant fringed chest scarf, a mosaic of gold and deep burgundy.

"It's from Germany. Mother still has relatives there, you know."

Jensine, remembering her mother's advice to give a gift which would remind Moveta of the giver in years to come, had decided on a crystal bowl, perfect, she thought, for fresh sliced peaches or cranberry sauce. When Moveta pulled back the white tissue, the cut glass was resplendent in the afternoon sunlight. It was lovely. For once, she was without words. "I don't know what to say."

"That's a first, Moveta," Frieda said, and they all laughed. It wasn't long before it was 4:00, and they had exhausted all the news from Lake Valley, including a few tales about the new home economics teacher. It was time to think about heading back.

"Suppose Emil'l be lookin' for me to put somethin' on the table for supper," Ella laughed.

"Oh, no you don't! You're not leaving here without coffee and a big piece of my cranberry cake. I'll stir up the hot butter sauce right now." Quickly, they found themselves sitting around the oak table, ready to enjoy Moveta's dessert. She lit the Christmas candle nestled in a centerpiece of spruce boughs, and Ella folded her hands for a brief prayer. Jensine was surprised when Moveta quickly crossed herself. She certainly hadn't expected her to convert, at least not so quickly. The table talk was light, plans for the holidays and such. Moveta seemed cheery, but there was definitely an air of hurt vulnerability about her. Finally, Ella had the courage to ask the question all three of them had on their minds. She reached over and covered Moveta's hand with her own.

"How's it goin' with your folks, Moveta? I suppose you'll be seein' them sometime over Christmas."

Moveta put down her dessert fork with a shaky hand. "Actually, I haven't seen or heard from them since Albert and I eloped. Dad sent us $50, but it was just a check, no message or anything. I tried to call home, but my mother hung up as soon as she heard my voice."

"I'm so sorry, Moveta, but don't let them spoil the happiness you and Albert have found," Frieda prompted.

"How about Albert's folks? I bet they're excited about bein' grandparents and all." It was beyond Ella's comprehension any baby wouldn't be welcomed and loved. To her, life was all about family.

"Oh, God no! Albert's mother won't even speak to me. She told Albert that I trapped him into marriage by getting pregnant. And can you believe this? The old bag never says a word directly to me or calls me by name, even when we're in the same room. Like last week, we bumped into them at the grocery store. She looked right through me and said to Albert, 'Hope you told *her* not to waste a lot of money on Christmas baking. You two don't have a pot to pee in the way it is.' Isn't she a sweetheart? God, I wanted to push her right on her fat rump! But you know what? Albert and this baby are my sunshine. I don't really give a damn about what Alice O'Connor thinks."

"Well, Albert's pa ain't that way, too, is he?" Ella asked in the futile hope someone in the family cared about Moveta.

Moveta laughed. "Ella, he's been henpecked for so many years, he doesn't even have a mind. It's just mush. 'Whatever you say, Alice' and 'Yep, Alice, I done it.' That's about the extent of his conversation. He spends most of his time in the machine shed or barn just to get away from the old witch."

"That woman'll be mighty sorry some day," Ella said, her voice tight with disapproval. She'll get her due. You mark my words. It'll come home to rest right on her shoulders."

The early evening was already dark, and the ride home quiet. Finally, Ella broke the silence. "And Moveta's such an easy person to love. It's just a darn shame. I might just write her folks and give 'em a piece of my mind." She blew her nose loudly and added, "Never heard of such a thing, turning out your only child. They're breakin' her heart; that's what they're doin'. I'm real worried about her.

But Frieda was optimistic. "I'm not, Ella. Moveta's the kind to make her own happiness, and she will."

Just as her own sister was bound and determined to make life miserable for herself, Jensine thought sadly. But she knew no matter what her parents were going through with Kirsten, nothing her sister could ever do would cause them not to love her.

Jensine was invited to Will's parents the next day. He picked her up in time to attend church, and as they slid into a front pew next to his parents, his mother reached over and squeezed her hand. Lottie Mosher was an absolute joy, but her husband was an odd duck. For one thing, he fussed about almost everything but didn't appear to do much of anything except lie stretched out on the davenport and mutter, "What's gonna become of me?" Lottie was a cheerful little woman, short and round, who hobbled around on her arthritic feet without complaint. She had the patience of Job, at least to Jensine's way of thinking. Her own mother would have grabbed Amos Mosher's ear and had him up on his feet in two jerks. She wouldn't have put up with that nonsense, not for a minute. Amos got a big kick out of testing Jensine's intelligence and was clever in the way he did it, making it seem as though he really wanted to the know the answer, while in fact he already did. He also seemed bent on getting her response to loaded philosophical questions. "Is there a heaven and a hell?" he asked her one Sunday over dinner. Even Lottie lost her patience a bit.

"Oh, for pity sakes!" she retorted, little red flags of color appearing on her plump cheeks, "You've been an elder in the church for twenty years. If you don't have it sorted out by this time, don't bother Jensine with your foolishness!"

"Don't get your dander up, Lottie," he grumbled. "Just askin' a simple question. Pass the pickles, will you, Will? No need for them to be sittin' in front of your plate the whole meal." He leaned back in his chair and wiped his hands on the sides of his vest. "Might as well serve up the pie. Looks like everybody's about done eatin' their meal." Of course, Lottie was quickly up, carrying the plates to the kitchen so she could serve the pie. Jensine got up to help and couldn't resist giving her a quick hug once they were in the pantry.

"Do you mind if I snitch a cookie? Your filled raisin are fabulous, just like everything else you make." It was true. Lottie's cooking and baking made even dear Ella's pale in comparison. Her cake doughnuts were simply wonderful, and her bread had a special taste, the result of using the water she had saved from boiling potatoes.

"You go right ahead, Jensine. Will likes them, too, but I think he's most partial to my doughnuts. And don't you pay any mind to Amos. He just likes to tease a bit. Everybody's got their ways, I guess." Besides being a good cook, Lottie Mosher was the least judgmental person she had ever met. Jensine looked around the small pantry and kitchen, thinking if things went as planned, in another year, she would be stacking her own dishes on the shelves and filling a cookie jar with crisp sugar cookies. Will's folks had bought an old home in Round Lake, just down the street from Jacob and Lizzie Bauer. It had a big garden spot and a small barn, so Lottie could have a few chickens and fresh eggs for her baking. The house wasn't anything special—no running water, an outdoor privy—and to be honest, more than a bit run-down. But Lottie said it would do just fine since she could walk both uptown for groceries and to the Presbyterian Church for Sunday services and monthly ladies aid meetings without any trouble. None of it mattered to her husband. According to Amos, he wouldn't be around long anyway. As far as Jensine could tell, there wasn't anything wrong with him a good swift kick in the behind wouldn't take care of.

Jensine and Will had set the summer of '30 for their wedding. His folks would move into town after the corn picking was done the previous fall, and Jensine, of course, would complete the year at Lake Valley. That would give her time to add to her savings, and Will could finish making payments on the machinery he was buying. After talking to Will's older brother Francis, who was a country schoolteacher and not interested in farming, Amos and Lottie had agreed to sell Will the farm with a small down payment and yearly installments on the principal due after the fall harvest. It bothered and surprised Jensine that her father had been lukewarm about their plans. "Not that I don't like Will, Jensine," he had said. "I do, but times are real hard. Don't think I'd be givin' up a good teachin' job to be a farmer's wife right now. Give it some time. You never know. Things might pick up after a spell. President Harding seems to think so."

"What's keepin' the pie?" Amos called from the dining room.

Lottie winked at Jensine. "Give him the small piece, Jensine. He'll be sure to grumble about it all afternoon."

19
DIRTY POLITICS

Jensine awakened to a cold, quiet house, not a sound of Ella stirring up the coals in the range and no smell of fresh coffee drifting up the stairs as it usually did that time of morning. Strange, she thought and then wondered if she had just imagined hearing the back door open earlier while she was still drifting in and out of sleep, pleasantly reliving her weekend with Will. "Ella?" she called from the top of the stairs. "Are you down there?" Jensine waited and then suddenly apprehensive, belted her robe around her and quickly went down the stairs. She found Ella, still wearing her worn winter coat, slumped over the kitchen table, her head cradled in her arms.

"Ella! What is it? What's wrong?" Jensine pulled a chair close and gathered the shaking woman into her arms. "My God, Ella, what is it? Tell me!"

"Oh, Jensine, somethin' awful's happened," Ella managed to sob. "It ain't true. Emil would never do such a thing. And to think folks would even believe a flat-out lie that that."

"What are you talking about, Ella? What's happened?"

By this time, Frieda was in the kitchen doorway, concern clouding her dark eyes as she pulled back a chair and reached across the table to cover Ella's hand with her own. "It's all right, Ella," she soothed. "It's all right. Just tell us what's wrong."

"I don't know if I can even talk about it," Ella said, lifting her head and wiping her nose with the handkerchief Frieda provided.

"Try, Ella," Frieda urged. "Just start from the beginning."

Ella struggled to compose herself. "Those new folks who moved into the old Anderson place south of the creamery are the ones

131

sayin' it. They got those two big girls in high school, couple of real homely ones, too, if you ask me."

"You mean the Angerhoefers, Ella?"

"Yah, them. I guess the mister is real tight with Voss, and you know how he don't like us on account of Emil sticks up for Mr. Kruse and don't kowtow to Voss like some folks do."

"I know that, Ella, but I don't see what it has to do with..."

Ella broke in with fresh tears. "What he's sayin' is nothing but a lie." She shook her fist to emphasize. "A damn lie is what it is!" Jensine looked over Ella's head at Frieda. Neither one of them had ever heard their housekeeper use even a mild expletive. Something was very wrong, and Jensine had the feeling if Clarence Voss had anything to do with it, it wasn't good.

"Friday noon, Emil went down to the furnace room like usual to get a mop for cleaning up the lunch mess, and there was those two girls, smokin' behind the boiler, Emil says, as big as you please. He told 'em in no uncertain terms to git on out of there, and they'd be called on the carpet with Mr. Kruse the first chance he got. Course, they beat it to Voss right away, and he hightailed it to Mr. Kruse 'fore Emil could even get there."

Jensine breathed a sigh of relief. "Oh, Ella, that's no big deal. They're the ones who are in trouble, not Emil."

"That's what I told Emil, Jensine, but he says they told Mr. Kruse Emil tried to grab 'em..." Ella's voice dropped to almost a whisper, "...and touch their private parts."

"That's absolutely ludicrous!" Frieda said sharply. "Mr. Kruse will never go for that bunk. They're just trying to save their own skins, Ella."

"I know that, too, Frieda, but still, folks like dirt, and you know it. Voss and Angerhoefer want Emil to answer to the school board at the meeting tonight. Emil can't take a thing like that. I know that for sure. His heart ain't so good as it used to be."

"Mr. Kruse'll never permit it, Ella," Frieda said with conviction. "Is Emil over at school now?"

"He can't even be there at the school. He's at home tryin' to make sense of the whole thing. Mr. Kruse says for him not to come in today, not until he get things worked out."

"Well, I'm taking you home, Ella. That's where you need to be, not over here waiting on us lazy ladies." Frieda tried unsuccessfully to lighten the situation. "Jensine, tell Mr. Kruse to cover my first hour class for a few minutes. I'll probably be a little late."

❦

There was an unmistakable undercurrent of tension at the school, a distinct polarization around opposite ends of the horrid rumor. Jensine noticed several high school girls sympathetically standing around the Angerhoefer girls, who normally were loners. Jensine had even heard them in the bathroom once, laughing and complaining about what a hick school Lake Valley was. Now, suddenly, the sisters were basking in newfound popularity. Then, there were others like Johnny Atzen who was obviously arguing with his classmates about the accusation. Their voices dropped as Jensine walked by, but not before she heard Johnny say, "It's bullshit, you guys, pure bullshit!"

"You got that right, Atzen," Glen Heinrichs agreed. "Both of my folks are coming to the meeting tonight, and they're going to bring up a few things old Voss might not want to hear. And as for the Angerhoefers, I guess they move around a lot and are nothing but troublemakers wherever they decide to squat."

"Yeah," Johnny added, "my dad heard old man Angerhoefer had sticky fingers the last place he worked."

At this point, Jensine felt she had to step in. "Glen…Johnny… get to class. This isn't the time or place for this discussion."

But Johnny wasn't willing to let it rest. "But it is, Miss Neilsen. Emil's gettin' screwed, and you know it!" Before she could answer, Frieda came up the steps and literally shoed the group along to class.

"Tardies will be reported," she said firmly. "I'll talk to you at noon, Jensine," she whispered as she closed her door.

133

It was a long morning and an even longer afternoon. Mr. Kruse came to her door shortly before the end of the sixth period to tell her there would be a brief faculty meeting in the library immediately after school. Frieda had told her at noon the school board had decided to question Emil at the board meeting even though Mr. Kruse had argued it was nothing more than a ridiculous accusation. Some of the board members said it would be best to bring it out in the open, so folks would know what really happened. Jensine felt sick to her stomach.

❧

The meeting after school was brief and without Clarence Voss. Mr. Kruse looked exhausted, as if he hadn't slept the entire weekend. After the elementary teachers trooped in together, he closed the door and sat down at the table, at first seemingly absorbed in the pen he held. Then he said, "It seems we have some unpleasant business to talk about. I don't believe what's being said about Emil, and I know you don't either, but the fact remains the Angerhoefers have made some serious charges, and there's a certain faction here in Lake Valley that seems to support them."

"You wouldn't be talking about Clarence Voss and his cronies, would you?" Frieda questioned caustically. "Surprise, Surprise!"

Mr. Kruse couldn't help a tight smile. "I know you know the score, Miss Bauer. It's been pretty much an ongoing problem since I came. But I didn't think they'd stoop this low, using Emil to get at me." He paused, and the room was quiet except for the corner radiator, which chose that moment to hiss and vibrate. "I would prefer that none of you attended the meeting tonight. Hopefully, most folks will be sensible and decide to stay home."

"I'm sorry, Mr. Kruse, but I don't think we can count on that, not with Voss trying to drum up support all over the district. I think we should all be there for Emil, in the front row."

"Amen to that!" Marjorie was nodding her head emphatically. "I know you're thinking this is a community concern, but we're part of this, too."

"I appreciate what all of you are feeling, but I think it's best not to add any fuel to the fire. Stay home and let the school board do its business."

"Like those nincompoops know anything," Frieda muttered. "This whole mess really scares me. Personally, I think Emil needs a good lawyer."

"Miss Bauer, please...Having some high-powered lawyer at the meeting could backfire. It might make people think Emil has some reason to defend himself."

⁂

Neither Jensine nor Frieda cared about having any supper. Jensine felt more like throwing up than eating, and Frieda was literally fuming about the whole affair, pacing back and forth in the chilly kitchen, her hands gripped tightly around a hot cup of cocoa. Jensine broke the silence. "I feel like we should ring up Moveta. Emil is one of her favorites, and she would want to know."

"You know, Jens, that's a good idea. She might even have Albert drive her over so she can strangle Voss. Let's ring her."

"Frieda, do you think Ella will go to the meeting?"

"Oh, God, I didn't even think about that, Jens; we've got to go no matter what Mr. Kruse says. We don't have to say anything, but we need to be there for Ella. Let's make a quick sandwich and head over to the school about a quarter to seven."

"I'll ring Moveta. You make the sandwiches."

Moveta's response was, first shock and then anger. "That bastard Voss!" she bit out. "I'll kill him with my own two hands. Call me the minute you hear anything."

Mr. Kruse was more than just a little naïve to believe Lake Valley folks would be sensible and stay home. By the time Jensine and Frieda walked over to the school, the gymnasium was already nearly filled. The school board and Mr. Kruse were seated behind a big table that had been brought in from the library. Ella and Emil, looking suddenly old and frail, were squeezed into the front row on the left side, their adult children surrounding them on either side, and across the center aisle were the Angerhoefers, their two daughters— without their usual makeup and short skirts—and, of course, Clarence Voss. The rest of Lake Valley seemed to have chosen a side according to their opinion.

"Let's find a seat toward the front if we can, Jensine," Frieda whispered. "Otherwise, we won't be able to hear anything."

"Mr. Kruse will see us for sure then."

"I don't really care, Jens. We're here for Ella and Emil."

As they moved up the aisle, an obviously pregnant woman stood up in the second row and waved, "Over here, you two." It was Moveta and next to her, Albert. Moveta patted the two chairs next to her. "Sit!" she said. "There's going to be some real shit kicking here tonight if I have anything to say about it."

Frieda leaned over to whisper, "I don't think any of the teachers listened to Mr. Kruse. They're all here, even the prune-face who took your place."

⁕

At seven o'clock, the board chairman, Art Dietz, tried to bring the meeting to order. Not even a sharp rap with the gavel made any noticeable dent in the noisy gym. Jensine remembered that these were the same people who came last Friday night to cheer on the basketball teams. Now, they seemed more like a mob ready to enjoy someone else's humiliation. What had Emil ever done to deserve this? To give him credit, the chairman did attempt to carry on the regular business of the board, but several farmers seated on the Angerhoefer side rudely interrupted him.

"We ain't interested in the minutes of the last meetin', Art, and you damn well know it!" one hollered out. "Get on with what we're here for." The chairman looked over to Mr. Kruse for help, but he just shrugged as though there were really nothing he could do about it.

Art Dietz was in obvious misery as he said, "Well, then, I guess we got some parents here tonight with a complaint. Mr. Angerhoefer, do you want to say what's on your mind?"

136

"It's what I come for, I guess." A heavy, unkempt man dressed in overalls got to his feet. "Most of you folks probably know we're new out here. The missus and I got two girls in the high school, and what they tell us is that the janitor over here put his hands in places they don't belong. I told the missus we gotta do somethin' about it before some girl who can't handle herself gets hurt. Looks to me like you got a dirty old man workin' right here in the school, and it ain't right." A mixture of cheers and boos erupted.

Moveta leaned forward to pat Emil on the back and whisper, "What a liar!" The board chairman seemed unable to quiet the room, and finally another member grabbed the gavel and pounded on the table.

"Shut up, all of you! Shut up! Or we'll take the meeting to the library, and you can all go home. That's where you should be anyway."

"You got no right to be doin' that, Cletus. This is community business. Maybe you shouldn't be on the board if you don't got the stomach for it." Jensine immediately identified the speaker as a farmer who hung out daily at the store, according to Ella, and complained about everything. Voss here says you're just a yes man for a superintendent anyway. Ain't that right, Clarence?"

"What's your part in all this, Voss?" Art Dietz asked, apparently ready to take charge again. "Emil's not on trial here. The board is just listening to a parent complaint."

"Well, these folks are new to the community, and they came to me because they didn't think they'd get a fair shake if they went to Kruse. I think the only fair thing to do is to ask Emil a few questions and maybe our fine superintendent, too. Maybe he's not cut out for this job. Seems like he doesn't know what's goin' on in his own school." Again, more cheers and boos.

Mr. Kruse stood up quickly, leaned on the table, and looked across the crowd. "Emil Ehrenberg has been a respected man in this community all of his life. Last Friday afternoon, he reported two girls were smoking in the furnace room, and he told them to leave. I have absolutely no reason not to believe him."

"Oh, sit down, Kruse!" a woman called out. "Let's hear from Emil. You don't know what went on down there."

Just as quickly, Frieda was on her feet. "And you don't either, Mrs. Varner. A good question might be why the girls were down in the furnace room in the first place?"

"Well, I know about your family, *Miss Bauer*, German Jews. That's what the Bauers are." There was a single collective gasp from the crowd.

"That's it! Let's move the meeting, Art," Cletus shouted.

"Without even giving Emil a chance to speak after you dragged him to this kangaroo court? Over my dead body!" It was Moveta, and she was steaming.

"If I could just say a word..." Emil asked, standing with Ella at his side to face the crowd. It was suddenly very quiet in the gymnasium. "I want you folks to know I treat your kids like they're my own, and if you don't know that by now, there's not much I kin say. Those two girls were smokin' in the furnace room, and that's all there's to it. The most I did was motion with the broom for 'em to git. And they did...no back talk or anything." He paused and reached over the back of the chair to take his mackinaw. "I think we'd better head on home and let you folks sort it out for yourselves. Come on, Ella, we'll go out the side door over here." Emil's family watched them go but remained seated.

"Now what?" Jensine turned to Frieda.

"Well, I know one thing," Frieda replied "I want my question answered. What were those girls doing down in the furnace room, if they weren't smoking?"

The board must have been thinking the same thing because Art Dietz pounded the gavel again and looked directly at the Angerhoefers. "All right if we ask your girls a few questions?"

"Hell no, it ain't all right! They're just kids and they been through plenty already. My girls don't lie. If they say they wasn't smokin', then they wasn't. If they say a dirty old man put his hands on 'em, then he did." There were murmurs of assent from that side of the gym.

"I usually stay home and mind my own business, but this whole thing's a pile of shit, if you don't mind me sayin' so." It was Bill Fuchs, leaning against the back wall, his voice loud and clear. "What we got here is a bunch of folks ready to lynch a man that's done nothin' but good for this community his whole life. Why don't you just get a rope and be done with it?"

"Oh sit down, Fuchs! What do you know about anything?" It was Mrs. Varner again.

"Oh, I reckon I know about as much as anybody here tonight, includin' you, Betty, or whatever the hell your name is. Nah, this whole damn ruckus was stirred up by Voss on account a he wants to be the superintendent 'stead of Kruse. If you ask me, he's a pretty low sonofabitch to do what he's doin' here tonight. He's the one who oughta be strung up, to my way of thinkin' anyway."

"Well, nobody askin' you, Fuchs! Or cares what *you* think!" Betty Varner looked ready to explode but sat down quickly as her husband gave the backside of her coat a solid jerk.

But Bill Fuchs wasn't finished, not quite. "Pay my taxes same as anybody else in Lake Valley, so don't see as how I can't say what I'm thinkin' same as the rest. Angerhoefer says his girls don't lie. Maybe they don't. Well, I'm purty sure my girls don't either. They know they'd be in for a good thrashin' if they did." The crowd on both sides of aisle grew very quiet; sensing something important was about to happen. Allthough Bill Fuchs was rough and had fathered more children than any of his neighbors thought sensible, he did possess a certain integrity that couldn't be denied. And his family discipline was common knowledge. "Just got one more thing to say, and then I'll shut up." There was loud applause from the Voss side. "My girl Ethel was in the bathroom, back stall, she says, last Friday afternoon when those two girls who don't smoke or lie come in. Course, they didn't have no idea Ethel was in there, so wouldn't you know they opened the window a crack and rolled a smoke. Then they laughed, big as you please, Ethel says, about tellin' Kruse Emil grabbed 'em. I guess the way they put it was folks here are so damn dumb, they'd believe almost anything." He pushed away from the wall. "Ethel's waitin' out in the truck. Be glad to go git her if you wanna ask a few questions.

If you don't..." he shrugged. "Air in here is kinda gittin' to me...a real rotten stink." When there was no response except a few quiet whispers, he pulled the flappers of his cap over his ears and walked out, as did several others on the Voss side.

Art Dietz suddenly awakened from his state of paralysis, pounded the gavel, and demanded forcefully, "Anybody else got somethin' to say?"

Jensine found herself suddenly on her feet. She had not intended to say anything, but the shaky words came out anyway. "I think this community owes Emil Ehrenberg and his family a huge apology, and it should start with LeAnn and Lola Angerhoefer and Clarence Voss."

"You tell 'em, Miss Neilsen!" Johnny Atzen's voice rang out from the back, where he and about twenty other high school boys were gathered. Then they started to clap and stomp, and the gym emptied quickly, but not before Art Dietz pounded the gavel one more time.

"We're expectin' you folks to fold and stack your chairs 'fore you go. Can't really expect Emil to do that when he gets here tomorrow morning, now can we?"

❧

Moveta quickly shrugged into her coat. "Let's all drive out to Emil and Ella's. I can't wait to see Emil's face when we tell him the good news. What a nightmare for him."

On the drive out, Frieda looked over at Jensine and commented. "I'm glad you said something in there, Jens. Otherwise, you were so quiet about the whole thing. It was almost like you had something else on your mind."

"Oh, I was just thinking about something that happened a long time ago and what my mother said to me."

"I'm listening."

"It's personal, Frieda."

The dooryard of the Ehrenberg farm was filled with cars as they followed Moveta and Albert to a parking spot along side the barn.

"How did people get here so fast?" Frieda asked. "We left right away."

But as they approached the open porch, which led to the front door, there were no sounds of any celebration, but rather an eerie quiet. Moveta frowned and then shrugged questioningly before she knocked. Emil and Ella's oldest son Percy opened the door. Jensine took one look at his pale face and knew something was very wrong.

Moveta must have thought the same, her voice shaky and feigning cheerfulness. "Where's your dad, Percy? Tell him Moveta is here to give him a big hug!" It was then they saw Ella sitting on the end of the saggy couch, head bent and hands folded carefully in her lap. She didn't even look up at the sound of Moveta's voice.

"God, what's going on, Percy?" Moveta asked, squeezing Albert's hand for support.

Percy's quiet voice echoed in the silent room. "All we really know is when Ma and him got home, he went out to the barn... I guess to check on the new calves. That's what he told her anyways." Percy covered his face with his hands to regain some semblance of composure. "I don't know what us kids were thinkin' of... lettin' 'em go home alone like that."

"Where is Emil, Percy?" Frieda broke in, her face pale.

"He's still in the barn, Miss Bauer. I called the coroner in Jackson, and he said to leave him there until he got out here." Then he sobbed, "I covered him with one of Ma's quilts."

"Oh, my God," Moveta whispered. Albert pulled her close with one arm and reached out for Jensine with the other.

"Was it his heart?" Frieda asked quietly. "I know your mother was worried about that."

Percy turned away as if he couldn't bear to speak the awful words. His wife Myrna rose quickly from her place by Ella and took her husband in her arms. "Let me, Percy," she said softly. "It'll be easier for me to tell them." She paused, took a deep breath and expelled it heavily. "I guess Emil swallowed some Paris green...that awful stuff he used in the barn to get rid of the flies. By the time Percy found him in the harness room, it was too late."

As Emil's sons bore his casket down the center aisle of the Lake Valley gymnasium, Jensine couldn't help but notice how the polished oak floor gleamed in the afternoon sunlight. What in God's name had happened in this place?

Then she remembered Emil's simple but ironic words of comfort. "It'll all come out in the wash, Jensine. Always does."

20

LET ME LOVE YOU

Things did come out in the wash, but not in any way that mattered a whole lot to Jensine and Frieda. They got through it; that's as much as could be said. And really, they had little choice since there seemed only a brief, though shamed, pause in Lake Valley before life went on as before.

Emil was gone, and nothing could change that, Jensine thought sadly whenever she looked across the windblown cornfield to the southwest corner of the old settler's cemetery. It was childish to even think it, but she was glad Ella had chosen that spot to be Emil's final resting-place instead of the Lutheran cemetery up the road. Two weeks after the funeral, Frieda and she stopped at the fresh grave. There was a single path through the snow to the mound of dirt, which wouldn't be leveled until spring, and where a frozen geranium, only recently searching for sunlight from a windowsill in Ella's kitchen, lay in humble tribute. Frieda broke the silence. "I can't stay here."

"I know. It's freezing!" Jensine agreed as she turned up her coat collar and moved to block the wind.

"I mean Lake Valley."

Jensine felt as if someone had just delivered a hard punch to her stomach. "But, Frieda…" Then she thought back to that awful night of the school board meeting. "Is it because of what Mrs. Varner said?"

"Oh, that's nothing, Jensine. Actually, I just have to laugh about it because I'm pretty sure Betty Varner, good Lutheran she claims to be, doesn't have even the foggiest notion of the difference between a Christian and a Jew."

"But your family's Presbyterian anyway, isn't it?"

"Well, Mother and we kids are. Dad just goes on special occasions. In Germany, the Bauer side of the family's Jewish, but since Mother is a gentile, we kids wouldn't be Jewish; in the strict sense of the faith, that is. But if Mother were Jewish and Dad a gentile, then we would be."

"Really? It seems like just the opposite would be true."

"It's because the mother's the heart of the home and the one responsible for observing Jewish law," Frieda explained. Then she paused and reflected, "Dad must have been mighty surprised to find synagogues so few and far between here. Actually, I think the closest one is in Sioux City, and that's over a hundred miles from here. Anyway, it's a life they left behind, and like Dad always tells Mother, "Turn the page, Lizzie. Turn the page.""

"But if that's not it, Frieda..."

"I don't know. It's a lot of things really. You'll be a farm wife as soon as Amos and Lottie move to Round Lake, and Moveta will be busy making babies like any good Catholic wife." Then she added, "And I think we both know Ella won't be back." Frieda paused and then stooped down to touch the earth at her feet. "Good-bye, old friend. I probably won't be back, but you'll always be here," she said softly and touched her heart in a silent gesture.

Jensine swallowed the lump in her throat. "But you'll finish out the year, won't you, Frieda? At least that."

Frieda rose and put her arm around Jensine's waist. "Come on. It's too cold to stay here. Don't worry, I won't leave you all by your lonesome for a little while. I've been accepted by the University of Minnesota for fall quarter to work on a degree in public health. That I know for sure. After that..." She shrugged her shoulders. "Lately, I've been thinking about missionary work, maybe with the Navajo in New Mexico."

"But you love teaching, Frieda, and I know you like the kids here."

"I'll still be teaching, and in a way that really matters, Jensine. Tuberculosis is a terrible problem on the reservation. They need both nursing and education. And don't kid yourself; we know the kids here will do just fine without Frieda Bauer."

"But they won't, Frieda, and neither will I!"

"Oh, pooh, you'll be so busy with Will, you won't even miss me. I need a change, Jensine. I really do. Right now, I feel bitter and angry, and I'm having a difficult time understanding and accepting how so many good people of this community could be fleeced out of their common sense by a fool like Clarence Voss and a few chronic complainers like Betty Varner."

"But how about Bill Fuchs and the Atzens? And at least Voss had the sense to resign. Marjorie said she heard he took a job in Iowa someplace. And the Angerhoefers, I guess they left in the middle of the night."

"But how does that really change anything, Jensine? Some things can't be fixed. It's as simple as that."

⁂

Jensine and Frieda were right; Ella didn't return to the teacherage. Percy stopped by one evening not long after they'd been at the cemetery to tell them his mother had gone to stay with his sister in Windom for the time being. "Mom's not doin' too well with this mess. Kind of disoriented," he apologized. "I'm thinkin' there's just too many reminders of Dad around here right now. But she said to tell you she misses you and…and another thing…" He couldn't help chuckling when he added, "She says to remember to close the damper on the range a bit, but not too much so as you draw smoke." Jensine and Frieda both laughed, remembering how they had done that very thing making a batch of fudge one Sunday evening and had to open windows to air out the kitchen.

"It'd probably be for the best if you ladies went on ahead and looked for someone else to help you out here."

"I know your kids are all in school. Would Myrna be interested?" Frieda asked.

He shook his head ruefully. "I already mentioned it to her. A few extra dollars wouldn't hurt nobody these days, but she won't have nothin' to do with it. I'm thinkin' maybe Grace Atzen might be a good one to ask."

145

As Percy put on his cap and turned to the door, Jensine put her hand on his arm. "It won't be the same without your folks, Percy. I hope you know that."

"Not for us either," he said quietly.

"I didn't realize Percy was so gray," Frieda commented as she closed the door behind him and turned off the porch light.

In the quiet of her bedroom, Jensine started a letter home but quickly gave up on the idea. No words seemed to come after the greeting. Really, what more could she say about Emil's suicide that would mean anything to her parents who had only met him once. And besides, her father's health was so fragile that even talking about death seemed tasteless. He was no longer able to see except for the fuzzy outline of things, and when he wasn't resting in the darkened bedroom, he spent his time in the big kitchen rocker with his leg propped up on a stool. The doctor told Johanne even if there wasn't improvement, they could be thankful the ulcer wasn't getting worse.

Kirsten's baby was due in early June, perfect timing so Jensine could stay with her father while Johanne went to help with the new arrival. At least she wouldn't have far to go; the couple was back in Albert Lea living with Thor's mother until the implement business picked up, if it ever did. Farmers just weren't buying anything.

Jensine was worried about Kirsten. She hadn't really expected her sister to go through morning sickness without vigorous complaint. That just wasn't her sister's way, but she seemed to grow more cross and apathetic about the baby as the months went by. From her letters, it sounded as though she and Thor spent most of their time quarreling. And Kirsten wasn't one to spare the intimate details of their arguments, which was unfortunate, because her family was left to worry about them long after the two of them made up. The marriage was definitely an on-again, off-again affair. Christian had told her privately at Christmas that he and Johanne had made more than one trip to Albert Lea, once even in the middle of the night, to try to sort out things. Kirsten had locked everyone out of the house and threatened to gas herself, but after a good hour of Johanne's pleading and, finally, threats to call the police, she opened the door and fell sobbing into her husband's arms. When Jensine told Will about it, he just laughed. "Everybody's afraid to call your sister's bluff, Jensine, and she knows it."

"Well, I hope you don't think I'm that way."

"Better not be. You'll find yourself out in a snow bank."

Jensine found it easy to talk to Will about almost anything. Her mother wouldn't have approved of her sharing family business, but it was such a comfort to curl up on the teacherage couch with him and just talk. She knew his presence helped her get through the emptiness she had felt after Emil's death. He had even driven over the same evening to be with her. At first, since Maurice Sheldon was at the board meeting, she assumed he had carried the news to Will. But it was Frieda. She had driven Jensine back to the teacherage and then continued on to Round Lake to spend the night with her parents, leaving Jensine alone, feeling hurt and totally abandoned. But within an hour and a half, Will was there. He hadn't even taken time to change his chore clothes. Jensine didn't care. All that mattered was he was there, and she was in his arms. "Are you okay, Jens?" he whispered, his breath soft against her hair.

"Oh, Will, it is so terrible! How did you find out…Maurice?"

"No, I was just finishing up in the barn with the new lambs when Frieda and Ma came out to get me." His hands begin moving over her back in strong soothing strokes. "God, I can't believe it about Emil. Ma just grabbed the pail from me, and said she'd finish up. Frieda pushed me out the door, and said, "Jensine needs you. I'll help your mother.'"

Gradually, Jensine's convulsive shivering stopped, and she was vaguely aware Will's hands had moved from her back to the soft underside of her breasts. It was an intimacy they hadn't shared before, but she didn't even think about stepping away. Will was warm, alive, and exactly what Jensine needed.

"Let me love you, Jens," he whispered. "Let me love you."

21

A Change in Plans

Kirsten's baby, a colicky but otherwise healthy girl, arrived on schedule the second week of June. The timing couldn't have been better, Thor home for the weekend, Jensine just finished with the Lake Valley school year, and the first session of summer school at Mankato not yet begun. As planned, Johanne went to Albert Lea to be with her daughter. Thor's mother, Beatrice, or Big Bea as Kirsten called her in private, was simply not up to coping with a new baby. The woman had numerous ailments, the details of which she loved to share with any willing ear. In Johanne's estimation, they were all in her head. "That woman'll live to be a hundred because she never does anything but sit and complain." With Thor on the road most of the time, Kirsten and her mother-in-law were forced into close and uneasy company, and even though Jensine knew Johanne was excited about her first grandchild, she wasn't looking forward to being in middle of a lot of squabbling.

For Jensine, however, it was a peaceful time; hours of visiting with her father and Christian on the front porch after the supper dishes were put away and then writing long letters to Will after everyone else had gone to bed. "By this time next year," she thought, "I'll be getting ready for my own wedding." Will and she agreed that it would be just a simple affair at the parsonage with her parents witnessing the ceremony. To begin with, there wasn't money for anything as extravagant as Kirsten's wedding, even though Jensine knew her mother would go without to be fair. "You should have a nice wedding, same as Kirsten, Jensine. We'll manage somehow."

But Jensine was adamant. "Oh, Will and I have the money to pay for it ourselves, but we think it makes better sense to buy furniture and get a few other things we need for the farm."

"It's probably for the best," her mother agreed, "but your father and I don't feel right about it. She stiffly embraced Jensine and added, "You're just as deserving as your sister." And then, "But I guess we both know a wedding doesn't make the marriage. Look at your sister and her mess."

At the end of the week, Christian drove them into Albert Lea to properly admire baby Alice and fetch Johanne home. It was quickly evident she was more than ready to leave. Her grip was sitting on the front step when they arrived, and she looked frazzled and tired as she came out to the car to greet them. As Jensine and Christian helped Peder out of the car, Johanne made her feelings abundantly clear. "I'm ready to go any time you are. This constant squabbling is almost more than a body can take. I'll tell you one thing. Thor needs to do some real housecleaning when he gets home. There's just no sense to it, those two fighting like they do."

Beatrice was nowhere to be seen, taken to her bed with another bad headache, according to Kirsten, who was walking the baby, shushing her as she paced back and forth across the living room. She took one look at Jensine and burst into angry tears, "God, I'll never know why anybody wants a baby! Nonstop bawling...and if I have to rinse out one more stinky diaper...Here, enjoy!" she encouraged sarcastically, as she handed the baby to Jensine and stormed into the kitchen. Then she added crossly from the other room, "And if Thor thinks he's going to be on the road and gone all of the time, he's got another think coming! It's his mother and his squawking brat!"

Johanne shook her head and watched protectively as Jensine put the baby to her shoulder. "Put your hand behind her neck, Jensine." Jensine wanted to remind her mother she had held a baby before, but then she caught her father's wink and knew there wasn't any point to being sensitive over such a small matter. Instead, she walked over to the davenport where Christian had settled her father, carefully nestled Alice in the crook of his arm, and went to find Kirsten.

Kirsten was leaning over the sink and didn't say anything until Jensine walked across the room and put her arm around her shoulders. "I'm sorry, Kirsten. I know it's got to be hard not having a place of your own and with Thor gone so much. But it'll get better. Just give it a little time."

"Oh, Jens, why can't anything ever work out the way I want it to?"

"But things will work out, Kirsten. And Alice is just beautiful."

Kirsten turned to her, tears welling again, "That's part of the problem, Jens. I don't know if I really want it to work out."

The ride back to the farm was quiet, Christian seemingly lost in his own thoughts and Peder napping almost before they were out of town. Jensine thought her mother seemed downright weary, and she was surprised at her mother's frankness when Johanne sighed and said, "Sometimes life's just too much." She paused and then continued, "Understand I'm not feeling sorry for myself, Jensine. Lots of people have it a whole lot worse. It's just with your father being so sick and the note coming due on the farm, I don't need this commotion with Kirsten every time I turn around. Seems like she's never happy about anything."

Jensine felt sorry for her mother. Hard work and constant worry, that seemed to be her lot in life. She wondered if they were really in danger of losing the farm. They had worked so hard to make a go of it, and now nothing seemed to be worth anything. If it weren't for the cans of cream Christian delivered to town twice a week and the egg money, there wouldn't be any cash to count on. But the creamery was still giving nice premiums, Noritaki china, so that must be a good sign, Jensine thought. Her mother had been able to collect twelve place settings for her, and it was beautiful, a delicate pink azalea pattern trimmed in gold, packed at the bottom of her cedar chest, just waiting to be used.

151

Will spent the Fourth of July in Ellendale at the Jensen family reunion. Jensine had warned him in advance about Cousin Enid and her obsession with nursing. Will had written back that she hadn't met his Aunt Tillie with her ear trumpet yet, so he'd give her relatives a little leeway until he could make an honest judgment. Will's sense of humor was one of the things Jensine adored in him. But from the moment he arrived, Will seemed quiet, not his usual self at all. It had been a hot, sultry day, so after the reunion at the farm, the two of them decided to drive over to Beaver Lake for a quick swim. The holiday crowd had long since departed, so they had the beach to themselves as they sat down and wiggled their toes in the still-warm sand. Finally, though, Jensine turned to Will and asked, "Is something wrong, Will? You seem so quiet and deep in thought."

Will picked up a flat stone and threw it easily, watching as it skipped cleanly across the water at least three times. Jensine clapped in appreciation. "The secret, Jens, is you have to find a really flat stone." Then he turned to her, "I don't know how to tell you, Jens, because I know how disappointed you're going to be."

"What? Just tell me, Will. What is it?"

He paused, reached for another stone, took a deep breath, and said, "I guess we aren't going to get the farm after all." This time he didn't skip the stone but threw it hard, hitting the water sharply.

Jensine was stunned. "But what happened? I thought it was all settled. Aren't your folks going to move into town in the fall?"

"I guess that's still the plan,"

"Well, then I don't get it" Suddenly she thought of what her mother had said and what Will had written in early June about how dry things were down that way. "Oh, Will, they haven't lost the farm, have they?"

"It's not that, Jens." He searched for another stone. "The thing is Francis didn't get his teaching job back out in Indian Lake, and he's decided to take over the farm."

"Decided! Francis has *decided* to take over the farm." Jensine couldn't remember ever having been so angry. "How does that work? You've been doing the farming all along, and now suddenly, Francis is coming home to farm. For God's sake, he won't even pull a weed in your mother's garden!"

Will pulled her close. "Shh, Jens, it's all right. We'll figure out something."

"You know, I can believe your father would pull a stunt like this, but not Lottie!" Jensine angrily shrugged off Will's arm and went to stand by the water's edge. "Why, Will? Why would your folks pull the rug out from under us like this?"

Will came to stand by her. "Actually, it's not Dad. He said Francis had his chance and turned it down, but Ma said Francis is married, and now that he's lost his teaching job, he and Eleanor don't have anyplace else to go." He lifted his shoulders in a tired shrug. "I guess Ma figured him being the oldest and all, he should get the farm if he wanted it."

"That's a lame excuse if I ever heard one! What about us, Will? What about us?"

"I'm working on it, Jens. There's an older couple, Nora and Paul Wickstrom, who want to rent their eighty west of town, so I've been talking to them. We can move our machinery and livestock over there when the fall crops are in." Then he paused before continuing, "The only problem is we can't have the house until they build in Worthington."

Jensine felt as if someone had doused her with a cold pail of water. "Then we can't be married next June?"

Will sighed. "I'm disappointed, too, Jens. But I think you'll like the Wickstrom place. Kind of tucked back in a big grove of trees. The house is old, but it's got a nice big porch and lots of flowers planted around. Nora said to bring you over to see the place when you get back to Lake Valley in August."

Jensine's disappointment stuck in her throat even after Will left the next morning. When she told Johanne and Peder, her mother simply said what Emil had always said, "It'll all come out in the wash, Jensine, always does."

Jensine couldn't help herself. "You know, I'm sick to death of that pathetic platitude, Mother. It means absolutely nothing to me."

"Well, feeling sorry for yourself won't help any either. That's for sure. This whole thing probably wasn't too easy for Will either." Then she added, "And don't go blaming Lottie. You don't know her reasons, Jensine."

Her father reached over to pat her hand and added, "Your mother's right, Jensie. And things could be a whole lot worse. You got a good job there in Lake Valley."

When Kirsten heard the news, she just shrugged. "It figures." And then somewhat smugly, "Oh, come on, Jens, you didn't really think the good fairy had touched your life with a magic wand, did you? Even you can get crapped on, big sister."

Will did take her out to the Wickstrom place her first weekend back in Lake Valley. Jensine had to admit that it was a lovely spot—lots of towering shade trees, big open front porch, and flowers everywhere. After Nora proudly explained how she had carefully planted her perennials so something was always blooming, she invited Jensine into the kitchen for lemonade and a frosted molasses cookie while her husband and Will checked out the horse stalls in the barn. The house itself was drab, and badly in need of fresh paint. Evidently Nora Wickstrom wasn't as interested in her house as she was the yard. She told Jensine about the cold upstairs and drafty front room. "But," she said, "we close 'em both off during the winter, so it don't bother us none. A body don't need a lot of space to get along. We got the bedroom down here and a nice warm kitchen what with the range and all." Nora paused. "About the only bad thing is you got to carry your water from out in the orchard on account of there's no pump in the house. We used to have a cistern, but it cracked and don't hold water."

But none of it mattered to Jensine except that Will and she would have a place of their own. "How is your house in Worthington coming along?"

154

"Oh mercy, we haven't even gotten around to that yet, but Paul says if the fall corn prices are decent, maybe we can dig the basement in the spring" Then she smiled at Jensine in quiet approval. "You know, we're real excited about Will and you gettin' the farm. Paul says Will's a hard worker, and he'll make a go of it if anybody can in these tough times."

As they drove down the dirt lane, Will pulled her over to his side. "What do you think, Jens? I kinda like the place."

"I do, too, Will, but do you think we'll ever get to move in? Nora says maybe, maybe, they'll start in the spring." Jensine couldn't help herself, "Oh, Will, I'm so disappointed. Now we probably can't even count on getting married until the following summer."

Will was silent as they turned onto the gravel road. "I'm sorry, Jens," he finally said. "Say, Ma says we should stop over for fresh pie before we head back to Lake Valley. Want to?"

"Not really, Will. I still think it's pretty crummy of your folks."

Will squeezed her thigh gently. "I was pretty down at first, too, Jens, but now I'm thinking this is probably for the best. We're going to be renting better land, for one thing. The Wickstrom place never floods and the soil's got a little more clay in it to hold the moisture in dry spells."

"I wished I could be more like you, Will. You always see the bright side," she said as she laughingly slapped away his errant hand.

"Fresh peach pie at Ma's?"

"Oh, I suppose."

Lottie embraced Jensine and Will at the door. "I was hopin' you'd come. Come sit at the table, and I'll pour the coffee." The pie was delicious, of course. Even Amos managed a compliment. But the conversation didn't have its usual spontaneity, and Jensine sensed the whole mess would have to be aired if they were to get past it.

After coffee, Will and Amos went out to the barn to repair a harness, and Lottie and Jensine were left alone in the quiet kitchen, Lottie busily stirring cream into her coffee and Jensine tracing the lines on the red checkered table cloth.

Finally, Lottie put down her spoon. "It wasn't a fair thing to do, Jensine. God only knows, Will's the one who's kept this farm goin'."

Jensine couldn't keep the bitterness out of her voice. "Then why, Lottie, why? Will's worked so hard…and then you do this to him. I'm sorry, but it is unfair. Francis doesn't care a fig about the farm, and you know it."

Lottie's face crumpled under her tears, and Jensine suddenly felt very ashamed. This woman's life wasn't easy, and she knew it. "Oh, Lottie, I didn't mean to sound so hateful. I'm sorry." She reached over to cover the knobby arthritic hands that had done far more than their share of work.

"No, I'm the one who's sorry, Jensine. It isn't right. It's just Will has always been such a go-getter, and folks like him right off. But Francis is different that way. People don't take to him the way they do Will, and things are always kind of a struggle for him. Amos says he's got big ideas, but they never amount to anything."

"But he doesn't even like the farm, does he?"

Lottie was quiet as she wiped her eyes with the back of her hand. "Not like Will, and I don't think being a farmer's wife is what Eleanor has in mind at all." She took a sip of the now-cold coffee and pushed it aside. "But it's about all Amos and I can do to help out. With no job, they'll be out in the street." Then she paused, "You know, my own mama used to say you end up helping the one that needs it. I never understood why she helped my brother Chet so much and welcomed him back with open arms when he just up and left his family every couple of years, but now I know what she meant. Francis is a lot like Chet. He just can't seem to make a go of anything, but Lord, I still love him!" Lottie sighed, tears again close to welling over. "I hope you and Will can forgive me, Jensine."

Jensine took Lottie in her arms and hugged her. "Oh, Lottie, you know I love you! Besides, we really like the Wickstrom place. Will and I will be just fine."

Perhaps, Jensine thought, every family did have a child that seemed to need more than the others just to get along. Like Kirsten.

She visited with Lottie while Will did the evening chores, and then he drove her back to Lake Valley. They made a batch of fudge together and curled up on the davenport to catch up on what they'd missed all summer, comfortable with their growing intimacy.

Jensine had just finished correcting the last spelling paper and was ready to head for the teacherage and a quiet October weekend with Will when the school custodian, Maynard, stopped in with the news. "Boy, ain't it somethin', Miss Neilsen?" Unfortunately, Emil's replacement liked talking more than he did wiping down the boards and mopping, so Jensine prepared herself for a lengthy and colorful visit before he got around to pushing the oil mop up and down the aisles of her classroom.

"What's that, Maynard?"

"Betcha you haven't heard the news. You sure as hell ain't gonna like it when I tell yuh the stock market's crashed...bottom dropped right out." Jensine felt suddenly chilled despite her warm sweater. "Yep, I'd say the whole country's got a tit in the wringer now!"

23
LAMBS DANCING...

The teacherage was a gloomy place with Ella, Moveta, and Frieda all gone. Frieda, who was finishing her nursing degree at the University of Minnesota, wrote frequently to Jensine and seemed excited about the possibilities of mission work with the Navajo in New Mexico. Thoughtfully, she always asked about Will.

Frieda's replacement at Lake Valley was a shy young man, so quiet even Maynard gave up trying to visit with him. "Never knew such a quiet fella," Maynard told Jensine one afternoon as he pounded her erasers over the wastebasket, sending up a cloud of chalk dust. "It's like he's got nothin' to say." Then Maynard dropped his voice and leaned toward Jensine at her desk. "If you ask me, it's kinda funny he rides up from Lake Park every day with an old gal like Florena. She bosses him around like he's some damn little kid." Then caught in his own chalk dust, Maynard backed up and coughed loudly before continuing. "Yah, they even eat their lunch together. See, she spreads this red tablecloth on her desk, and they just have their own little picnic right there."

Jensine asked, even though she knew the answer. "And how would you know that, Maynard? You weren't peeking, were you?"

"Oh, you betcha, Miss Neilsen. At least 'til she put that construction paper over the window. Well, hell, somebody's gotta keep an eye on Ole Florena, you know. Damn if she's not old enough to be his ma."

Meanwhile, Moveta, in a well-intended effort to patch things up with Albert's mother, had quickly converted to Catholicism and was already expecting her second child, but it did nothing to soften her mother-in-law's heart. Mrs. O'Connor still refused to speak directly to Moveta or even hold "the little heathen," as she called her first grandson; this according to Moveta who sent Albert over to Lake Valley every month or so to bring Jensine to Sunday dinner.

Jensine saw Ella in church one Sunday with Percy and his family, but the Ella she knew was gone, lost in a faraway world of her own. Now, she was an old, thin woman with empty eyes who bore little if any resemblance to the energetic, compassionate housekeeper who clucked over her girls at the teacherage.

Still, Jensine was glad she was at Lake Valley. Her teaching kept her busy and she was careful to save as much of her salary as possible. Knowing it would offend her mother if she knew, Jensine waited until Christian took her to meet the bus after her visits home before tucking some money in his pocket. "Use it for Dad or to pay a bill," she told him. "I know it's tough."

Johnny Atzen was still a handful. On Halloween, during his junior year, he and a few friends somehow managed to put a young heifer and an outhouse on the school roof. Maynard was beside himself. When Jensine walked across from the teacherage early the next morning, he and Mr. Kruse were staring up at the roof in disbelief. "I know it's that asshole Johnny Atzen and his crowd. Now how in the hell am I gonna get a cow and an outhouse off the damn roof?" Maynard complained.

"You don't have to, Maynard," said Mr. Kruse calmly. "I think we'll just wait until whoever put them up there decides they should come down. I don't think we'll have to wait too long. Someone's bound to miss their outhouse, probably their cow, too." He was right.

Martin and Louella Kruse left at the end of Jensine's fourth year at Lake Valley. The new superintendent, E.B. Logue, was an old, retired math teacher from Minneapolis, recently widowed and still bent over in his grief. He kept a bottle of liquor in his bottom right-hand drawer, according to Maynard, that is. Jensine doubted it.

"Well, I seen it with my own eyes, Miss Neilsen. I was in askin' what he wanted to do about the spot in the gym floor that's bubbled up on account of the water leakin' in from the roof. 'Well, Maynard,' he says. 'I guess we'd better fix the roof before we do anything.' Then he opened a drawer and took out this bottle of hooch. He didn't try to hide what he was doin' or nothin'. Nope, just pulled out the cork and took a big swig. Didn't offer me none though."

Mr. Logue wasn't a fireball, that time of his life long over. He did have a surprisingly blunt manner of speaking, though, and wasn't afraid to season it with a few *hells* and *damns* which caused Florena to loudly clear her throat in censure. But he was fair and taught an advanced math class, calculus, for interested juniors and seniors like Johnny Atzen, who said Mr. Logue was a math whiz. And unlike Mr. Kruse, he wasn't disapproving when teachers came to him with discipline problems and handled them with a real knack for understanding human behavior. Maynard said it was probably because he was used to "dealin' with all of those hooligans up there in Minneapolis."

Jensine found out for herself about Mr. Logue's bottle and his discipline one October afternoon when she had trouble with one of the Hayenga boys in afternoon study hall. Norman Hayenga was a huge kid who took delight in passing gas openly, the noisier the better. Finally, Jensine had had enough and told him to get out. He just laughed and passed even a bigger stinker, so rotten Johnny Atzen fell out of his seat in mock asphyxiation, sending the whole study hall into an uproar. For the first time in over four years, Jensine left her study hall unattended, and in tears, and went to get Mr. Logue.

He sat so small and frail at his desk that Jensine wondered if she shouldn't have gone down the hall to get the new manual training teacher instead.

"Mr. Logue, I want Norman Hayenga out of my study hall...and right now. And I don't want him back! He can sit and pass gas somewhere else!" She waited for him to get up and follow her back to her study hall. At first he didn't move, but then he shoved back his swivel chair and bent down to pull open the bottom desk drawer. He took a half empty bottle from it, and paused after uncorking it to say, "Sorry about Norman, Miss Neilsen. We'll get his ass right out of there." He took an enormous swig, enough to make his eyes water, and generously offered the bottle in her direction. Jensine was almost tempted.

The noisy study hall quieted down quickly as they entered, all eyes glued to the white-haired man whose task was to remove big Norman from the room. E.B. didn't say anything, just looked at Norman for a long minute, beckoned with his finger, and waited. "I got plenty of time, Norman," he said. "You just sit there until you're good and ready." It wasn't long before Norman got up and followed him out of the room, a docile, lumbering, red-faced giant.

When Jensine left Lake Valley at the end of the year, Mr. Logue stopped by her room with a beautifully wrapped gift. "Open it," he said. As she unwrapped the slender crystal vase, carefully folded in white tissue, he added. "It's like you. Lovely." Then he embraced her tightly. "You love that man of yours, Missy, and let him know it."

Even though Will ploughed the Wickstrom eighty in the fall of '29 and planted the spring crops in '30 and '31, it was March of 1932 before Nora and Paul Wickstrom finally had their farm sale and moved to Worthington. By that time, both Jensine and Will had learned to accept the inevitable delays and disappointments as part of the times. To be fair, they couldn't complain about their circumstances as they watched the old couple's hopes for a good auction that would tide them over in their retirement years fizzle in one brief afternoon.

Concerned there would be a poor turnout, Will passed word to the neighbors that it would help out if they could manage to buy even a small item or two, just a tool or a couple of Nora's extra canning jars. As he explained to Jensine, "It would be nice to send Paul and Nora into town with a little extra cash."

There was a good crowd, despite the blustery day, no doubt about that. Of course, some always came for the lunch and the opportunity to gossip and gawk, but there were few serious buyers. Throughout the auction, Paul just shook his head and accepted the low bids. But when his team of work horses was trotted out of the yard for a measly fifteen dollars, he turned to Nora with tears in his eyes. "Hard to let old Jim and Betty go for so little, ain't it, Mother?" Indeed, the proceeds of the sale were so meager the auctioneer didn't even take his usual cut, saying that whatever the lunch wagon brought in would be good enough.

With the house finally empty, Will and Jensine spent the weekends cleaning, painting walls, and varnishing woodwork. Will sponge-painted the drab kitchen in a celery green and cream. In April, Jensine withdrew her five years' worth of savings, nearly five hundred dollars, and they went to the buyers' market in Omaha with Will's friend Walt. Besides playing the saxophone in Will's band, Walt operated the local hardware store with his father and sold a few dining and bedroom sets as well. He suggested they might get some good prices because of the business he gave the wholesaler. Jensine doubted the small amount of furniture Walt sold would be enough to influence anybody. In her estimation, he wasn't the big cheese he thought he was...always tooting his own horn, pardon the pun, and, as her father would have said, was just a big toad in a small puddle. But Will said it wouldn't cost anything to look and the trip to Omaha might be fun.

As it turned out, Jensine threw caution to the wind and almost bought out the market—a cherry bedroom set, an oak dining table and chairs, Copper Clad range and a coal burning stove, a small maple kitchen table and chairs, a davenport and matching chair of durable frieze, a colorful oriental rug and kitchen linoleum, lamps, an extra bed and dresser. She even splurged on a red accent chair for the front room. At the end of the shopping spree, only seventy-three dollars and some odd change was left, which they agreed would go into their savings account at the Citizens State Bank, a little rainy day cash. The furniture was delivered to the Round Lake railroad depot in mid-May, and with the loan of Walt's store truck and the help of Walt, Francis, and Amos, was carefully moved to the Wickstrom place. They waited until the weekend because Jensine wanted to be there. Amos, of course, fussed about wasting a nice day on moving furniture when Will should be planting corn instead. Everything went smoothly until they tried to slide the heavy range across the last foot of kitchen linoleum, which had been freed from its tight roll but not yet quite flat. The back range foot caught on a small swell, and before Will could holler stop, there was an ugly rip in the linoleum. The room was suddenly quiet except for Jensine's "Oh, shit!'

Then Will's laughter filled the room. "Damned if just hearing you say "shit" isn't worth a hole in the linoleum."

Amos even stopped his complaining to remark, "I didn't think you had it in you, girl." Then he chuckled. "A little starch is good in a woman."

The wedding was set for June twentieth. Jensine had a rare sense of contentment. Her house was filled with beautiful things. There was a little money in the bank. And there were celebrations even though she and Will had not wavered from their simple wedding plans. Grace Atzen hosted a huge shower for them at Lake Valley. Jensine knew many of the gifts of beautiful crystal and linens came from the cedar chests and china closets of the women whose children she had taught over the past five years. And there was Lizzie Bauer's community shower at the Presbyterian Church, and, of course, Aunt Maren and Aunt Mena's huge family get-together which included both the Jensens and the Neilsens. Yes, she had to admit, everything was coming out in the wash, just like Emil and her mother had both said.

"You must have special connections with the man upstairs to get a day like this, Jens," Will said appreciatively as they made last minute preparations before their drive to the Methodist parsonage in Ellendale. Jensine agreed that it was a perfect June afternoon, pleasantly warm but without the humidity that always seemed to wilt everything come July. Her only regret was that her father was not able to come. Peder had taken a turn for the worse in March, was now bedridden most of the time, with his vision completely gone and the festering ulcer on his leg growing larger by the day. He seemed to sleep more than he was awake. Johanne had told Jensine at Easter she shouldn't count on her father being able to witness the small ceremony. "Best you ask Christian, Jensine. I think he'd be proud to give you away."

And Christian was pleased. "Hey, Sis, somebody's gotta kick you out of this family. Might as well be your little brother. How about if I bring Hannah along so as you can throw your bouquet to her. She's havin' a hard time sayin' 'yes.'" As much as Jensine wanted to include Hannah, she knew she couldn't without incurring Kirsten's wrath. Her sister was positively livid when Jensine told her there would be no guests. "My God, Jens, I know you get sick of my complaining, but I can't believe I'm not even invited to your wedding."

When Jensine finally came down from her bedroom in her wedding dress, Christian and Will both whistled. It was a striking blue silk afternoon dress with a matching bolero, the fitted empire waist skirt falling from an attached long-sleeved, cream satin blouse. Jensine thought she saw tears in her mother's eyes, and Will cleared his throat suspiciously as he reached for her hand.

"I want to say good bye to Dad before we go. I know he can't see me, but…"

Peder was napping when Jensine leaned over to whisper, "Dad, we're going now. Wish us luck."

Peder's eyes didn't open, but his voice was steady and clear. "Wing and a prayer, Jensine. Wing and a prayer." And then to Will, "You take good care of my Jensie, you hear. She's always been special to me." Then he reached out to touch Jensine and felt the wetness of her tears. "Don't you be cryin' now. This is your big day."

Jensine looked around the kitchen as they prepared to leave. "I guess that's everything, Will."

"Sure hope so, Jens. Good thing your mother and Christian are following us in their car. Otherwise, we'd have to tie 'em to the rumble seat."

"Probably a good place for a bossy mother-in-law," Johanne retorted, caught up in the teasing mood. "Wait, I almost forgot..." She disappeared into the pantry and came back with a bouquet she had fashioned from a few white garden lilies and a piece of blue lace. It was perfect.

As the minister prepared to read the words of the simple ceremony, Will put his arm around Jensine's waist and pulled her close to whisper, "I told him to forget the line about you obeying...just be a waste of words."

Jensine moved her elbow to deliver a hard jab to his ribs. "Will, be serious!"

It took less than five minutes to tie the knot and bind them together, in every possible way...until they were to be parted in death.

After coffee and cake in the parsonage dining room, Jensine and Will headed west on Highway 16. They wanted to be home by dark even though Amos had said he would go over to their place and check come chore time. "You might just decide to pull over at the hotel in Fairmont to do a little honeymooning and not get home till morning, right Lottie?" he said as he playfully pinched his wife's round behind.

Will laughed but Jensine could feel herself turn red. Lottie apparently saw little humor in his remark and was sharp in her response as she turned to deliver a swat. "Mind your tongue, Amos!" Then she turned back to her big crock of bread dough and kneaded vigorously. "What kind of a thing is that to be sayin', you old goat!"

It was dusk when they drove up the lane and into the dooryard. The day lilies had closed their blossoms, and only an occasional impatient bleat of a nursing lamb broke the quiet. "Oh, Will, isn't it just perfect?"

"It will be if I can ever get you out of the car and into the bedroom. It'll just be my luck to have everybody show up for a shivaree."

"Shivaree? What are you talking about, Will?"

"Don't they do that where you come from? You know, people show up in the middle of the night banging pots and pans and keep on until you invite 'em in for something to eat."

"I've never heard of such a thing! Your mother never said anything about it."

"That's the thing, Jens. It's supposed to be a surprise. They want to catch you in your nightgown. Course, so do I. Oh, don't look so worried. I didn't tell anybody except my folks that we'd be back tonight. You didn't tell anybody, did you?"

"Well, just Moveta, but..."

"Moveta! God, Jens, you might as well have put it on the front page of the newspaper." Will put his head down on steering wheel, sighed and then laughed. "Moveta! You've got to be kidding! Come on, let's go. Maybe I can get you in bed before they come."

There was a note from Lottie propped against a frosted angel food cake on the kitchen table. "Welcome home. I put a little supper in the ice box."

Afterwards, Will went out to check the livestock and let the sheep out to graze the yard during the night while Jensine put away the dishes and unpacked her small grip. On the very top, was an unexpected gift neatly folded in white tissue, a beautiful hand-stitched muslin nightgown, the neck of the pin-tucked top interwoven with blue ribbon. Jensine felt a stab of homesickness as she buried her face in the soft gown and took a deep breath of the soothing scent of lavender, her mother's favorite. "Oh, Mama, I do love you," she whispered.

Will had just turned down the lamp and convinced Jensine it was way too warm for a nightgown when car headlights beamed up the lane, and the loud, persistent honking of horns pierced the silence. "Oh, Christ," Will said in exasperation, "here they come!" He pulled on his pants and headed for the front door. "Just put on your nightgown, Jens. The more we protest, the longer they'll stay."

As people piled out of their cars, Jensine spotted Moveta immediately, hugely pregnant and beating on a copper boiler with all her might. Albert was right by her side, of course, laughing and banging two big pots together. "Hot springs tonight!" he yelled, and everybody hooted and made even more noise. Jensine couldn't believe the crowd—Amos and Lottie, the Bauers, Grace and John Atzen from Lake Valley, Nora and Paul, and all of their neighbors, everybody... except Francis and Eleanor. After the noisy celebration, which seemed to go on forever, the women brought out picnic baskets and crowded into the kitchen to put their offerings on the table.

Moveta hugged Jensine. "Bet you'll never guess what I brought" And she dramatically placed a crystal plate stacked with homemade fudge at the dessert end of the lavish spread.

It was 1:30 before the last car left, honking down the lane, and Will and Jensine finally turned back to their interrupted lovemaking. Afterwards, they fell asleep, spooned together, the summer breeze lifting the white lace curtains.

Later in the night, Jensine awoke with a start to the sound of a sharp staccato noise which seemed to come from the front of the house. Then there was silence and again the staccato. "Will," she whispered. "Something's out there."

"Nah, it's just your imagination, Jens. Cuddle in here," he persuaded, drawing her close to his warm body. "I'm tired."

"Will, I'm serious. There's something outside. Listen!"

Will sighed and listened. "Yeah, something's out there all right. I'll take a look." He left the bed and disappeared into the front room. Then he called softly, "Come here, Jens." As she came into the front room, he put his finger to his lips and pulled the curtain back from the window. "Look." There in a moment of magical moonlight, Will's arms wrapped around her, they watched the spring lambs, bobbed tails flagging and little hooves tapping in mystical rhythm, dance across the old wooden porch.

24

SETTLING IN

Jensine's stomach had been queasy all morning, so a little break from her bread-making was more than welcome when Will came into the kitchen and plunked down the small bag of groceries he had picked up in town. She liked it that he didn't seem to mind stopping at the store, and in truth, it had become a bit of a game, as he always found some little treat to add to the ordinary things on her list. Not much, of course, maybe just a few lemon drops or a peppermint. "What's this?" she asked, immediately searching the bag and finding a red and white wrapped candy bar. "It must be new."

"Called a Cherry Bing, I guess. Sid said he gets them from the Sioux City vendor. Anyway, thought I'd better try one and take another home for the missus."

"Did you eat yours?"

"You bet. I needed something sweet. Anything left in the pot?"

"Not much I don't think, mostly grounds." Flour up to her elbows from kneading, Jensine unwrapped the bar and sat down at the kitchen table to enjoy her first Cherry Bing. It was absolute perfection, no doubt about it: a rich, solid mound of cherry nougat dipped in creamy milk chocolate and crushed peanuts. "Oh, Will, this is wonderful! Just as good as Fanny Farmer's. I could eat the whole thing."

"Go ahead. You probably won't care much about it later."

Jensine was tempted, but over the past few days she had quickly learned not to trust her stomach, especially in the morning, so she rewrapped what was left of the bar and tucked it for safekeeping under the dishtowels in a pantry drawer. Then she turned to Will, who was dumping his coffee in the slop pail before straightening to gaze out the kitchen window. "Man, that was some wicked brew!"

"Something's wrong, isn't?" When he didn't answer, she reached over to rub the spot on his back, just below the right shoulder blade, that always liked a little attention. "You can tell me, Will," she said as she gently massaged.

"The bank's closed, Jens."

The queasiness returned, this time so strong that she instinctively covered her mouth before she replied, "Maybe it's just an audit, Will. They do that sometimes, don't they?"

"It's just wishful thinking, Jens. I watched Harold and Ralph board up the door myself. They weren't talking to anybody, just put up the sign, pounded the nails in and went around to the back. When Leslie Hanson asked what the hell was going on, they didn't say a word."

"But our savings, Will! It'll still be there when it reopens, won't it?"

Will spoke sharply without his usual patience. "Wake up, Jens! Don't you get it?" He took off his cap and raked his hand through his dark hair in frustration. "If you didn't get your money out yesterday, it's gone."

"You mean everybody who had money in the bank lost it?"

Will was quiet before he said, "I guess some folks knew ahead of time it was going to fold and took their savings out. Leslie says it seems a little funny they're the same folks who are buyin' up the farm foreclosures around here before the rest of us even hear about 'em." Then he slapped his cap against the table so sharply Jensine's bread crock literally jumped. "God dammit anyway! We probably can't even afford a load of coal for the winter!"

This time there was no holding back her turbulent stomach, and Jensine rushed by Will, out the back door, and made it to the cold outhouse in time to lose her breakfast and half a Cherry Bing. Still gagging, she heard Will at the door. "Are you all right, Jens?" She finally turned and slumped down on the empty space between the two holes, putting a foot against the door to keep him out while she searched for something besides a catalog page to wipe her mouth and vomit spattered shoes.

Will pushed on the door. "Come on, Jens. It's not the end of world, you know." Then he laughed. "We've still got the Mason jar in the pantry. Must be at least fifteen bucks in there, so I guess we're not dead broke."

Jensine took her foot off the door and let it swing open. Will just stood and stared, trying desperately not to grin. Then he whistled in mock appreciation. "Well, what?" she asked crossly as she pulled her apron loose, wiped her mouth and then moved down to her stained shoes. "What are you grinning about?" She took her time, hoping he'd have the good sense to leave her alone in her misery. No such luck! He stayed planted at the door until she wadded up the soiled apron and fired it right in his face. God knows, it wasn't exactly the way she planned to tell Will he was going to be a father.

Will was openly thrilled with her news and Lottie, too, when they stopped over after church for coffee, but not Amos, which came as no surprise to Jensine. "Awful poor time to be bringin' a child into the world. Poor Will! Now he'll be havin' another mouth to feed along with everything else." As if "poor Will" had nothing at all to do with it. Usually, she kept her thoughts to herself, mostly out of affection for Lottie, who was constantly embarrassed by her husband's ill-timed remarks. But this was one Jensine couldn't let go.

"Well, rest assured it'll never be a dime out of your pocket, Amos." He snorted a little in surprise at her sharp response and then gave his wife a sheepish grin. But Lottie would have none of it and literally had him out of his chair by the ear and into the dining room before he could so much as utter an ouch.

"There you go again, Amos. Why can't you ever learn folks don't give two cents for what you think? That's their business…not ours."

If Jensine hadn't been so irritated, she would have laughed. Will did, all the way home.

"Don't you love it when Ma gets tough?" he asked as he pulled her close and then reached down to cup her breast with his free hand.

"Will, watch the road!" Jensine unwrapped his arm but took time to kiss his hand before placing it on wheel.

Nora Wickstrom had been right when she told Jensine that carrying water from the orchard got tiresome. More aptly put, it was a royal pain in the rear, especially on wash day, and became increasingly that as Jensine's pregnancy advanced. Though she knew Will would have been quick to help, she just couldn't bring herself to ask him to lug the pails for her. So she usually waited until he was out in the barn doing the morning milking before she headed for the orchard to carry the eight or so pails needed to fill the Maytag washer and rinse tub. But first, of course, it all had to be heated in the copper boiler and range reservoir. Washing clothes was an unpleasant, all day chore and especially during the winter months when everything had to either be hung out to freeze on the clothes line or draped over clothes racks. The sharp smell of bleach hung in the house and the windows fogged with the excess moisture.

One cold Monday when she was bundling up for her several trips to the well, Will said in exasperation, "It wouldn't kill you to ask, Jens?"

"I guess I'm like my mother that way, Will. I don't like to ask others to do my work." And she was off down the path to the orchard, a five gallon pail in each hand.

Will followed, shaking his head. "Just hope I don't find you layin' out in the orchard with a bucket over your head some day." Then he walked off, throwing his hands in the air and muttering, "Go ahead then if you're so hell bent on doin' it yourself!" Jensine stooped down for a big handful of the wet March snow, formed it quickly into an icy ball, and heaved it in his direction. She never expected her aim to be so perfect; the snowball hit him squarely in the back of the head. He turned quickly, shaking the snow from his collar. "Woman, you sure do like to throw things at me! I think maybe you need a little snow down your neck." He wrestled with her gently and ended up kissing her instead, his hand slipping under the old mackinaw jacket to caress her swollen belly.

Willl's orchestra still played at area dances most Saturday nights, but standard admission had become "pass the hat," and not many people had anything to put in it. Once, when he came home with only a quarter, his share for the night's work, she couldn't help but ask as he joined her under the covers. "Why keep on with it, Will?"

"Oh, it's a little break. Making music makes me feel good, Jens…always has. Folks get out and dance a little…seems like they forget the bad stuff for awhile." He snuggled her against his chest, spoon fashion, and tucked her nightgown around her feet, saying, "God, woman, but you've got cold feet!" and then adding, "You should come along once in a while, Jens, like Ted, instead of sittin' home here by yourself every Saturday night with your nose in a book." Ted was Rosie's husband; he seemed to never tire of listening to his wife's piano playing and thumping the heel of his hand on the table to the beat of the music. Jensine had gone a few times, but she didn't enjoy dancing with the sweaty strangers who always asked her and felt conspicuous sitting alone or with Ted who didn't talk much and didn't dance at all. She knew Will was disappointed, especially at first, but then one late Saturday afternoon, as he was struggling with the collar button of his dress shirt, he came to stand behind her, softly nuzzling her neck. "How about comin' along tonight, Jens? I'll get a table right up close to the orchestra."

"That tickles, Will!" And she moved quickly away without answering.

"Up to you, I guess." He never asked again.

But Will was right about the bad stuff; there was plenty of it. He had hoped to sell a few pigs in the fall at the livestock pavilion in Worthington, but when he drove into town to arrange for the trucking, he came home frustrated and angry. "God, Jens! It'll cost more to truck 'em to market than they're worth. But the thing is I can't afford to feed 'em through the winter either." Then he shrugged.

Guess we'll be eatin' lots of pork, and if worse comes to worse, I'll do what Gerald Anderson says he's gonna do…dig a pit and shoot the damn things!"

In the end, they butchered three of the barrows, another for themselves and one each for both Francis and his folks. Lottie and Amos were living on a shoestring. Francis hadn't made a farm payment in nearly two years, and if it weren't for Lottie's garden , and the railroad workers and teachers she boarded, they wouldn't have been able to scrape by. Will had said more than once he hoped his brother wasn't getting in over his head taking out loans right and left on the farm with the bank in Worthington. But Francis told Will he needed to do considerable fixing up before Eleanor was willing to stay put in the old farm house. Amos was typically outspoken in his disapproval. "Puttin' all that money in the place and they don't have a pot to piss in!" And for once, Jensine had to agree with him.

Even Lottie, so usually nonjudgmental, was worried. "It'll be a sad day if he loses the farm. I don't know what he'll do…or us either." But still, Lottie tried to press a few quarters in Jensine's hand. "It's not much," she said, "but maybe it'll help buy a little gas so you can get home to see your pa."

"Oh, Lottie, we can't take your money. We're planning to go before spring planting."

Lottie's soft brown eyes unexpectedly filled with tears and she took Jensine in her arms. "I know you don't want to see your pa like this, but some things just don't wait until spring." And Lottie was right. Some things didn't.

Peder Neilsen died as a late winter snowstorm howled through Southern Minnesota, drifting across fields and highways and choking off all travel between Sioux Falls and Albert Lea. As the bad weather moved out and eastward, Will's brother-in-law Ernest walked across his eighty in the bitter cold to bring the news. Kirsten had been able to reach the local operator, and thankfully, Alvera, who openly rubbered on everyone's conversations, was also kind enough to walk over to the grocery store and leave the message for anyone who might be going out in the direction of the Mosher farm.

Jensine knew she had denied the inevitable. Her father's leg had been amputated nearly to the hip the previous fall in an effort to stop the gangrene, and her mother had told her that if Will and she could see any way to do it, she should probably try to come. Kirsten was more direct. "Dad's not going to make it, Jens, so if you want to see him before he goes, you'd better get your fanny home." Will had encouraged her, too, saying he would find the money for gas somehow.

When the township finally ploughed out the back roads, Will took Jensine into town to call home from the back room of Sid's grocery store. Alvera said she was more than welcome to use her switchboard phone, but Jensine didn't trust her emotions, and even though she knew Alvera would rubber no matter whose phone she used, at least her tears would be private.

The connection was poor, a clear indication that everybody on the line at both ends was listening in. Johanne's voice was faint and tired when she answered. "Mother, it's Jensine."

"I know who it is. And don't you even be thinking of coming for the funeral what with the storm and you expecting. It would be downright foolish!"

"But Mother..." Jensine broke down then. "I didn't even get to say goodbye."

Jensine was carrying Monday's wash water from the orchard when she felt the warm gush between her legs. She dropped the pails, hands holding her belly, and watched as the pink liquid stained her rolled socks. "Will!" she screamed. "Will!" Will was hitching up the team down by the barn but quickly looped the reins over a corner post and headed for the orchard on a dead run.

He needn't have hurried. Rob was born two days later, a big baby, weighing nearly eleven pounds. Dr. Paget apologetically told an exhausted Jensine, "We let him get a little big on us. Probably should have taken him a couple of weeks ago." The baby had a mop of straight black hair and was beautiful except for his cone-shaped head and several skull depressions from the forceps that were necessary to deliver him.

"Never again," Jensine swore. "Never again!" Will brought her a dozen red roses and a Cherry Bing.

Two years later in January, John was born, followed by a sister Charlotte in December of the same year. Irish twins, Johanne called them, openly disapproving of Will's obvious lack of control. Amos shook his head and wailed, "Poor Will! All those mouths to feed."

25

DOUBLE TIME

It seemed to Jensine that the first few years of her married life were remarkable, not in the sense of being singularly wonderful, but rather that each was lived so separately and deliberately, like stepping carefully to a slow, gliding waltz. The family album recorded the children's baby years, even in months: black and white photos of Rob arriving home from the hospital, swaddled tightly enough to please even Johanne; John, barely able to walk, staring wide-eyed through the fence at the big Duroc boar; Rob and John holding little Charlie between them, sleepy and cross from her afternoon nap, soaked diapers drooping to her fat knees.

Then, without giving notice, the measured dance slipped into double time, and much too quickly, at least for Jensine, Rob was five years old and ready to start first grade at Shady Nook, the one-room school just a half-mile down the road. The Kosters, who farmed just to the north of the Moshers, said their two older girls would be more than happy to stop for Rob, so he wouldn't have to walk alone. Jensine knew they meant well, but Rob was such a little boy, and he barely knew the girls. She knew he was bound to be scared. No, it would be best to walk with him, at least the first week. Surely Will could stay with John and Charlie for a half hour, or if not, she could pull them in the little wagon. But when she asked him, he frowned and said impatiently, "Don't baby Rob, Jens. You gotta cut the apron strings some day. Might as well be now."

"But, Will…he's so little…"

"Jens, he'll do just fine."

"What if he cries?"

"That won't be the end of the world either, Jens. He'll get over it…quicker than you, I'm thinkin'."

On the first day, Jensine checked Rob's lunch box, loosened his bib overalls at the shoulder a bit, and combed his hair one last time; then with Rob, John, and Charlie in tow and the Kodak stashed in her roomy apron pocket, she walked down the lane to wait for the Koster girls. The boys chased each other in and out of the ditch until Jensine told them to stop before their pant legs were all wet from the morning dew. They laughed and made one more trip into the ditch before Jensine grabbed them by the arms and spotted the leftover jelly in the corner of Rob's mouth. She pulled him close and firmly holding his chin, dampened her forefinger and rubbed off the offending pink stain while he squirmed to get away.

"You don't have to wait, Mom. I'll be okay. I don't want the kids to think I'm a baby…like Charlie."

"I'm not a baby," wailed Charlie.

"Baby! Baby! John teased, dancing around Rob until the elder swung his lunch pail and narrowly missed clobbering his younger brother in the head.

Jensine quickly gave up on her plan to get a snapshot of Rob and the neighbor girls on the first day of school. Instead, she lined up her own three, took a quick photo, kissed a reluctant Rob on the cheek and walked back up the lane, carrying Charlie and dragging John along. Inside the back porch, Jensine watched until Rob and the Koster girls started down the road. Rob didn't seem a bit frightened, swinging his new lunch box in big circles until it opened unexpectedly and scattered wax paper and jelly sandwiches on the dusty gravel road. She heard them laugh and saw the three-some stop to pick up the ruined lunch. Jensine sighed, already tired and the day scarcely begun.

❧

By the time John and Charlie started school, the country school was in the midst of a heated squabble about consolidation with nearby Round Lake. The Shady Nook neighborhood was divided.

Some parents, including Jensine, were pleased with the little school; it was small—only eleven students—close to home and thereby safe. Folks who no longer had children of school age were generally opposed, not wanting to pay any extra taxes for somebody else's kids when it cost next to nothing, only one teacher's salary and a few supplies, to keep Shady Nook open. Still others said their kids weren't getting much of an education at the country school and lagged behind other students when they went to town school after eighth grade. Jensine didn't believe that for one minute. It was just plain bunk, and she was quick to share her opinion in hopes of persuading the neighboring Hansons who lived across the section and were still sitting on the fence.

It miffed Jensine that Will didn't seem to care much about the outcome. He was more interested in helping get a county library in Worthington and piloting a new cash crop, soybeans, for the U of M School of Agriculture. "Far as I can figure out…" he said, "doesn't make much difference one way or the other. No sense fightin' about it with the neighbors, though, Jens. That's for sure."

"How can you say it doesn't make much difference, Will? I don't want Charlie and the boys riding all over the country in some old bus for a good hour every morning with a bunch of high school kids. Lord knows the ideas and language they'll pick up."

"What kinda ideas you talkin' about, Jens?" he teased, pulling her onto his lap and squeezing a nipple through her housedress. "You gotta wean 'em, Jens. You gotta."

The matter was settled when the new farmer next to the school property decided to square off his section and offered some hard cash the Shady Nook board couldn't refuse. The final vote was close, but in September—Rob, John, Charlie, and the Koster sisters climbed on the school bus and went to town school. Jensine didn't talk to Margaret Hanson for the next year.

From the beginning, the two boys were inseparable. They hurried home from school to listen to "Sky King" on the old radio in the kitchen and then left with a fistful of oatmeal cookies to play in the barn or out in the grove where they'd built an elaborate tree fort. On Saturday nights, they listened to the "Hit Parade" and exchanged bets on the top tune of the week, mimicking the silly songs that won week after week like "Buttons and Bows" and "I've Got a Lovely Bunch of Coconuts." Except for the family, Rob and John were simply the Mosher boys, two very different boys somehow blended into one soul. It wasn't that they looked alike. Rob was tall and dark like his father; John was smaller and favored the Neilsen side of the family. Rob was the risk-taker. Jensine would never forget the time he jumped out of the hay mow expecting to land in a pile of alfalfa Will had just forked down, only to miss it completely and land on his behind on the frozen ground beyond it. He walked gingerly for a week or two, but the close call didn't scare him enough to keep him from climbing the silo chute one fall day when he was fourteen to stand on the very top and wave his cap to a waiting world. Even Will hollered that time as he ran from the pig barn, John trailing behind. "Get the hell down, Rob!" he shouted. Jensine watched from the kitchen window, her heart in her throat, until Rob dropped to his knees and crawled over to the chute to begin his descent. Trembling, she went outside to stand on the back porch. Will, as angry as Jensine had ever seen him, waited at the bottom of the chute to grab Rob by the jacket collar and shoved him toward the barn. "Grab that fork over there and pitch down some silage if you're so damn hard up for somethin' to do." After Will headed back to the pig barn, Jensine heard John and Rob laugh as they each took a fork and disappeared up the silo chute.

Jensine found out later in the day from Will that John had told on his brother, racing into the pig barn to yell, "Come quick, Dad! Rob's goin' stand on the top of the silo!" When she asked John about it, he said, "Don't worry, Mom. I'll watch out for Rob." And he did, even in little things like giving up good shots in a basketball game to unselfishly feed the ball to Rob and adding more than his share of carefully saved nickels and dimes so they could buy their first Schwinn bike. In high school, the Mosher boys were a duo—on the football field, the basketball court, in the trumpet section of the band, and on the piano bench pounding out their own renditions of "Heart and Soul" and "Chopsticks."

All three of the children were musical, and Will had looked for a piano, so they could take lessons. The old upright he'd found was cheap but so huge that it crowded the rest of the front room furniture into a less-than-attractive arrangement. Jensine didn't much care for it, but for once, she kept her opinion to herself, mostly glad her tin ear hadn't been passed on to her children because music was such a big part of Will's life. Rob caught on quickly and soon discovered he could play by ear, but the teacher wasn't impressed when he substituted his own chords and runs in his Bach recital piece. "But it sounds good," Rob argued when his father told him to stick to the notes on the page, and he never did discipline himself to learn the scales like John and Charlie or complete the music theory exercises his teacher expected of her students. But Rob could sit down at the piano and pick out any tune, improvising as he went along. And he was right. It sounded good!

Jensine always thought Charlie was truly a middle child…not by birth place, but because she always managed to be in the middle of things. The only place she wasn't successful was when it came to her two brothers. Not even Charlie could wiggle her way between them. She was her dad's girl, no doubt about that, traipsing after him in her brothers' old bib overalls, a feed cap pulled down over her ears…and she had Lottie's soft brown eyes, which she could fill with tears or bat with feigned innocence whenever it served her purpose.

Usually happy and always creative, Charlie played school for hours, read countless books, drew pictures—even on the wall behind the hard coal stove—practiced her piano lessons without any reminder from her mother, and was content with wearing her cousin's hand-me-downs. But that all changed the morning she discovered a spot of blood on the crotch seam of her pajamas when she was eleven. Without the slightest balk, Charlie embraced adolescence and her emerging womanhood as if it were a grand personal epiphany.

When Jensine complained about Charlie's obstinacy and downright sassy behavior, Johanne sniffed and said she shouldn't expect much...spoiling a perfectly good name like Charlotte with a horrid nickname. And Will agreed in a rare criticism of his favorite, that Charlie was a "handful."

Even Rob, certainly no angel himself, complained. "You'd better do somethin', Mom. Charlie's gettin' wild."

When Charlie started dating, Jensine made it clear that she had to ask permission and be home by 9:30; exactly one half-hour after the movie was over. And there was to be absolutely no parking in the driveway. Jensine saw to that. If Charlie sat in the car more than ten minutes, Jensine flipped on and off the yard light until her daughter scrambled out of the car and stormed up the steps.

"Honestly, Mom, why don't you just come out to the car and sit with us!"

"Well, behave yourself then, Charlie. When I look out there and don't see anybody in the car and the windows are all fogged up, I know what's going on. I wasn't born yesterday."

❧

There was bound to be some worry, anger, and frustration—raising two handsome boys and a rebellious daughter, but if Jensine could have gathered up those years to freeze in time and then stretched them out for the rest of her life, she would have been content. Will, Rob, John, and Charlie—home, happy,...and safe.

26

DIFFERENT PATHS

The first time the Nobles County Republican Party came calling in '56, Will was at the kitchen table having his morning coffee, one of yesterday's sweet rolls, and looking over the feeder steer market prices in the *Sioux City Journal* while he waited for the first cutting of alfalfa to dry enough to rake. Jensine was kneading down her bread one last time before she shaped it into loaves and rolls. When the expensive Buick turned into the driveway and stopped at the end of the sidewalk, Will downed the last of his coffee and went to the screen door. "Looks like three of 'em in the car. Suppose they're either out sellin' somethin' or want directions." Then he went out.

When he didn't come back in after a few minutes, Jensine's curiosity got the best of her and she went to the small window in the pantry. Will was leaning against the car, talking with two businessmen, from the look of their clothes anyway, and a tall, well-dressed woman. It made Jensine conscious of her own worn housedress, which Will said should have been tossed in the rag bag a long time ago, but she thought it plenty good for the garden weeding she always did on Tuesdays. "I hope he's not buying any encyclopedias. I should have gone out. They'd have been on their way in no time." She shook her head and returned to her bread-making. "Will always thinks he has to listen, no matter how foolish it is. I hope he's got the sense not to invite them in."

Jensine was slapping the last loaves to get rid of the air bubbles and brushing the tops with a little melted lard for a soft, brown crust when Will came back into the kitchen. Charlie had asked once in grade school why she couldn't have Wonder Bread sandwiches like the rest of the kids instead of Jensine's thick, homemade slices. But is was a different story now that she was in college and her friends begged her to bring back Jensine's caramel rolls and Swedish coffee cake when she was home for a weekend. John never cared one way or the other as long as it was bread, but Rob had shared her delight in the crusty heel of the bread still warm from the oven, slathered with butter and rhubarb jam.

"Well," she asked. "What'd they want?"

"Wait 'till you hear this, Jens."

"You didn't buy any books, did you, because they're going right back if you did."

"Any more coffee? I probably got time for another cup before I hook up the rake."

Jensine knew he was deliberately stalling. She set his coffee down in front of him, so hard it slopped over onto the table. "Will...!"

He wiped across the spilled coffee with his shirt sleeve and looked up with a grin. "You won't believe this, Jens. That was the Nobles County Republican Committee. They want me to run for State Representative in the fall." At her shocked expression, he added, "Course, they said they'd give me a little time to think it over."

Jensine knew he had already decided; that was Will. And she was furious. "Haven't you had enough, Will? Do you have to be gone every night of the week to be happy?"

"Where's this all comin' from, Jens? I think it's really somethin' they asked me."

"How in God's name are you going to fit this...this running for public office in with everything else?" Then she added sarcastically, "Why don't you just rent a room in Worthington. Then you'll be handy for the meetings at the Co-op and the elevator, and the ASC...not to mention your weekly practices with the male chorus." She paused in pretended thought. "Oh, but I forgot about the new church manse, didn't I? How will they ever build it without you?"

"Jens..."

"No, I mean it, Will. You never quit anything. You just join and join and join some more." She grabbed his half-finished coffee and dumped it in the sink. "Don't expect me to be a part of this because I won't. I'll do the chores, so you can gallivant around the county, but I'm telling you right now I'm not sitting in any booth at the county fair shaking hands and smiling at people I don't know and probably wouldn't like if I did."

Will didn't seem the least perturbed by her outburst. Instead, he grabbed the white dishtowel hanging on the refrigerator handle, twisted it quickly and then let it go with a sharp snap. It would have caught her squarely in the rear if she hadn't jumped. "You're soundin' more like your mother every day, Jens." Then he added, "Hey, I quit the band, didn't I? That made both you and Ma happy."

"You didn't do that for me or Lottie, Will, and you know it. You quit the band because you had too many other things going on Saturday nights."

"But this is something I've never done before, Jens. You'll be proud of me if I get elected, won't you?"

"See, you've already decided to do it." Jensine opened the door to the basement and took her dirty garden shoes off the top step. "Do what you want. You always do." And then as she slammed the screen door shut. "Funny you didn't join the Ku Klux Klan when your nutty Cousin May from Sibley wanted you to. Not a black person within a hundred miles, but she was hell bent to chase all the Irish Catholics out of Osceola County. A hundred percent American…isn't that what she called herself?" Will just laughed.

The strawberry patch was wet with morning dew, and Jensine's shoes quickly caked with mud as she bent over to pull the crab grass, careful not to step on the young plants. June berries were always the best, sometimes small, but always sweet. As she headed back down the next row, she glanced up to see Will head for the alfalfa field. He waved and shoved the clutch forward until the tractor popped and then jumped into a faster speed.

It was the one thing, Jensine thought, where they truly didn't share a common ground. While she drew back from being involved, even with her neighbors sometimes, Will was energized by it. Oh, it wasn't she didn't belong to anything; she did. She went to Ladies Aid and taught Sunday School, even was superintendent once. And she joined the Home Extension Club. Will still laughed about one of their projects. They were supposed to collect wild plants to make bouquets, the project leader suggesting that roadside ditches were a wonderful place to find an assortment, so Jensine spent a good afternoon wandering the ditch along the road side in search of plants that might offer real beauty after they were dried and sprayed gold.

She found plenty but especially liked the tall plants with an arrangement of three serrated leaves at the end of each stem. Back at the house, she tied several plants together with short pieces of twine and hung them from the ceiling of the side porch to dry. Jensine was setting the table for supper when she heard Will open the porch door and suddenly break into laughter.

"God, woman! Are you plannin' on smokin' happy weed all winter or what?"

"What are you talking about, Will? They're for my extension project."

"You know that's marijuana you got hangin' there, don't you? Sure as hell hope the minister doesn't come callin' tonight."

Will teased her about it for weeks, and he must have told Amos and Lottie because the next time they stopped over for coffee and pie, Amos sat down beside Jensine and said, "I hear you're takin' up smokin', Jensine." Then he chuckled and said she was "startin' to make a real good cherry pie."

Jensine pretty much lost her enthusiasm for Extension Club after that and dropped out after spending two afternoons with a hammer and nail, pounding her initials and a floral design onto a huge round tin platter; copper repoussé, the extension leader called it, except they were using tin instead of copper because of the cost. Will took one look at and said it was the ugliest thing he'd ever seen. Eventually, he took the platter out to the barn, cut it up with the tin snips, and nailed the pieces over holes in the feed room where he thought the mice were getting in.

Several times she had thought about going back to teaching when the kids were in school. The Round Lake superintendent had even tried to persuade her to take a fifth and sixth grade position once. Will said she should do it if she wanted to, but there was always so much to do on the farm, and Jensine was comfortable with her books and sewing. And with Will gone so much, somebody had to be around the farm.

⚜

Will won the election and left for St. Paul after Christmas and didn't come home except for an occasional weekend. In the end, Jensine did sit with him in the county fair booth and celebrated his victory with a small glass of wine as they waited into the night for the elections results. And she was proud, but she stayed home and did the chores as she'd promised and even delivered an early spring calf or two before the session was over and Will was home again, excited and eager for the next legislative term. They fell back into the routine of farm life, but Jensine sensed there was a part of his life she no longer shared.

27
FAMILY MATTERS

Jensine was picking green beans in the garden by the house when Will's sister turned into the lane and stopped by the mail box. She opened the car door enough to wave and holler: "I'll get your mail."

"Now I'll never get the beans picked and snapped. Once she gets here, she never knows enough to go home," Jensine thought crossly. In the many years she had known her, Irene never stopped over unless she had something on her mind, and without fail, her visits left Jensine irritable, fuming, or hurt...sometimes all three. She had never understood it. At first, Jensine thought it was spite but finally after thirty years, she decided Irene was just too dumb to know better. For whatever reason, her sister-in-law had the notion it was her duty to promptly report anything she or Ernest, her know-it-all husband, heard about Jensine and Will. Most of the time, it didn't amount to a hill of beans, but still..."

After Rob's birth, Irene brought a lovely crocheted blanket and the news that Francis and Eleanor thought Rob was a homely little mutt, with all his black hair and funny-looking head. And another time... "Ma says you don't know much about canning if your jars don't seal." Apparently, Will told his mother she had to open several jars of pickles and reheat the brine because they started to cloud, a sure sign they hadn't sealed. Jensine was more than a little put out, and after Irene left, she didn't waste any time getting down to the pig house, where Will was castrating and vaccinating the young pigs, to tell him so.

"Whether my pickles seal or not is none of your mother's business, and I don't appreciate your running over there with everything that goes on in our house."

189

Will looked up in surprise at her outburst and reached over to rinse his bloody hands in the can of disinfectant by the pen gate. "What the hell are you talkin' about, Jens? You get in a damn stew every time Irene drops over." Jensine knew he was disgusted when he swore. "God, Jens, you know how she adds on to everything. Why do you even listen to her?" Then he held up the scalpel he was using. "Want to hop over the gate and hold the pigs for me?" Jensine fled back to the house, annoyed at how quickly Will could get her boil back down to a simmer.

The most hurtful of Irene's visits was after Jensine and Will moved from the Wickstrom place to the farm north of Round Lake in '35. About six months after John was born, Will bought his first tractor, a Model B John Deere, and started talking about finding more land to farm. Jensine had balked at first. "But, Will, I love this place!" And it was true—the open porch, the huge cottonwoods, Nora's beautiful flowers, which had flourished over the past four years, and her own huge garden north of the grove.

"But here's the thing, Jens. We can't make a living farming eighty acres with a team of horses anymore." Then he put his hand gently on her rounded belly. "Especially with another one already in the oven," he said jokingly.

She shoved his hand away. "You know how I hate that crude expression, Will."

Jensine wasn't surprised in early November when he came home from hauling corn to the elevator with news of a farm north of town up for rent after the harvest. "It's one of Bill Reinhart's places...guess the renters have decided to call it quits. It's almost three hundred acres, some of it nice pasture. There's a little low peat ground, but Bill says we can tile that out and maybe get a ditch dredged to take the water."

"What's the house like?"

"You'll love this, Jens. It's on the main road, so they've got the REA. You can finally use that pretty lamp you bought in Omaha.

The house looks big. Four bedrooms and a big hall upstairs, Bill says, and another down. If you think we can handle it on such short notice, Jens, we can probably move in after Thanksgiving and be settled before the baby gets here. Or we can always wait until March, but it'd sure be nice to have the spring farrowing over there in the new pig house.

They drove by the farm after church the next Sunday. Will said the folks living there probably wouldn't mind if they stopped and looked at the house, but Jensine shook her head. "No, I'm sure it's fine, Will, what with electricity and all and five bedrooms. Just think," she teased, "with all that room, we won't have to squeeze three cribs into our bedroom when the baby comes or watch your dad shake his head in despair every time he looks in our bedroom." Then she added somewhat nostalgically, "I think it looks a little like the teacherage, except the front porch doesn't wrap around." Will was more interested in the farm buildings—the red, hip-roofed barn and a roomy machine shed and new pig house. Jensine thought the whole place had an untidy look, but she was probably expecting too much; it was November, and harvest and manure hauling took its toll on the dooryard of any farm.

When she wrote her mother they were moving, Johanne responded more quickly than usual with her advice. Jensine laughed when she read it. "Be sure you leave the house clean, Jensine. You don't want the next folks to spread it around the neighborhood after you're gone that you kept a dirty house." She would have nodded her approval as Jensine, ready to deliver in two weeks, got down on her hands and knees to wipe up the kitchen floor one last time. In the end, besides being hard on her knees, it was a waste of time. No one ever lived in the house again, and eventually the farm site was bulldozed for a few more acres of tillable land.

As they drove away, she thought of the summer night they had watched the spring lambs dance across the open porch. Will was getting out of the sheep business; no money in it, he said. Jensine would miss the lambs, even the old ram that butted a terrified little Rob up against the orchard fence. "What he should do" she thought, "is get out of the chicken business...except for a few layers, and, of

191

course, the spring fryers." She wouldn't mind that at all. Cleaning the eggs every week with a soft cloth and a little vinegar water so they could be crated for Will to take to Worthington was a disgusting chore—the worst, except for picking the eggs, that is. The strong ammonia smell of the chicken house made Jensine's eyes water and nose run even though she drew her apron up to cover her face. It was like Christian always said, "Feathers and poop! That's about all a chicken amounts to."

On moving day, they left Rob and John with Lottie. Amos met them at the door, fussing about how the baby cried too much, Rob got into everything, and how it wouldn't work out with the boarders and all, but Lottie quickly shushed him and said sharply, "Quit your fussin', Amos. And don't worry, the little boys won't be botherin' your nap none." Then she added under her breath, "Lord help us if that should ever happen! You might as well be dead all the sleepin' you do, Amos Mosher."

Irene said she wanted to help, but there was a Christmas cookie exchange at Swedish Baptist she hated to miss. She was Johnny on the spot, though, as soon as the work was done and managed to be right at Will's elbow when he unlocked the kitchen door for the first time and moved back to let Jensine inside.

Irene gasped and shook her head. "My Gawd! Look at the cobwebs! When they're black like that, it means the chimney isn't drawin'. Look, Jensine," and she pointed to the solitary light bulb in the ceiling, "there's even a big one hangin' up there."

Jensine's hands went to her belly. It felt like the baby somersaulted and then kicked for emphasis. "My, my," Irene scolded, "she sure left a dirty house…my, my…and if that doesn't beat all! There's the slop pail under the sink, full up and frozen solid." She looked sympathetically at Jensine. "And you being so pregnant and all. Bet you're wishin' you'd stayed put."

Jensine's legs were suddenly wobbly. "I need to sit down somewhere, Irene." Her hands went to her belly to soothe the dull ache that was gathering force.

"I'll get Will."

Will brought in two chairs, set them in the dining room, and surveyed the cobwebs and litter the previous renters had left behind. "Pretty bad, I'd say, but guess it's nothing we can't clean up. I think I'd better take you to Ma's when we go for the next load. Just sit tight a minute and visit with Irene."

"The French doors going upstairs are nice," Irene offered. "If you can ever get them clean…" She smiled and paused before saying in obvious enjoyment, "I guess quite a few folks wanted to rent this place. Ernest heard in town you got it because Toots Reinhart is sweet on Will. They say her husband must be blind not to see it, especially with her goin' to all the dances Will plays at…hangin' around hopin' she'll get to dance with him." She looked at Jensine's stricken face and reached over to pat her knee. "And you sit home waitin' for another baby. Ernest says it don't look good, no matter how you slice it."

"Please get Will, Irene."

"Is it the baby?"

⚜

"We'll never make it, Will," Jensine whispered in agony. "I feel like I need to push."

"For God's sake, don't push! Get in the back seat and cross your legs. We'll get there."

Six miles down the road and halfway to Ochedyen, Jensine screamed and delivered her baby. At first, there was just Jensine's quiet weeping and Will's "Holy Christ;" then the mewling cry of a newborn.

"Don't pull on the cord or anything, Jens. Put the baby on your belly…anything you can cover it with?"

"Will?" Jensine asked feebly, "Are you sweet on Toots Reinhart? Irene says Ernest…"

At first, there was nothing except the hum of the car motor. Then Will's laughter filled the car. "Irene and Ernest…I should've figured…Jens, do you even know who Toots Reinhart is?"

"No, just they've got money, that's all."

"Jens, she's pushing sixty and weighs at least two hundred and fifty pounds. But I'll say one thing…she's light on her feet…a damn good dancer."

Jensine couldn't think of anything to say except, "Oh." And then…"I think it's a girl."

Dr. Pagent kept her in the hospital eight days, said she needed the rest, but Jensine was restless and worried about the boys even though her mother had come from Ellendale to help. For one thing, John was barely weaned and just starting to use the cup. And the house was filthy. How could she bring a new baby into such a pig sty? Will seemed to sense her anxiety as he settled her and the baby in the front seat for the ride home. "What's wrong, Jens?"

"Oh, everything," she wept. "The house is filthy. John is still a baby, and Rob is into everything."

"Listen to me, Jens. The house is fine. John took his first steps, and your ma's got Rob toeing the mark. Me, too, I think."

Johanne met them at the door and immediately took the baby. "You should have swaddled her tighter, Jensine. She could take a cold." Then she added, "Charlotte's a nice name. I hope you don't go callin' her Lottie or…"

"We were thinkin' about Charlie," Will said, winking at Jensine.

The house had been transformed. It sparkled and smelled of Pine Sol. "Will, it must have taken an army to clean up this place. Who? Not Irene?"

"Oh, I guess Ma told Lizzie Bauer, and she told Nora Wickstrom, so the three of 'em showed up with their brooms and mops and gave the place a real goin' over." Jensine started to cry.

Johanne looked over her head at Will. "She's just a little weepy from havin' the baby. It'll pass."

Irene and Ernest came over the next Sunday with a pink crocheted blanket for the baby and Francis' opinion that Jensine was going to be all worn out having one baby after another like she was.

Yes, Irene's visits had gotten pretty tiresome over the years. Jensine sighed, "I might as well forget the beans and find out what *Ernest* heard in town." She gathered her apron around her picking, and walked up the row to greet Irene.

"Not much mail, mainly just the paper," Irene said as she handed it to Jensine. "Can't stay long, but thought I'd drop by."

"*Well, spit it out, Irene,*" Jensine thought to herself as she waited for whatever news was on its way.

After asking about John and Charlie and wondering if it weren't a little late in the summer to still be freezing beans, Irene finally got down to business. "Ernest says he heard in town Will probably won't get reelected in November because he voted for Daylight Savings Time. People just don't like it, Jensine."

Jensine bristled immediately, and for the first time in three decades she openly confronted her sister-in-law. "Ernest and you don't like it, you mean. I suppose you're like the rest of the nincompoops who actually think their tomatoes won't get red because there's less daylight! Well, Irene, you and Ernest can vote for anybody you damn please. And from now on, just keep your news to yourself."

Irene looked like she was going to pass out on the spot. She got into her car, made a sharp U-turn in the driveway and squealed down the lane in a cloud of dust. Jensine marched back down the row of beans and picked with such a vengeance that before Will was home from his campaigning at the county fair, she had picked, snapped, and frozen thirty pints of August beans—Irene's opinion be damned—carried ground corn to the steers in the feedlot, and made a double batch of fudge.

28
REMARKABLE LIKENESS

"Don't be wishing your life away," Johanne Neilsen always warned whenever Jensine complained, which was fairly often, about the demands and worries of motherhood and how wonderful life would be once the babies were out of diapers, or all three children were in school, or then out of school and off to college, and of course, finally married and settled down. "Just you wait," Johanne scolded, "the older you get, the faster the years fly by. You'll be an old woman like me before you know it."

"Like me"…there was more truth in those two words than Jensine liked to admit, even at eighty, when acceptance or, more truthfully, resignation was so much a part of the fabric of life. She remembered her father's advice about planting her own garden and her own naiveté in believing that it was actually possible. She had decided long ago that life was more of a dot-to-dot affair…a time and an event leading to another time and event, an uncertain graphing at best and certainly no clear picture at any point, even at the end.

"Like me"… Jensine thought about Johanne's words often. The remarkable thing was that she could name the exact time and place when she became her mother. It was March of '58 when Charlie called from college to tell them that she was going to spend spring break in Florida with her boyfriend. "Not if you plan to live in this house!" Jensine told her in no uncertain terms.

Charlie had laughed and said, "Oh, Mother, be serious. I'm not your little girl any more. We'll just be gone a week."

"It's just not proper, Charlie, and I know your father won't like it one bit either."

"That's a laugh! Dad won't care, Mom, and you know it. You're the one who's always so stuck on being proper. That and work."

"Good thing somebody is. When will you get it through your head we're not here just to have a good time, Charlie? It's time you realized that."

"Who says, Mom? I mean…where is it written we're not here to have a good time?"

Jensine was about to elaborate when she heard Charlie's exasperated sigh and scolded, "Don't give me that long-suffering sigh of yours, Charlie. I know what goes on down there, drinking and sex. And last year I read about some fool who jumped out of a window and broke his neck."

"Oh, my God, Mom! I'm not like you. You're so scared of dying, you've missed living. See you…" And she hung up.

Jensine had been so angry, she'd grabbed one of Will's chore jackets off a hook in the entry way and headed to the machine shed where he was changing the oil in the new John Deere. She was irked about that, too. Why he needed another tractor was beyond her.

"Oh-oh…" he said as she came through the open door. "Somethin' tells me you're not bringin' me my afternoon coffee."

"I just got off the phone with your daughter. She's going all the way to Florida with that boy she met from Duluth."

"Charlie's twenty-one, Jens. Let her live her own life."

Jensine literally trembled as she angrily shook her finger at him. "Oh no, you don't, Will Mosher! You're not giving me that line of B.S. ever again. That's what you told me when Rob went off and joined the army and…"

Will didn't let her finish. "Don't get started on that, Jens. It's over and done. Let it be."

"Maybe for you, but not for me!"

"Jens…" Will warned.

Jensine knew better than to push it any further. "Well, what if she comes home pregnant? Then what?"

Will just shrugged and said, "Then I guess she does. We gonna have coffee this afternoon or not?"

"I suppose. Don't we always?" she answered crossly. Then as she left to go back to the house, Jensine sniffed and added, "I really don't know what this world's coming to."

Will tossed his wrench up on the work bench with a bang and laughed. "Goddamn, Jens! If you don't sound just like your mother! You oughta hear yourself."

Back in the kitchen, Jensine put on the coffee and cut two big pieces of the raisin spice cake she had frosted earlier. It was Lottie's recipe and one of Will's favorites. She thought of Lottie. Such a loving and patient heart that woman had. And work…Lottie never sat. It seemed right she had died in her sleep. Jensine was convinced she was probably just too tired to go on and it was the only way she could think of to escape and finally get some rest. But Amos, the old poop, even found cause to complain about that: "I married a young woman to take care of me in my old age, and then she up and died on me."

But what Charlie said about her not living, that wasn't true, Jensine thought. It wasn't true at all. To hear Charlie talk, Jensine arrived on this earth old, a postmenopausal woman with a thickening waist…who still awakened to pajama-drenching night sweats. Oh, she had lived all right, and it wasn't any damn spring break in Florida either; that's for sure. And Charlie…well, that was a laugh. Falling on her rump in a patch of nettles and crying bloody murder for her father was probably the closest she'd ever come to real living.

The more Jensine thought about Charlie's accusation, the more it really bothered her. She went into the bathroom and stared at herself in the mirror above the sink. "Good God, Mother! I even look like you!" And she did look like Johanne, the same tight lips and the two little lumps of sagging flesh that were starting to form along her jawbone just up from her chin. Where had her lips gone? Good thing she never wore lipstick because there wasn't any place to put it. It would bleed into the wrinkles like Iona Jensen's did and make it look as if she had pretty much missed her mouth all together.

Jensine opened the kitchen window a crack and hollered down toward the shed, "Are you coming or not? I'm not bringing it down there." Often she did. Over the years, they had shared afternoon coffee sitting against a warm tractor tire out in the alfalfa field, leaning on an old fallen cottonwood in the pasture where Will was fencing, and even once, in the hay mow where privacy and fragrant clover had led to other things.

As she sat down at the table to wait for Will, Charlie's accusations lingered like the unpleasant smell of recently peeled hardboiled eggs. Oh, she could tell Charlie about living…about how, despite everything, somehow they made ends meet and made it through the Depression. And it wasn't just the money part that had been so hard. It was little things, too, like turning over the plates and cups on the table so they wouldn't be covered with the fine red dust that blew across Oklahoma and Nebraska into Southwestern Minnesota. It was the anguish and unspoken fear of Lottie and Amos when Francis lost the farm, and Kirsten's bitterness when Thor left her for a floozy he'd met somewhere in Wisconsin. He must have been doing more than selling farm machinery when he was on the road.

Jensine sighed. If Will didn't get a move on, his coffee was going to be stone cold. And that was one thing he was willing to grumble about, cold coffee. She added a little milk to hers and thought again about Charlie. Well, she'd find out soon enough living was a whole lot more than a shopping spree in Minneapolis and necking in the back seat of her boyfriend's car down by the plum grove, which, by the way, Jensine had known all along. When Will laughed about all the used rubbers he found down there when he was fixing the fence, she never told him it was his own daughter who parked there.

Of course, Charlie had gone to Florida, regardless of what Jensine thought about it. And she didn't jump out a window or get pregnant. Instead she taught fifth grade for a few years and then married a serious fellow from South Dakota who wasn't much fun but knew how to make money. It was a good thing, too, because Charlie liked to spend it.

There was nothing to tell about Rob...his life was over before it began.

John took a job in Dallas as soon as he finished his engineering degree at Brookings. His wife was nice enough, a successful lawyer, who never wanted a family. She usually didn't come when he visited a couple of times a year. "Gloria needs her own space," John explained. Jensine suspected the farm was definitely not Gloria's idea of "space." The few times she had been persuaded to come along, she kept her nose in a book the whole weekend and quickly declined Will's invitations to look at the crops or inspect the pig nursery or feeding pens. And it was too bad, Jensine thought, because the farm was a wonderful place, so full of life and satisfying even in bad years. She remembered how often Will and she had prayed for rain one week and spent the next praying that it would stop before the peat ground flooded out. Will always said farming was nothing but a big crap shoot.

29
LEAVE IT ALL QUIETLY

Mercy, how she missed Will and the farm! The cancer had been quick, and Jensine was grateful for that. It seemed funny Will hadn't complained about feeling punk or anything, at least not to her, and he was always good about his yearly check-ups, even those nasty colonoscopies. Then for the doctor to say it was already into the liver. How could that be? Of course, Charlie rushed home from Sioux Falls and they went to Mayo, but, in the end, there was nothing to be done. And to think, Will was only seventy-three.

John came home in February and helped her set up a hospital bed downstairs in the living room. He seemed unable to talk to his father about anything except the weather, and Jensine felt relieved when he went back to Dallas. After he left, Will chuckled weakly and said. "I never knew John was so interested in the weather." Gloria sent flowers and a card, hoping, she said, that Will was well on the way to a speedy recovery. And Charlie wasn't a whole lot better. Whenever she came, she kept busy in the kitchen…whispering to Jensine, crying, and wiping her nose, conveniently distancing herself from her father in the other room.

So it was Jensine and Will who were left to talk about the dying. It was probably better that way. Near the end, she climbed up on the bed to lie beside him, to be near him as he struggled through the long restless nights. They held hands and talked about everything, except the weather—their first dance, the old Wickstrom place, Will's years in the State Legislature, the old dog Shep who bolted over the barn door at the first roll of thunder, and, finally, even the pain of losing Rob. For the first time, they were able to laugh and cry together over the pictures Jensine had carefully mounted in the family album. As they pressed their hands in a gentle caress over Rob's smiling high school graduation picture, Will said, "I thought if I didn't talk about Rob, the pain would go away. It wasn't fair to you, Jens."

"But you never forgot how to laugh, Will. It was the only thing that kept me going some days."

Then he covered her left hand with his. "I didn't ever get you that big ring I promised, did it?"

In the morning, Will usually fell into an hour or two of exhausted sleep, and it was then Jensine worked in her garden, frantically weeding and weeping at the same time. His death was easy. He turned over on his back, sighed, and was gone. It was the dying that was hard.

Mildred Anderson was there the next morning before ten o'clock with a bowl of potato salad. "I don't have time to come in this morning, Jensine. I wanna get over to Fleet Farm for that sale they're havin', but I brought over a little somethin' to let you know we're thinkin' of you." Then she patted Jensine on the arm. "We have to accept it as the good Lord's will, Jensine. I had to do that with Bill, too. But the Almighty never gives us more than we can handle. I guess we can all be thankful for that." At that moment, more than anything, Jensine wanted to push Mildred Anderson off the back steps on her fat behind.

Frieda's letter came after the funeral was over and everybody had gratefully gone back to their living.

Dear Jensine,

We stand in awe and reverence before all creation as we view it—as we live our lives, becoming part of it, yet at times seemingly unable to understand the why of so much of it. We plan; we speak of the tomorrows as if there will always be time to accomplish the many things we want to do. I find great joy in living each day to its fullest—just filling my being with the beauty of God's handiwork, in all its perfection, at every turn of the eye. Why the exquisite variety in the form and color of flowers? Why the gorgeous plumage of the birds or the ever-changing beauty of landscape and sky? We can't explain or answer any more than we can comprehend the great love shared by humans, ever-increasing as years unfold and continuing on in spite of the unwelcome appearance of death. To have one we love say "auf Wiedersehen" to us and the world brings sadness and many lonely, difficult hours. It is then the words of the Psalmist so well express a way of peace and comfort, "Leave it all quietly to God, my soul."

I think so often of our meeting and becoming friends at Lake Valley; your marriage to one of my dearest friends and into a family who were old friends and neighbors, and then as the years went by, all bound together with love and friendship. Remember when Mother said she wanted Will to sing at Dad's funeral and at hers? He did, you know.

I think of the many good visits and particularly the last two times I was back—coffee at your house. It was nice. There is so little one can say in sympathy and understanding—only this: I love you and your family and am happy you have beautiful memories of one who lived a full life. I loved Will, too.

Love,
Frieda

Jensine put Frieda's letter in her cedar chest on top of the folded flag and beside a pressed garden lily from her wedding bouquet, a Cherry Bing wrapper, and an old stained envelope with a recipe for homemade fudge scribbled on the back.

30

SET IT FREE

She hadn't intended to go at all. When the invitation arrived in early June, Jensine read it with a bit of nostalgic interest, but really nothing more. After all, who would she even know at an All-School Lake Valley Reunion? It had been more than sixty years since she closed her classroom door for the last time and left with Will to be a farmer's wife. And really, nothing much remained of the community she once knew. Oh, the Log Cabin was still drawing crowds. That didn't surprise her much. Even her own children, especially the two boys, but sometimes Charlie, too, under the guise of going to a movie in Worthington, had wound up out there and come home smelling to high heaven of cigarette smoke, cheap aftershave, even beer. She wasn't fooled.

But the beautiful old teacherage was long gone, and the school had finally closed last year, the few students remaining in Lake Valley and the surrounding small towns bused to a central location in an attempt to make at least one decent-sized area school. Jensine had read in the *Globe* that some well-meaning and apparently wealthy farmer from out that way had bought the old building but hadn't decided what to do with it—maybe a community center...mainly just "it'd be a shame to let all of those beautiful oak floors go to hell." How Emil would have applauded that sentiment! The creamery, too, had not survived the changing times or the bulldozer. The few farmers who remained worked two or three sections instead of eighty acres and had long ago sold off their Holsteins, pigs, and chickens in favor of cash crops and winter vacations in Arizona. In truth, lambing, slopping the pigs, and picking eggs were just as much a thing of the past as the ash pile and running to the outhouse behind the shed

207

in the dark and cold, the last being a perfectly appalling thought to her grandchildren in their three-plus-bathroom homes. Now that she thought about it, Charlie had insisted on five in her new place in Sioux Falls and then was forever complaining about having to clean such a big house. It wasn't exactly the truth because her husband paid for a cleaning lady to come in every Tuesday. Jensine remembered how excited Will and she had been to finally get one small bathroom in the old pantry off the kitchen on the farm. The boys were already in high school by then.

Anyway, it would be entirely too much fuss to go. For one thing, Jensine no longer drove. The children had insisted she permanently park her old sedan in the garage where it gathered dust and sparrow poop and had even taken the keys with them as an extra precaution. Well, they hid them in an old vase up in the cupboard the first time, but she used that as an occasional hiding spot herself, so it hadn't taken more than a few minutes on her kitchen stool to retrieve them once they were down the road and out of sight. She had been put out at first, to be so treated like a child, especially since she had never made a claim on her auto insurance, not a single one in all the many years. Most everybody she knew, including her children, had a fender bender from time to time and sometimes even more than that, and nobody took their keys away. Jensine suspected the nosey young neighbors across the street had probably said something to Charlie about the little mishap down at the filling station. She hadn't intended to pull out so sharply that she caught the back bumper of the rusted out car parked at the other pump, but the driver had been just fine with her offer of cash. Jensine wasn't naïve enough to believe the car would ever be fixed, the twisted bumper being fairly minor in the whole scheme of things.

Of course, there was the ticket for driving too slow on I-90, but she didn't know how Charlie could have found out about that. She had given the officer a piece of her mind. For pity sakes, why wasn't he out looking for speeders and drug dealers instead of ticketing law-abiding citizens for going thirty-five, a foolish waste of taxpayers' money in her estimation! Then he had acted so smart when he said, "You're sitting pretty small in there, even on that pillow, Ma'am. Sure you can see out the windshield?" Well, she'd never heard of anything so stupid! Of course, she wouldn't be driving if she couldn't see, would she?

It was a nuisance to ask people for a ride here and there; it was enough that Will's nephew down the street drove her to Worthington occasionally to shop for items they didn't stock at the local grocery. The shelves were daily more empty, single cans and boxes pushed to the front to hide shrinking stock. It was just a matter of time, Jensine knew, before Stuart, the last of several brave souls, would give up his ill-thought business venture. He told Jensine the state inspector said he had to tear up his wood floors to meet some code, and he couldn't afford to do that. Too bad because he was a nice enough fellow, and it was a shame he couldn't make even a meager living at the store. But then, there hadn't been much loyalty to local businesses for a long time. Oh, people wanted the grocery there for a gallon of milk or a loaf of bread when they needed it, but otherwise, even the old timers, who should know better, Jensine thought, drove to Worthington to shop at the big Hy-V out at the mall.

And the more Jensine thought about it, she just wasn't up to it. She was tired, "all played out" as Amos Mosher used to say. Back then, it hadn't meant much, just another complaint from someone who had truly mastered the art of belly-aching. But now, she had to admit, it aptly described how she often felt. Lately, she had been having little spells; it was hard to describe them in a way that made sense, so she didn't bother. Besides Charlie would probably schedule an appointment and haul her off to the Mayo Clinic if she heard about it. That girl seemed obssessed with making sure her mother never died. Jensine had asked her doctor about it, though, a young fellow in his fifties whose father had delivered her last two children. "There's sort of a buzz and then everything just stops for a moment," she explained. "Not long, you understand, but enough so I know something isn't right."

"Hmmm," he murmured, clearing his throat and flipping through the last pages of her chart quickly. Then he smiled tiredly, "Probably not too uncommon at your age, Mrs. Mosher. But let's get you in here a little more often for blood work. It'll minimize the problem of clots." He paused, then carefully closed the folder on sixty years of medical notes before adding, "By the way, I see we haven't had our Pap smear or mammogram for a while."

There was that infernal "we" again. Once she had reached eighty, it seemed that no one could talk to her without using that pitiful collective pronoun. Ye gads, did everybody really think they were somehow a part of everything she did? "How are we doing today, Mom?"…"What would we like today, Mrs. Mosher?"…"How did we like our sermon this morning?" Now, even her doctor had fallen into the jargon reserved for old people.

She laughed and couldn't help asking, "Do we really want to have our Pap smear and mammogram?" At least his ears had the good sense to turn a bit red, even if his brain was clueless. Then she added apologetically, "Oh, we'll do it in the fall if I'm still around. Nothing special about those parts anyway. They might as well wear out with the rest of me."

Yes, all things considered, it would put a real clinker in the works if an old teacher keeled over in the midst of an otherwise happy reunion celebration.

Jensine had just finished pulling the crab grass out of the perennials and was setting her muddy garden shoes on the basement steps when the phone rang. "Oh, poop! It's probably Charlie, calling again for the third time today to remind me not to stay out in the sun too long. Mercy, but that girl gets tiresome! And now that she has those unlimited minutes on that little phone she carries everywhere, there'll be no end to her foolishness."

But it was a man's voice, maybe that salesman selling cemetery markers again. How many times did he have to hear "no" to understand the meaning of the word? Good grief, the last time she'd been out to Will's and Rob's graves with geranium pots for Decoration Day, it looked as if the saints were getting ready to march in. Everybody in town had apparently fallen for the good deal, which included a free package of Omaha Steaks, and bought a marker even though most of them were a long ways from "being in that number;" and, Jensine sniffed, probably shouldn't count on it anyway. When they set Will's stone, she had her name engraved alongside his, not a death date, of course, although she just as well could have to save fuss and expense later on. It wouldn't matter much in a few years what was on it anyway, or that it had been badly chipped by a backhoe preparing a nearby grave site. Of course, Charlie thought it was awful, and the city ought to pay for a new one.

The speaker was tentative. "Hope I'm not bothering you, but I'm looking for a Miss Neilson who used to teach in Lake Valley...oh, at least sixty years ago or so. Don't even know if she's still around or even alive, but I'm pretty sure she married someone from Round Lake. His name doesn't come to mind, but one of the Ehrenbergs, a great grandson of the fellow who used to work at the school, I think, and still farms out there seems pretty sure it was a Mosher. Well, you're the only one in the phone book, so I thought I'd give it a try."

"My word," Jensine thought and then asked, "Who is this? I hope it's not another sneaky way to get me to buy a new monument. I said 'no,' and I meant it."

"No, no...I'm not selling anything. My name's Finnern...Duane Finnern. I'm planning on coming up that way for a school reunion later in the summer and just thought it would be kind of fun to see if I could connect with her somehow. She was always one of my favorites." Then he cleared his throat and added, "Thought I could at least tease her about the trouble we gave her in study hall and how all of us fellows thought she had such good lookin' legs."

Jensine wished her red stool was closer to the phone. She needed to sit down. For pity sakes, Duane Finnern! He had to be past eighty himself. She knew he ended up being a professor at Iowa State; Frieda told her that years ago. "Duane?" she asked, "Duane Finnern?"

"Yes…" Then Jensine heard a familiar chuckle. "Say, I wouldn't be talking to my old study hall teacher right now, would I?"

"Oh, my! Just a minute. Don't hang up, Duane. I just need to pull my stool over to the phone. What a wonderful surprise to hear your voice!" The receiver clunked against the wall as Jensine left it dangling and went to get her stool.

Duane hadn't lost his persuasive charm over the years because after ten minutes he had her talked into attending the school reunion. He and his wife would pick her up at around five the night of the affair, and they would go for a little drive around Lake Valley before going to the school for the banquet and program. "We'll get you home by 10:00…seems like Marie and I need our beauty sleep, too," he assured her. "Unless, of course, things get so lively we don't want to leave early."

"Now why did I agree to such a dumb thing?" Jensine thought as she hung up the phone. "For pity sakes, Duane Finnern! She should really just call Duane right back and tell him she couldn't do it, but then as she dragged her stool back to its place by the side cupboard, she put her mind at rest. "Oh, well, I may not even be here come August."

But what in the world would she wear? Everything in her closet had seen better days. Charlie would have to drive over and take her to the Mall to shop…maybe a light suit. She wasn't looking forward to that. The last time she shopped for a dress, Charlie's daughter Emily volunteered to drive over from Sioux Falls to help her find something "really cool," but at the end of the day, they came home with nothing. Everything drooped on her small, thin frame which had become quite stooped; osteoporosis, the doctor called it. According to him, she should have been drinking more milk. Well, why did he wait so long to tell her? A lot of good his ill-timed advice would do her now! Besides, it was a lot of nonsense. No one liked ice cream more than she did, and any darn fool knew that was a milk product. Some days it was all she had, that and a piece of chocolate broken off from the Cherry Bing or 7-Up candy bar she always kept in a kitchen drawer under the dish towels. Charlie's little grandson Ned teased her about it but said he wouldn't snitch as long as she shared with him.

She'd call Charlie after supper when the rates were cheaper. Jensine knew the children laughed about her being so tight. John had all but scolded her about it when he came from Texas last Christmas. "Mom, you don't have to pinch pennies like you do, you know. For God's sake, spend some money on yourself. Nobody has one of those wall phones anymore." Well, what did he know about it anyway? Just because he was lost without having one permanently attached to his belt didn't mean she needed one. Good grief, last Sunday one of those foolish little things rang during the communion prayer, and she was pretty sure it wasn't the good Lord calling!

If John had struggled like Will and she were forced to during the Depression...just to make ends meet, he probably wouldn't be so free with his cash either. She knew both Charlie and he were dying to know exactly how much she actually had, but their curiosity made her all the more tight-lipped about it. They'd find out soon enough. Too bad she wouldn't be there to see their surprise when they opened the safe deposit box down at the bank. She didn't think they'd be too disappointed. The CDs had stacked up over the years, and she had been lucky to have her money in the right place when interest was up to eighteen percent in '81. She wondered what they would do with the extra money. It would be spent quickly; she was sure of that. Maybe Charlie could put in another bathroom.

Jensine didn't feel like any lunch, but that wasn't anything new. Her appetite had pretty much disappeared. Sometimes just a piece of her homemade bread and a sliver of chocolate was enough to get her through the day. She decided to freshen up and sit on the porch while her hair dried. Her long hair was a nuisance now that her arms were so stiff, but she had never been able to bring herself to cut it.

Mostly, she was happy with her simple hairdo, a fat white braid neatly wrapped around her head instead of the thin frizzy curls her few remaining friends and Kirsten had. There was nothing attractive about that, to her way of thinking.

The screened porch was pleasant, warm, with just enough breeze to be comfortable. As Jensine settled back in the worn old rocker that had been her father's favorite for so many years, she thought about Duane's call, Lake Valley, and the past, something she rarely did anymore simply because she didn't have the energy and more often than not, it was painful.

She could never think of Johnny Atzen without remembering the day she and little Charlie had walked down the lane to get the mail and the *Weekly Globe*. Charlie chattered and stepped on her shadow while Jensine visited a bit with Donny at the mailbox and as he drove away, quickly read the bold headlines about the war. Then her eyes drifted down the page and suddenly locked on a familiar face…Johnny Atzen. Her first reaction was numb denial. It couldn't be! Surely God wouldn't take both of dear Grace's sons. But it was Johnny; there was no doubt about that, handsome and jaunty in his officer's uniform. "Area Man Killed in Pacific Action." Jensine would never forget how she stumbled into the ditch and fell to her knees to vomit until there was nothing but bitter bile. Then she wept and screamed for the incredible waste—bent over in the weeds, grass, and wild daisies, until Charlie ran to get Will, and he lifted her to her feet and helped her back to the house. Years later, Jensine thought perhaps it was God's feeble attempt to prepare her for Rob's death, somewhere in the skies over Korea. Nothing could have prepared her for that.

Will had been out in the dooryard someplace and John and Charlie still in school when Pastor Ed from Zion Presbyterian had called to say he was going to stop out for a bit. "Is Will around?" he asked. Jensine put a fresh pot of coffee on and then went to find Will. He'd been down by the machine shed, getting the driller ready for spring planting.

"Pastor Ed's coming out. He wondered if you were around. Must be some problem at the manse. Suppose the basement's leaking again?"

"Wouldn't think so. It's been a dry spring. Coffee on? I'll be up as soon as I get this sprocket greased."

Jensine had just moved the coffee pot to the back burner when she heard the car pull up. "Mercy, that was quick!" She'd pulled back the curtain at the kitchen window and watched as Pastor Ed got out of the back seat and waited for whoever else had driven out with him. "Good thing I baked a pan of brownies this morning," she'd thought. It was then two uniformed men moved away from the car and waited while Pastor Ed walked down to meet Will who was coming toward the house. Jensine watched as the minister held out his hand in greeting and then pulled Will into his arms. The reason for his visit was suddenly clear.

⁂

In the wrenching sorrow that followed, after the memorial service was over and the folded flag wrapped in tissue and placed in the cedar chest, Jensine went through the motions of living. Charlie and John deserved that. But she lay sleepless in the dark endless nights and moved away from Will's warm body for the first time in their years together, turning toward the wall as she frantically tried to remember Rob's face and hear his voice, but there was nothing. She tried to explain her torment to Will. "I can't see his face. I can't hear his voice."

Finally, one night, Will sighed and pulled her back tightly into the curve of his body. "We've got to let it go, Jens. We've got to." Then they wept and clung to each other...and later made love with such fierce urgency they felt apart exhausted but somehow cleansed of their grief.

⁂

Jensine toed the painted floor, setting the old chair into gentle motion. It really was a grand day. "Glad I didn't let Charlie talk me into that three-season porch," she mused. "I'd miss all this nice breeze." Her thoughts turned to the spent peonies by the front steps. The hard rain earlier in the week had laid the heavy pink blossoms flat. She could just as well snip them off and be done with it.

༄ৡৈৢ

She thought of Moveta, dying of breast cancer and not out of her fifties, leaving a weeping Albert and seven sturdy sons who absolutely cherished her. And to think, she ended up having to take care of Albert's mother after a stroke left her bedridden and crankier than ever. Jensine knew it had been a miserable six years for Moveta. And all the while, she was having babies and somehow squeezing them into that little place because Mrs. O'Connor wouldn't have "that woman" living in her house.

And there was Moveta's mother, the old biddy who never forgave her daughter for marrying Albert and becoming a Catholic. Funny how some people went to the grave without giving an inch. If anybody deserved to be stranded in purgatory, Jensine thought, it was Agnes Ogilire.

Of course, it wasn't any picnic having Amos Mosher live with them after Lottie died either. Like Will said, "For someone who's always talkin' about dying, it's takin' him a helluva long time to do it."

"Ninety-eight years," Jensine thought, "and twelve of them under my roof." In the end, he reversed the days and nights and wandered around in his nightshirt hollering, "Lottie... Lottie!" And Charlie certainly hadn't appreciated his peeing off the front step one evening when her boyfriend came to pick her up. But that was Amos.

"Ah...Moveta. A little piece of your fudge would really hit the spot right now!" She wondered what Moveta would think if she knew what a great comfort her recipe for homemade fudge had been to Jensine over the years—countless pieces of creamy chocolate, celebrating good and bad times, joys and sorrows, life and death. Now she thought about it, maybe Moveta did know all along about the power of a batch of fudge.

༄ৡৈৢ

Of course, Jensine could never go back in time without remembering Ethel. She was the first Fuchs to graduate from high school and go on to college. That was a happy ending, Jensine thought, if there ever was one. Ida and Bill's baby-making machine apparently broke down after number twenty-one. Years before, Jensine sent a card for their fiftieth wedding anniversary when she saw the announcement in the *Globe*. Their hard work must have paid off because Will's nephew told her once that the Fuchs owned most of Jackson County.

❧

And Frieda…no spring chicken either, by any means, but, well, Frieda was Frieda.

❧

There was that buzzing again. It really was getting to be bother-some. And today, when Mildred stopped and asked if she needed anything at Hy-V, for the life of her, not a word would come out. It was embarrassing; that's what it was.

❧

The rocker stopped. Jensine rested her head against the high back and closed her eyes. Life was a strange affair all right. There was no getting around that, but the more she thought about it, she guessed Emil and her mother had been right. Things did pretty much come out in the wash…oh, not usually the way they were planned, but still, sorted out as best some things can be….

❧

And there had been wonderful blessings—her strong mother and gentle father; the friendship of Moveta, Frieda, Emil, and Ella; her students, especially Johnny, Duane, and Ethel; the passionate love of Will; the fleeting gift of Rob, so like his father in his love of music and life; the pleasure of homemade fudge, a Cherry Bing, and, yes, Jensine thought…even lambs dancing.

❧

The buzzing was louder now and persistent, almost like a winter fly caught between the windows, demanding someone raise the sash and set it free.

ABOUT THE AUTHOR

Mary Ellen Johnson grew up on a farm in Southwestern Minnesota, one of six children, and attended a very small school much like the one in her book. After graduating from Mankato State with a degree in English, she married, raised a family of five children, and taught school for twenty-nine years. Mary Ellen and her husband Carl live on Lake Pulaski in Buffalo, Minnesota.